The Designated Twin

Drew Taylor

Taylor Made Publishing

Ebook ISBN: 979-8-9863426-9-6

Paperback ISBN: 979-8-9863426-8-9

Cover and Interior Design by Drew Taylor

Character/Object Art by Callie McLay

Edited by Leah Taylor

warning

What's In This Book?

If you like to fully experience a book for what it is, then skip this section

TDT is a twin switch royal romantic comedy that follows the journey of an autistic woman who likes life the way it is. Through this book, she will discover that she can indeed face change, and she will do so in the way she sees fit. Please remember that Lorelei's experience with autism is hers alone. This is not meant to represent every single person's experiences. Autism is a spectrum, and this is where Lorelei falls on it. The male main character is a flirty sweetheart who, once he's aware of Lorelei's preferences, changes his approach to best serve her. This is totally a "he falls first" situation, and I pray you enjoy the sweet innocence of this little fairytale.

TDT is spice free. There are, however, kisses, attraction, and longing stares. Why? Because these two are exploring this slow burning chemistry between them as they learn each other on an emotional, mental, and physical level. Furthermore, attraction and lustful thoughts are a natural, human thing that we battle. I seek to showcase that while also having my characters learn to take their thoughts captive.

TDT contains a wine-drinking scene as these are grown adults who can make their own decisions knowing the consequences or lack thereof for their actions.

TDT is spice-free and written from a Christian perspective. I seek to write characters who are flawed and sinful, yet, they recognize their need for Christ and seek forgiveness, repentance, and redemption. I wanted to read a romance where faith wasn't the main storyline, yet the characters were Christian and operated from that worldview...so I wrote it.

Read at your own risk. And I pray you LOVE this story. Please leave a review if you do :)

To the girlie looking for an escape – I pray this book sets you free.

Also, hi, Mama and Dad.

This one is for you. Somehow your personalities ended up woven into all the parental figures in this book. The good and the bad. I'm thankful for our successes and our struggles together. I couldn't ask for better parents. Thanks for everything you do for me. I **lava** you both.

Korsan Translations

Here is a helpful guide to Korsan words! Reference as needed.

Haalaa = greetings/hello

Attaans = a Korsan curse, similar to "Dang"

Riiksdaag = Korsan parliament

Broor = Brother

Systeer = Sister

Kryaa paa diig = Feel better/Get Well

Mysaa = think hygge

Prisaa Guud = Praise God

Taak = Thank You

Vaarsaagood = You're Welcome

Before

Once upon a time, on a tiny island country south of Norway and Sweden, a jet-setting second-born prince was visiting the palace to celebrate his father's fifty-ninth birthday when he learned horrid news: his brother, the crown prince, was diagnosed with a disease that rendered him unfit to succeed the king. The second-born prince was splintered; his love for his brother caused him to grieve what the coming years would hold for his sibling. On the other hand, the prince now had to grieve the loss of the life he lived—a life of freedom, exploration, and fun. The prince knew he had to shoulder the unwelcomed responsibility, so he vowed to himself, to his family, and to his God that he would do whatever it took to become a good ruler, the type of ruler he knew his brother would have been. The prince was urgently racing against time to become the monarch he envisioned himself to be as the Laws of Succession stated that the king's reign was to come to an end by his sixtieth birthday, just a mere year away. However, the prince had one last hurdle to jump over. According to the Laws of Succession, the ascending prince or princess must be married. The queen had picked out a beautiful princess of a neighboring country for her son, but the young prince was a romantic and desired to marry for true love. He bargained and pleaded with the king and queen to allow him time to find a woman who would love him and marry him. After an eventful and heated discussion, the king relented and gave the young prince three months to find a wife. If after three months the prince was still unattached, he would marry the princess and begin shadowing his father in order to learn how to be a good king. The once-spare prince hopped on a plane and flew back to his hideout, a small cabin tucked in the woods in a foreign country. For there he already knew of a lovely woman with fair, freckled skin, warm, coppery hair, and a bubbly personality that would rival his own. She would be the perfect candidate to become his wife and the future queen of his country.

If only she would fall in love with him as much as he already loved her...

CHAPTER ONE

LORELEI

Weird things are widespread in this world.

Why do women love wearing animal print clothing (looking at you, Hadley Dawson Rawls)? What is the point of a keto diet? Who decided daylight saving time was a brilliant idea? Where does one joyfully put together a 5,000 piece puzzle in an apartment that she shares with her messy twin sister? And how do I turn down my sister's absurd request to twin swap for her date tonight without breaking her fragile, romantic heart?

"Lucy, you know I've never been on a date before. I would only fumble this up for you."

Lucy lies on her back across the cocoa-colored loveseat with our shared ice bag—the one *she* picked out as it's imprinted with little crowns and hearts—over her left eye. She'd burst into the apartment ten minutes ago—knocking a few leaves off my Bird of Paradise plant that was innocently basking in the late afternoon sun under the window by the front door—in hysterics because a kid threw a tennis ball at a wall and it bounced back and hit her in the eye earlier today at the Juniper Grove Community Center where she works.

"But that's why you should go! It can be practice for your first real date when you meet that special someone." She says the words as if it's the most obvious solution, but she doesn't understand how the idea of a date sends my nervous system into a rebellion.

I have no idea how to behave romantically. In fact, the few times I've been interested in a guy, I've hidden and buried it until I got over the strange feelings. That's another question: how in the world does Lucy enjoy those types of feelings? The sweaty hands, hard and heavy heartbeats, the stomach knots, the uncertainty... It's all too much. But she lives to fall in love it seems.

Which makes my mission all the more impossible because her scheduled date tonight is with an actual, real-life prince. It's the type of scenario she writes about.

"Just slap one of the many makeup products you horde like treasure onto the bruise." It *is* a nasty bruise, and the swelling *is* atrocious. I smothered the injury in arnica gel immediately when she arrived home.

She removes the ice bag and sits up, leaning against the armrest while crossing her legs. "Look at this." She points to her eye, her pink-polished nail inches away from accidentally touching the monstrosity. "Regardless of not having a product thick enough to cover the intense bruise, this eye will be swollen shut by the end of the night. I'm already having trouble keeping it open."

I'm quiet as I sit on the recliner, the same chocolate color as our couch, rocking slowly while I process my sister's request. I love her. Dearly. And normally I would find a way to move mountains for her and her happiness. But this request is too much. And ultimately, I would only decimate her chances. There's no way Prince Finley Andersson would ask her out again after a night with me. I'm the awkward, socially clueless, brainiac, autistic woman who lacks the normal female warmth, sensitivity, and grace that my twin exudes, even if she has her more dramatic moments like right now.

"Please, Lor." Lucy sighs as if she's already been defeated. Which is true as of this moment. "We've switched before. And we've had a lot of fun doing it in the past."

"But that was when we were young. And it was innocent pranks on our teachers and friends." I think back to the times we switched in order to try each others' high school elective classes, to trick our friend group (minus Hadley who has always had a special gift to tell us apart), and occasionally, we even fooled our parents. It was... *fun*. And to be honest, I haven't had time for fun in my attempt to climb the ladder at my law firm, Donwell Family Law. Work has been my life for the past two years, and I still have a long way to go to make partner one day. I don't have time for silliness like this. And I have never switched with Lucy for a date or to trick a guy she was into. Frankly, she never asked.

"You've been working nonstop, Lor. You take care of me. You put everything and everyone else before you. I know I'm asking you to do this for me, and I also know it's an extremely selfish request." She crawls to the other side of the couch to be closer to where I'm sitting and grabs my hand. "But this is two-fold. Yes, you would be rescuing me, but this would also be good for you. You're twenty-five and have never been on a date. Which in itself isn't bad, but you should get this experience with someone we can trust."

I scoff. "How can we trust him? We've only met him once at Hadley's wedding, and to be honest, I didn't care for him much." The arrogance that dripped in his walk and the smirk that danced across his lips, even as he ran into me and spilled a drink down my bridesmaid dress, flickers to mind. The way my skin crawled at the wet, sticky fabric clinging to my body still haunts my nightmares.

"Hadley trusts him. And we trust her."

Valid.

"But still. Can't you simply reschedule the date?"

Lucy lies back down and places the ice bag over her eye. "He's a *prince,* Lor. I am lucky to have this date. I can't just reschedule with a prince."

"Why not? If he's here in Juniper Grove, Mississippi, he must not care too much about his title and position." *Though that haughty air around him at the wedding tells me his feathers would be tickled if something didn't go his way.*

"Hadley told us why. He isn't the crown prince, and he wants to pave his own path in life."

I stare blankly at my twin, who can't see me as she still has one eye covered and the other fixed on our white, textured ceiling. "Exactly. So he wouldn't be against rescheduling."

Lucy shoots up, dropping the ice bag, and turns that pointed glare right to me. "He is still a very rich, very mannered prince. Even in Mississippi. I don't have it in me to reveal I have a black eye from a kid while working at a job I can't stand because I'm not a successful romance author yet. I can't tell him all that. I need him to *like me* first. *Then* I can confess all my failings to him."

The anxiety and worry in her voice balls into a pit in my stomach. She doesn't often show how much she's struggling not having "made it" as an author yet, but I know it's killing her. She lives and breathes writing, and furthermore, I don't think the fiercest heartbreak would turn Lucy's idealist love sour. Though she has her head in the clouds at times, she's the purest, kindest soul I know. And again... I would move mountains for my younger-by-one-minute sister.

"But like I said, Lor. You work every day only to come home and work every night. You don't even watch documentaries these days, which is still boring, but I know you consider that fun. You stick to this rigid routine and never allow yourself to step outside the parameters you've set. Which I get. It calms you and makes sense to you. But you can't let autism dictate your life. You need to do something new. Different. Fun. Insane." Her words sting because, well, they're true. Since graduating from law school and accepting a full-time position at Donwell Family Law, work has become my identity. Occasionally I hang out with the girls, but even then, I retire early and shut myself in my room to work.

I've known I'm autistic since I was four, and I've constantly looked for ways to trick my brain into normalcy. I'm not ashamed by any means, but I also know that I can get... *stuck.*

And I am very much stuck in life right now.

As if sensing my change of mood, Frizzle, one of our two twin Abyssinian cats, jumps into my lap, rubbing her furry cheek against my hand. Not to be left out, Frannie, the other cat, jumps on the edge of the couch by Lucy's feet and then springs, using Lucy's face as a landing pad. She screeches and jolts up, throwing her ice bag onto the floor, but then she swoops Frannie into her arms, mumbling something about losing her good eye to cat claws.

"Why are you like this?" Lucy asks her, but then Frannie purrs and Lucy rubs her face against the cat's short, reddish-orange hair. "Yeah, you're my favorite. But don't tell Frizzle."

I chuckle. It's true. Frannie and Lucy are best friends while Frizzle prefers me. We swap occasionally, but for the most part, we've bonded with the cat that is most like ourselves.

Speaking of swap...

"Lucy, even if I went on this date in your place tonight, it wouldn't turn out the way you want. You know me. Finley would never text you or request a second date. I'd ruin your chances." Frizzle's sandpaper tongue licks my fingers, and I find the sensation oddly calming, which is *not* the feeling I get when I'm forced to wear clothes of that same texture.

"Lorelei, look at me." I turn my gaze from Frizzle to her. Lucy's head is tilted, strawberry blonde hair thrown over one shoulder, her bangs pinned back to keep the hair strands from poking her injured eye. "Yes, you're logical and uptight and sensible and all those good things, but you are also flexible and fun and have the ability to let loose every now and then. Though you don't show it often, you are witty and humorous. You simply let your fear of what people think get in the way of living, which results in you getting bogged down walking a tightrope of a life. And I know I'm preaching to the choir, but you can't keep being scared of how people perceive you. I don't believe you will bore Finley or scare him off. I wouldn't ask you to do this if I didn't believe in you."

Tears well in my eyes, and I hug Frizzle a little closer. She doesn't like that, so she wiggles out of my grasp and sprints off. Much like me. Closed off to affection. Running away at the first sign of intimacy unless it's with someone I've grown up with like my sister, my best friend, my parents, and Grandma Netty. I'm not even completely comfortable with my downstairs neighbor who has been frequenting my life a lot more recently, though Karoline is wonderful. It just... takes me a while.

"Do you really think I can achieve a second date with him for you?" I sniffle, pushing back the tears.

"Yes, I do," she declares. "Of course you'll have to play into who I am some so that he's not confused when he actually goes on a date with me, but I do want you to have this night. Even if it's just to practice for the real thing in the future. Even if it's just a night you can have fun and go on a date with a prince and lay all your uptightness aside. You can just go have a good time. I trust you, Lor."

As I contemplate her words, she relaxes back into the couch and Frannie stalks off, probably to find Frizzle. I lift myself out of the chair and squeeze onto the couch so I'm laying on my side facing Lucy. "You promise it's just this once? And you won't be mad if I do scare him away?"

Lucy grins and flops to her side to face me, shifting the couch a little with her movement. She uses the hand not tucked under her head to play with a strand of hair that has fallen out of my ponytail. "Yes and no. Just this once, and I won't get mad. If it's not meant to be, then it won't be. Simple as that. I'm trying to live in that mindset these days."

She blinks, though the injured eye remains halfway closed. Her hazel irises, often set in a beautiful green color, sparkle. At least, the one I can see.

I don't know if I believe her, but she seems to have faith in me. That notion alone is enough to bolster my spirits and confidence. I have zero plans to make this night about me, but at least I could get a good meal out of helping my sister. Also, it gives me the chance to vet this man out for myself to make sure he is worthy of my sister. Prince or not, if he doesn't measure up, I will find a way to push him out. I'm tired of seeing my sister heartbroken over loser men who think she's so naive and innocent that they can have their way with her heart.

I inhale deeply until my lungs scream for me to let it out. I tuck my face into my arm so as to not blow the hot air onto Lucy. Then I say, "Fine. But just this once. And I am not giving myself bangs to match yours..."

Lucy rolls over me until she hits the floor, then she stands beside me. I take her previous position of lying on my back and staring at the ceiling. Well, she's leaning over me now, so I'm mostly staring at a blackened eye and pearly white teeth. "But you'll need to borrow my wardrobe. Yours is too... corporate."

I groan and verbally digress, but internally, I'm curious to see what I would look like in Lucy's feminine flair and soft makeup. Will I pull it off as well as she does?

"Just no wool or polyester or other scratchy fabrics. Or satin. It's not quite like silk."

Two hours, tons of bickering, and eight outfits later, I have my answer.

Yes.

I don't recognize the woman staring back at me in the mirror. She's not Lucy, but she's also not Lorelei. My strawberry blonde waves fall gently over one shoulder. The blush pink, cap-sleeved dress somehow compliments my freckled skin without bringing out the red underneath. The waistline fits perfectly, and the hemline rests snugly below my knees. Matching pink closed-toed heels adorn my feet, and I know I'll regret letting her win that round by the end of the night.

"You look..."

"It's too much, right? I should change into pants."

Lucy places a hand around my waist and leans into my side. "No, Lorelei. You should never wear pants again. You look like a true princess. Polished, professional, and pretty."

I squirm at her words, and everything inside me screams to strip off the dress and grab my trusted black pants and white collared shirt. But tonight's goal is to be someone other than me, to be Lucy. And to *be* Lucy, I have to dress like Lucy. This dress is made of a silky material that doesn't cause my skin to crawl, which is the only reason I am agreeing to wear it.

"Seriously, Lor. I look like a twelve-year-old girl when I wear this dress, which is why I don't wear it anymore. But you? It's in the way you carry yourself. You make this dress look hot. Oh, and here's my ring. Wear it. You know I always have it on."

She gives me her silver band that she wears daily on her left index finger. I don't quite like the hard metal around my finger, but I'm doing this for her.

After I slip the ring on, Lucy slaps my butt, effectively ruining the moment between us. I side-eye her before returning to the woman in the mirror.

If I had a tiara, I might mistake myself for a princess, too.

Shaking the thought away, I grab my black purse from my dresser (I refused to use one of Lucy's pink ones. There is only so much pink a girl can wear), fill up my white to-go cup, tell my cats and plants goodbye, and head out the door.

Lucy stands on the balcony of the apartment, waving frantically and blowing kisses my way. Her show of affection doesn't end until I've pulled out of the parking lot and lost her in my rearview mirror.

I type in the name of the restaurant I'm supposed to meet Finley at. (I had Lucy text him during the two insufferable hours of constant changing to let him know the plans changed from him picking me up to me meeting him.) It's forty minutes away, and that puts me arriving thirty minutes early.

I have an hour and ten minutes to morph my brain into Lucy and calm my nerves.

Grabbing my phone, I turn on Taylor Swift's *1989* album. I'm not a fan, but Lucy is, and this is her favorite album. As lyrics about a tall and handsome man, staring at sunsets, red lips, and wild dreams play, I'm lost in a fantasy where I can freely shed my responsibilities, uptight premonitions, and odd brain.

A fantasy where I can simply be and freely feel.

As I arrive in the parking lot of Club Paris, a high-end french restaurant that I rarely go to, my phone dings with a text from my sister.

> Oh, I forgot to mention. Finley doesn't know that we know he is a prince. Keep it a secret. I want to see how long it takes for him to tell me.

Crap.

"I'm too logical to lie, Lucy. I don't see the point of lies. You know that." I croak to the screen. Then I mumble, "Why do you think it is hard for me to pretend to be you?" One of my autistic traits is that I mimic those around me, but when I'm masking, I hardly realize I'm doing it. When it comes to actively living a straight lie, well, I don't think I can do it.

Tucking my phone into my purse, I get out of the car and shut the door. Before I walk away, I use the side mirror to smile, altering it until it's like my twin is smiling back at me from the mirror, somehow trying to capture her warmth and sweetness and gentleness.

"Lucy?" a masculine voice calls. I ignore the sound, trying to fix my face to reflect my sister's. We might be twins, but the way we carry ourselves is opposite as can be.

"Lucy, is that you?" Oh. Right. That's supposed to be me...

Crap. Crap. Crap.

I snap my head towards the voice and spot Prince Finley Andersson waving to me as he leans on a dark-colored mustang from three cars over. My stomach drops at the sight of him walking towards me. Why is he here thirty minutes early? I arrived this early to give me time to adjust to my surroundings and morph into Lucy.

Precious time he's now stealing from me.

Why did I let my sister talk me into this? How can I pretend to be Lucy when her world is hues of pinks and purples while my world is one giant blob of black and gray? I'm going to crush her chance with this guy, and I can only pray she doesn't hold a grudge against me for my lack of socialization in a dating situation.

Finley stands in front of me wearing an admittedly dazzling smile with gorgeous blue eyes, a white button-up, and feather gray dress pants that fit him well. His blond hair is styled yet loose as it falls in front of his perfect face. He doesn't move like a man from Mississippi; his shoulders are set firmly back and the upward tilt of his knife-edge sharp jawline gives him that air of superiority I remember from Hadley's wedding. His gait is confident and stiff.

Yes, focus on that. Now, breathe. *What would Lucy say?*

"Oh, hi, Pri—" I cough, already screwing this up. "Finley." My voice sounds like an off-brand Barbie, and I hate myself for it. Finley, however, seems to think my greeting is adequate enough. Lucy might not question it, but I have to... "What are you doing here thirty minutes early?"

He snickers, and the sound grates against my bones. What's so funny about asking why he's here early?

"I could ask you the same thing. Seems we both value being on time. I have a reservation. Are you ready to go in?" He bends his arm at a ninety-degree angle out beside him. I've seen enough romance films alongside Hadley and Lucy to know I'm supposed to loop my arm through his, but I stare at his arm as if it might set me afire if I get too close.

I don't touch people unless I am super close with them. I've never touched a man outside of shaking hands and the occasional hug of my father when I see him. This feels... *intimate.*

"Are you coming?" Finley Andersson has the nerve to wink at me at that moment, a smirk forming on his perfectly symmetrical face. I swallow the bees swarming my throat and loop my arm through his.

And set me afire, it does. Where the bare skin of my forearm touches the sleeve of his crisp, white button-up shirt, it's like a star exploded, radiating burning heat that spreads through my arm, up my neck, and floods my cheeks. Highly uncomfortable at best and immensely embarrassing at worst. Though, I don't feel the instant revulsion or prickly feelings that I typically experience when I touch someone I'm not ultra familiar with. *Curious...*

Finley must notice the blush through my fair skin. The smirk on his face deepens, and he boasts an expression as if he's used to this sort of reaction from women.

But little does he know that this isn't because I'm enamored with the man. It's because it's the first time I've touched a man in this capacity. Why did it have to be an arrogant, cocky prince?

Oh, Lucy May Spence. You owe me big time.

Chapter Two

Finley

Dense man. You never told Lucy that she looked beautiful.

More accurately, she resembles a pastel pink angel, but that is perhaps too forward for a first date.

"Reservation for Andersson," I say to the young, male host. I glance at Lucy who's standing at my side, once again completely enthralled with her simplistic, refined beauty. The lady is sporting a constant blush. Coupled with the way she averts her eyes and clenches her hand into a fist—instead of resting it on my forearm like other women would do—reveals the blush is from a nervous innocence instead of *other* thoughts.

It's the most adorable and endearing thing I've seen.

"This way, please," the host says, leading us into the private room I reserved. One can never be too careful, even in a small town like Juniper Grove. Smells of warm bread and butter and stews and herbs infiltrate my senses as we walk through the small restaurant.

The circular table for two is elegant—a white table cloth with a candle centerpiece surrounded with rose petals. Two wine glasses, a bottle of Cotes du Rhone, and half a baguette with a ramekin of butter are immediately set onto the table before I have the chance to pull Lucy's chair out for her.

Her hand rests on the back of her chair as if she's about to get it herself, so I place mine over hers to make my intentions known, my long fingers swallowing her petite, clear-coated fingernails. I observe her reaction, gauging how she receives this minimal contact. Her hazel eyes widen as she stares at our hands, then she yanks hers out from under mine. The motion sends the solid, wooden chair rocking onto its back legs, the thick backrest slamming into my...

"Agh!" I groan, doubling over and instinctively sticking my hands between my legs, my stomach threatening to allow lunch to make a reappearance. My vision blurs for a brief moment as dizziness sweeps over me, and I grab the offending object to steady myself.

"Finley? *Finley!* Are you okay? I'm so sorry!" Lucy places a hand on my shoulder, but then the warmth of her touch disappears as quickly as it came.

I nod once and focus on taking deep breaths, trying to collect my composure as pain radiates through my nerves and my stomach rolls. After a minute or so, I'm able to stand straight, the pain still present but slowly dulling. Lucy stands off to the side, clutching her black purse with a death grip, her face contorted with concern as if she feels my pain. I release a long, slow, stabilizing breath and smile reassuringly at her.

"I'm so sorry," she says, but she remains as still as the King Erik statue of my great-great-great grandfather in the entryway of Stjarna Palace. "Are you okay?"

I nod curtly. "Yep. I'm okay. That was…"

"Painful?" She tilts her head, the grip on her purse relaxing.

"Yes. And embarrassing." I manage a snuffed laugh as the pain and nausea continuously subside.

Lucy, however, doesn't laugh. She takes two cautious steps in my direction, evaluating me through narrowed eyes and furrowed brows, and says, "It's a normal male reaction to that sort of incident. Are you sure you're okay?" The compassion and understanding in her voice surprise me. I've seen women laugh at men in similar situations before. I dare to believe it's a coping mechanism, but I'm glad to see Lucy doesn't respond that way. She genuinely cares about my well-being, not the awkwardness of the situation.

"Thank you for your concern, Lucy. Yes, I'm in pain, but it's easing up and I will be okay in a few minutes. Why don't we take our seats?"

She reaches for the back of her chair once more, but I take hold of her wrist, freezing her mid-movement. I stare into her wide, hazel eyes. "Please, allow me to be a gentleman and get your seat for you tonight."

"O-okay," she stutters. I release her wrist and slide her chair out. After gawking at the chair for a few seconds, she finally sits down.

I'm left wondering if Lucy has never experienced chivalry before. What is with these American men?

I take my seat opposite Lucy. "Would you like wine?"

She nods, and I pour her glass then mine.

"Cheers," she says, holding out her stemmed glass. I smile at the sound of her deeper but innately feminine voice, and we clink our glasses. "Did you know that in medieval times, people clinked their glasses together to ward off bad spirits? And we say cheers as a whispered prayer for gladness. It's funny how we willingly consume a product known for inebriation, which in turn breeds bad behavior, yet we feel the need to toast and clink first. It's like we know, deep down, that we probably shouldn't drink it."

The rim rests against my lips as I process her words. The longer I wait to speak, the pinker her cheeks grow, and it tempts me to stay silent forever to keep that butterfly blush painted across her cheeks and nose.

"Interesting." I sip the wine, trying to remember this informative side of Lucy from the wedding. We flitted through various conversations that afternoon while we danced and ate, but it was mostly Lucy agreeing with what I said, not adding in her own thoughts.

"I'm sorry." She covers her mouth with her hand for a moment before moving it to speak again. "I tend to ramble when I'm in an uncomfortable situation that I can't escape from."

I choke on the liquid and feel a dribble down my chin. I set the glass down gently and dab the wetness on my face with a black cloth. "You, uh, want to escape from me? You're uncomfortable?" I've been accused of many things, but never of making a woman uncomfortable.

"No, no, no," she protests. Her shoulders rise with a deep breath and fall as she slowly releases it. She leans across the table and lowers her voice like she's going to let me in on a secret. "I just mean that this is my first date ever, and I don't know—"

"This is your first date ever?" I stare agape. How could Lucy Spence go twenty-five years without dating a man? This woman is—a weird American term, but I'm going to use it—a bombshell. At Hadley's wedding, I couldn't get enough of her flirty banter, slight touches, and focused attention. She seemed experienced to say the least. "Oh, I'm sorry. I didn't mean to interrupt you. That truly took me by surprise. You're," I gesture to her with an open palm, "absolutely gorgeous."

She frowns. "There's more to a woman than her looks, you know."

Way to go, Fins. Stick that big foot of yours in your mouth, why don't you?

"I do know, Lucy. And you are correct. Yes, you're gorgeous, but I can already tell you're intelligent, and I anticipate discovering so much more. Which begs the question: how has no man taken you out before?"

She cocks her head to the side as if contemplating the validity of my words, then her eyes widen as if she remembered something important. She lightly shakes her head, sitting back in her chair with a slump before whispering to herself, though not quietly enough that I can't hear it.

"You are not doing this wrong, Lucy. It's your first date. That's okay. It means I shoulder the responsibility of making sure it is the best date the world has ever seen."

She laughs forcefully and a little too loudly. Then she straightens in her chair and begins twirling a strand of her hair around her finger, except instead of looking cute like I think she intends, it looks awkward. Especially when the strands get tangled in the simple silver ring on her index finger and she tugs it hard enough that her hand knocks into the table after it breaks free from the now-frizzed strand.

Lucy clears her throat, the permanent rose color across her cheeks intensifying. “Thanks, Finley. No, I have been on dates before. Plenty. My sister, Lorelei, has not. I was thinking of her, apparently, when I said that.”

That’s right. She has an identical twin. I met her at the wedding, too, except she was not as tolerable as Lucy was. I did spill a drink down the front of her dress, though, so I can be lenient when dissecting her personality and behavior. I’m sure she is just as peppy and joyful as Lucy is when her dress isn’t soaked through.

“Whew, pressure’s off, then.” I wink and take another sip of wine. It’s rich and sweet with hints of plum, cherry, and chocolate. It reminds me of the French imports we receive in Korsa. The silence stretches painfully for a few minutes.

I need to find a way to save this date. I trusted Hadley when she said that Lucy and I would be a great fit, and frankly, I liked what little I learned about Lucy at the wedding, though most of the conversation *was* flirty banter. Let’s see... *She said she was a writer!*

“How is that book of yours coming along that you told me about at the wedding? Did you break through the block you were having?”

She freezes, her fingers pinching a piece of bread to the edge of her lips.

Stupid man, you should have asked her after she’d bitten and chewed the bread.

“I, uh...” She drops the bread on the appetizer plate. “I need to use the facilities.” Lucy scurries out of the room, purse in tow.

Odd.

While she's gone, I think of ways to salvage this night. At the wedding, she told me she was a writer, she enjoyed swing dancing, she loved to read, though mainly romance, and...

There had to be more, right? Or was I simply into her because of the warm affection and attention she gave me? Did I enjoy her flirty banter and touches a little too much and it clouded my perception? My life three months ago is completely different from the life I'm attempting to build now. Three months ago, I wasn't in a rush to...

"So sorry," she says, sliding back into her chair with renowned ease and grace. That was quick. "Now, where were we? Oh, right. My book. Yes, it's going well. I broke through my writer's block and am currently drafting an urban romantasy about a merman prince and a female pirate. It's enemies to lovers."

"That sounds..." *Weird.* "Exciting."

"Mhmm," is her only reply.

Quiet ensues around us again. I almost wish I had social media so that I could find her profile to get an idea of what to talk about. She doesn't seem to want to tell me more about her book, but she was quite animated when talking about the history of "cheers" earlier.

I take another shot at conversation. "Did you know that the word 'cheers' itself derives from the French loanword *chiere*, which translates to 'face.' That's how it came to mean 'happiness' in the eighteenth century."

For the first time tonight, I watch Lucy Spence's face light up like Christmas lights in the palace gardens. Her smile stretches wider than the length of the Mississippi River. "Technically it came to symbolize one's spirit, so you could cheer to sadness."

"Nothing gets by you, does it?" I shake my head, bewildered by this woman.

She shrugs then lifts her glass to her lips. "Wow, this wine is excellent," Lucy comments, staring into the glass like she has x-ray vision to see each individual particle.

"It's French. Of course it's excellent. Though, you should try wine from my home country. We don't export it since we are small, but it is a delicacy within Korsa."

"The first wine is thought to have come from Iran. The Middle East is known as the breadbasket, so it makes sense. Bread and wine." She chuckles at herself, holding a buttered slice of bread in one hand and her glass in the other. I can't possibly stop the grin overtaking my face. This brainiac version of Lucy is plain sexy. The animation in her eyes, the nervousness laced in her voice, the way she tucks her hair behind her ears like she's not used to wearing it down. I'm entranced.

"Are you still uncomfortable with me?" I tease, and she covers her mouth momentarily with her hand again before dropping it.

"No, that one just slipped." She laughs, but it doesn't reach her eyes. Speaking of, are her eyes brown or green or blue? Obviously it's hazel, but they have shifted colors multiple times tonight depending on the lighting. I do remember a stark green present at Hadley's wedding, but now they seem to linger on the bluish-brown side.

Either way, Lucy's eyes are the eighth wonder of the world.

"Hey, Lucy?"

"Yes?"

I place my hand on the table, palm out. She stares at my open hand as if it might bite her, but after a moment, she places her dainty hand in mine. I give it a squeeze and look into her lovely eyes. "I like this side of you. Don't ever apologize or hide it. I'm always in the market to learn, and it's easy to learn if you are the one educating me."

Something akin to bewilderment flits across her face, but then she rips her hand from mine and proclaims that she needs to use the facilities again.

Since I feel better about the direction of the date, I sneak a glance at my phone while she's away. Thankfully, it was on Do Not Disturb mode, or else I would have thrown it at a wall. Five missed calls from my little sister, Astrid, pepper my screen. I send her a quick text.

What do you need? I'm on a date.

That's the problem, Prince of Hearts. Mamma's livid.

Why did you tell her I was out with someone?

Astrid sends a picture of Lucy and me sitting at this table. Thankfully, Lucy's back is to the camera.

The photo isn't in the news yet. But it was sent directly to Mamma's business phone.

Who sent the photo?

We don't know, but be careful, Fins. Johan and I are trying to track down the source, but Mamma is too busy freaking out that you're with a woman that's not Karin.

Blood boils beneath my skin, and I stand abruptly and exit the private room, scanning the open floor for anyone suspicious looking. I eye my two PPOs, Gabriel and Anders, sitting in a booth across the restaurant. They begin to stand, but I toss my hand up to stop them, then I forward them the texts from Astrid. They text me back saying they will scan the perimeter, but then they also reminded me there isn't anything they can do regarding paparazzi shots.

How many people are obsessed with me and my love life, anyway? Every time I move to a new place, all my dates are photographed and end up making waves and forcing me to move again. It's won me various headlines labeling me the Prince of Hearts. Yes, I've dated plenty over the past two years, but I refuse to settle for a woman I don't love. *For now,* my brain solemnly reminds me. *Because now there is a deadline.*

At least this one hasn't made the news yet. I would like a little more time to see if I could fall in love with Lucy. I trust Hadley, and I trust her judgment to recommend Lucy to me. Though Hadley is clueless as to why I truly need Lucy. Some cards have to remain close to one's chest.

I continue to sweep the room, but I see no one misplaced or anything out of the ordinary. I do, however, see Lucy walking my way, so I lean against the wall and wait for her.

"Waiting for me? How sweet," she coos awkwardly.

"Checking to make sure you did not get lost." The moment the words leave my mouth, I hear it. Literally anything else would have been more appropriate to say...

And she lets me know.

"I'm perfectly capable of remembering the path from this room to the facilities, thank you very much." She huffs and stalks past me into the room.

Way to go, again, Fins.

I follow after her. Moments later, Lucy is back in her seat across from me. I smile as if nothing happened while she pegs me with a rightfully-earned scowl.

But deep down, I'm planning the phone call I will have with Mamma later. One, I have been perfectly clear that I will *not* marry Her Royal Highness Karin Nilsson of Vespen, our neighboring country. Two, Father, and Mamma by proxy, allowed me these three extra months to search for a love match. I need to remind her of that. Three, we have someone to track down, and it must be someone that we all know for the picture to have been sent directly to Mamma's business phone.

An insider stalker. *Fantastic.*

I take a sip of wine and apologize to Lucy for implying she couldn't find our table on her own, hoping my smile conveys my sincerity. She's independent, and that would serve her well in the palace.

She nods with acceptance but frowns. "Is everything okay? You seem distressed."

How is she seeing right through me? I have a poker-face, and I manage it well. "Yeah, everything is fine. My sister texted with news from home, that's all."

Lucy begins to speak, but then clamps her mouth shut before taking a deep breath and beginning again. "Oh, you have a sister? What's her name?"

I hesitate. If I give her too much information regarding my personal life, she'll easily be able to identify me as the Prince of Korsa, and if I can have it my way, I'd like her to stay far away from that search. I need the opportunity to tell her who I am instead of her finding out on the internet. She'd run far, far away if she learned of my dating past.

Lucy stares expectantly at me, waiting for an answer. I guess I can tell her my sister's name. Plenty of girls have that name in Korsa. And if she ends up searching me online, I pray she'll give me the chance to explain myself.

"Astrid," I finally reply. "Mamma is worried about me. I haven't called her since I arrived back in town a week ago." Half-truths for the win.

Lucy's eyebrows pinch. "You should call your mama. Treat her well."

I snort a laugh, thinking about how my conversation with my mamma will go later tonight...

"What's so funny?" she asks, but the waitress appears with our food and her attention shifts fully to the young woman. I'm stunned at the way Lucy makes the waitress feel seen, like she isn't a backdrop in a scene. The entire time Lucy is focused on her, I am making heart eyes at Lucy. She's intentional, another quality that would bode well in Korsa.

Even with the mishaps that have happened, I'm intrigued by this woman. I've been trained to read people well, and I've already gathered that Lucy is intelligent, straight-forward, logical, and kind, if only a tad bit awkward and weird when she tries to act like, well... clueless. Would that be the right word?

Then it dawns on me. Is she trying to diminish her intelligence because she thinks that would be more attractive to me...?

"What was so funny about me telling you to call your mama?" Lucy's voice is stern, interrupting my thoughts. Before I answer, she takes a bite of her Blanquette de veau, a veal stew, and sighs, her voice lightening. "Oh, this is delicious."

"I'm glad you like it." I stuff my face with a bite from my plate, Tartiflette, a potato and cheese-based dish. Heaven in my mouth. But I better answer her question. "I laughed earlier because I found it cute that you told me to call my mamma. Is family important to you?"

After another large bite, which is refreshing seeing as women often eat the slimmest of pickings on a date, she says, "Family is the glue of society. You've got to love and cherish who God has given you through blood."

"Are you close with your parents? I know you have your sister. What was her name again? Oh, yes. Lorelei."

I pause because at that moment, Lucy coughs like she's choking on her food. I quickly pour a glass of water for her, and she chugs it between coughs.

"So sorry." Lucy stands and turns, her hip knocking against the table as her hand flies over her mouth. "I need to run to the facilities again." And with that, she's gone.

Goodness. I hope she's okay. I use the time she's away to check my phone again, and there are no more missed calls or texts. I also peek to scan the room again—still nothing. Gabriel and Anders are back in the building, and both shake their heads when I question them with the tilt of my head. I return to the table and wonder if the paparazzi will tire of me once I'm—

"Again, I'm sorry." Lucy sits down, smoothing her dress. Another record-breaking restroom run for a female.

"Don't apologize. It happens to us all. One time, I—" I trail off, realizing I was on the verge of telling her an embarrassing story from a state dinner a few years back that involved an emergency dash to the bathroom with barely enough time to get my pants down. "Well, it's happened to me before."

She grins softly, and I notice her lipstick is smeared in the corner of her mouth. Without thinking, I lean across the table and wipe it away with my thumb. My heart stutters and the tips of my ears burn hot. I quickly retract my hand. "Um, sorry. You had a little lipstick there." I gesture to the corner of her lip.

A blush coats her cheeks, and she glances away shyly. "Oh, thank you. Is it still there?" She turns her face to me with wide, innocent eyes. In this particular moment, they look like sparkling gold with a touch of blue.

"No," I whisper, not trusting myself to say anything more because of the overwhelming desire to kiss her.

"Lipstick usage dates back to over five thousand years ago with the ancient Sumerians..."

Lucy continues to indulge me with the history of lipstick, and it's the most fascinating story I've ever heard—because it's told by her. The way her eyes light up with hues of blue and brown when she talks about history is enchanting. We continue to eat and talk, and every now and then, between talks of history and philosophy and law, it's like her eyes dull to a muddied color and she grows quiet. After a few seconds, she snaps back into an awkward flirty person, but then I mention a random topic, and she's animated and brainy again, which I find way more attractive than her bad attempts at flirting and acting girly. Growing up enriched in history, I find it arousing that Lucy can match me fact for fact, and I can already imagine her face as she steps foot in Stjarna Palace for the first time.

Beyond that, I learn that she's passionate about reading (particularly law reviews and the occasional murder mystery), cats, holistic living, and her family (her mother and father are busy traveling the country in a van, and by the way her voice softened when speaking about them, I can tell she misses them). I like her determination and her optimism. I like her careful and intentional approaches to conversation. Countless times I've almost slipped and told her something that would give away who I am. Talking with her, at least the version of her I've gotten to know during the second half of this date, is like breathing—the most natural thing in the world.

As I walk Lucy to her car three hours later, I've forgotten about the photo, about my mother wanting to choose my wife, and about how this was only the first date.

When I lean down in an attempt to kiss her goodnight, she turns her head, and I plant my lips on her soft cheek. Initially, a shocked expression covers her face, but then she throws the first realistic flirty smile of the night my way and says, "You'll have to work harder to earn that from someone like me." My head spins like the oxygen flow has been cut off. Women are always trying to kiss me first. Once again, Lucy Spence is shorting my circuit.

I smirk and repeat a phrase I once heard my roommate, Mason, tell his fiance, Karoline, while she was toying with him. "I'll work like a dog to earn a kiss from you." And man, I mean every word.

Though it began awkward and rocky, Lucy loosened up over the date and showed me who she truly is. And I want *more...*

Lucy slips into a 1970s powder blue Mercedes Benz that looks like it's seen better days, and I close the door for her while contemplating if I could give this car a facelift one day. I stand outside on the driver's side while she cranks the vehicle and turns on the lights. She waves at me and blows a kiss as she begins to leave, and in one small glance back at me after her car inches by, Lucy frowns.

My heart feels as if it has been ripped from my chest because that frown can only mean that everything I've felt tonight was completely one-sided. The night already begins to play like a record on repeat, and I'm stuck wondering where I went wrong other than the two instances I know I put my foot in my mouth. I still plan to ask for another date, but will she say yes? Or has this been just another failed date to potentially flood the headlines and diminish my chances and time to find love before returning to Korsa?

Once I slip into my midnight blue car, I check my phone, a missed call from Mamma on my screen. Remembering Lucy's words to call my mamma, and the fact that I need to set her straight about Karin once again, I take a deep breath and hit the call button. I crank my 1960s Mustang and head out, the familiar black sedan with my PPOs tailing me. I'm lucky they let me drive myself.

The drive back to the cabin is long, and I know my roommate, Mason Kane, is going to pester me like a girl about every detail of this date. Mamma droned on about how I was living up to my Prince of Hearts reputation by going on a date with a woman who was not Karin. We have people looking into where the picture came from.

The most prominent thought on my way home: Lucy Spence did not have a good time with me tonight.

And that is a shame because I'm smitten with the intellectually stimulating woman.

Lucy's Journal

Friday, March 12th * 8:22pm * Sprawled on the living room floor holding ice to my swollen eye

*I sent my twin on a date tonight. With a prince. In my place. Yeah, that's right. I should be sitting across from literal royalty at this moment, staring into the bluest eyes I've ever seen. Seriously, those eyes have haunted my dreams since Hadley's wedding. I can't believe she actually nudged him to ask me out on a date. And I can't believe he wanted to! *Cue squealing and kicking my legs in the air as I write this entry.* But reality has to drop at some point, right? And the reality of this situation is that I am not on that date because I have a huge, monstrous black eye given to me by an uncoordinated youth at the community center. If only I had already made it big as a romance author. It feels impossible to sell clean romance sometimes, and I often wonder if I should just write smut under a different pen name. But I've struggled with sexual addiction enough in my past. I don't read smut anymore, though, I have to admit, in my loneliness, I've been tempted. God, are You happy with me? I hope so. Oh, Lorelei just texted me! She says the date went well and that I should have a* *chance to date the prince for myself. Hehe. Ah, all is well in the end. I should go write now, but I know I'll be too distracted waiting for Lor to get home with all the details. She called me a few times from the bathroom freaking out, but I got her back to a level head. I hope my twin did me justice. And I hope she had an overall good experience for her first date ever. God, will You bring a good man into her life? I worry about her.*

Chapter Three

Lorelei

"You did it!" Lucy, wearing a green face mask, hugs me tight enough to collapse my lungs. "I can't believe it! Look." She releases me, touches her phone screen a few times, and shoves it in my face. I step back so that I can see appropriately, and it looks like Finley texted her early this morning, letting her know he had a wonderful time last night and would like to go out again.

I smile, then finish gathering my paperwork to bring to the office. Yes, I'm aware it's Saturday, but I didn't get the work finished that I wanted to last night because I was shipped off on a date that I had no business going on.

I can't believe he said he had a wonderful time. With *me.*

"Your eye should be healed enough for regular concealer in a few days. Make sure to plan the date then." I pick up my brown leather briefcase and swing my little black purse over my shoulder. "I'm going to the office. See you later." I open the door, but turn around. "Oh, and don't forget to rub more arnica cream around your eye."

Lucy waves, already reading Finley's text again, or so I'm assuming. She does that often when it comes to men who show interest in her. But the thing is, I did a horribly awful job at impersonating Lucy. Finley kept encouraging the real me, and I kept releasing her out into the wild.

And he liked it.

He liked me.

I walk down the two flights of stairs, finding I have a little more bounce in my step than usual. The morning sun is bright, the wildflowers in the grassy patch across from the complex are beginning to spring up, the humidity in the air feels revitalizing for once, and the indigo buntings nested in the large oak tree sing a lovely tune.

I pause at the end of the steps and inhale.

My favorite season has officially arrived.

As I hop in my car and drive the short distance to the law office, I recall my conversation with Lucy late last night. Naturally, I didn't tell her of my abysmal behavior. I simply said that I slipped up a few times and spilled random facts, but overall, it was a normal experience. I absolutely did *not* tell her that I accidentally flung a chair into his man bits. She'd kill me for that. But in the grand scheme of things, I'm positive Finley will enjoy her as he did me, if not way more.

He enjoyed me.

Why does that thought keep resonating inside my head?

Must be because it was my first experience going on a date, and outside of my awkwardness when trying to act like my love-struck sister, I had a great time. It was fun to chat with him. He's knowledgeable, enjoys listening to my random facts, and puts me at ease, weirdly enough.

If Finley does marry Lucy, at least I know I'll like and get along well with my brother-in-law. I have decided that I will co-captain the shipping of their relationship alongside Hadley.

The parking lot is empty, and it's my favorite sight. Getting to work in the office alone is like waking up to presents on Christmas morning as a child. I haul my belongings inside the small, gray-brick building, ride the elevator to the second floor, and pass by all the floor-to-ceiling frosted windows covering my coworkers' offices until I reach mine at the end of the hall.

I enter my little nook, which I've brought to life with plants. A string of pearls hangs in front of my window, accompanied by a thriving pothos. An English ivy crawls on a bamboo plant ladder in the corner of the room, and I can't forget about the three little ghost cacti on my L-shaped metal desk. Not to brag, but my office space is the most peaceful in the building with its cream walls, forestry calming light covers over the two obnoxiously bright ceiling lights, and the aromatic diffuser nestled between two African violets on the plant ladder. To top off the cuteness? A picture of my cats nestled inside of their little brown cat bed back at home is displayed in its rightful, prominent position to the immediate left of my two desktops. It's in the perfect position to view when I need to look out the door or when I'm talking with a client across the desk.

After turning my computers on and filling my diffuser with eucalyptus, lemon, and sandalwood, I sit down and get to work.

At least, I try to. Curiosity gets the best of me, and I want to learn more about Finley's country and his family. He danced around details about his home life, but I understand it's because he's a prince. If I were a princess going on a date with an average non-royal for the first time, I wouldn't disclose that information either.

Though I have to admit, I'm glad Lucy has obsessive, stalkerish ways and researched Finley before she agreed to a date with him. Especially since I had to be the designated twin to go on the date in her stead. I don't like to walk into situations without having all the facts if I can help it.

I open a tab on the web to research the country of Korsa, effectively distracting me from annotating client files. I click on the government's page.

A scan through the website reveals Korsa is a tiny island country north of the United Kingdom and south of Norway and Sweden. It was originally native to Norwegian and Swedish peoples, but through various battles, a Viking subgroup known as Korsans took the land and claimed it as their own in the mid-1500s.

Next, I turn my attention to the ruling family, skipping over the king and queen for now. Finley is second in line to the throne and is one of three siblings—an older brother and a younger sister. Looking over their official pictures, my gut twists. They are all... *perfect.* Perfect jawlines, perfect noses, perfect hair, perfect eyes. All the siblings sport blue eyes and blond hair of similar shades. Comparing Finley to the crown prince, as they are the closest in age, subtle differences catch my eye. Where Finley's eyes twinkle with mischief, even in this official photo, his older brother, who looks to be named after their father, Erik Johan Andersson, is steady and regal. Finley's hair, though styled, still has a tousled wave to it while his brother's is slicked back without any evidence of a tousel.

Overall, Finley radiates effervescence; the crown prince commands order and seriousness.

Astrid resembles Finley over the crown prince, though she has a seraphic quality to her sharp but light features. Scrolling back up the page to the king and queen, I realize Finley and Astrid resemble King Erik while the crown prince takes after Queen Sylvia. The queen has long, silvery hair and darkened eyes. She looks like the embodiment of ice. The king sports darker gray hair cut short and, regardless of his aged state, his eyes are bright windows to what I assume would be a shining soul.

I smile while looking over the king's picture; he doesn't frighten me like the queen does. In fact, I imagine Finley will age like the king, keeping his twinkling eyes.

I close out of the tab as if that shuts down the nonsensical thoughts of twinkling eyes and reach for my bottle of water. After taking a big gulp, I steady my breathing, open my client files, and focus back on work I desperately need to attend to before Monday rolls around.

A couple of hours later, I stand up to stretch my legs and refill my water bottle. As I'm taking a quick jaunt around the building, I notice my boss's light is on.

I rap on the door, and within moments, the frosted glass entry opens.

"Hi, Mr. Austen," I say with a wave, greeting the man who looks like he could be my much older sibling. His hair, which resembles a deep reddish-orange sunset, is combed back with a wave that dips in the front. He has freckles dotting his face like I do, but unlike me, he's tall and brawny. Perfectly proportioned, if I do say so myself.

"Lorelei." He nods his head in greeting. "Fancy meeting you here on Saturday." He grins, and I return the smile. He says this to me every Saturday when I come in to work and he's here. It's kind of like our inside joke.

"How's the mayoring coming along?"

He shrugs. "Pleasing the majority of my constituents and ticking the rest off. You know how politics are."

Mr. Knightley Austen not only developed and now runs this law firm, but he's also the mayor of Juniper Grove, which explains why he's here on Saturdays quite often. He lost his wife in a freak snowmobile accident while they were on their honeymoon in Alaska. That was eight years ago, and I sometimes still catch him with tears in his eyes in his office. I think he works so hard to take his mind off her. Sure, they were only married for a short time, but before that, they had dated for a few years.

"At least the majority still supports you. Speaking of," I lower my voice even though we are the only two in here, "are you going to run for reelection this year? It's already March, and I haven't seen you announce your candidacy."

He shoves his hands into his jean pockets. "I plan to announce it in May on my birthday."

"I'm glad to hear that. You've got my vote, of course."

We exchange goodbyes after a minute, and I head back to my office to get to work on the last two case files that need my attention before Monday's client meetings.

I'm back at my computer and staring at my dual monitors; I have a case file displayed on one while the other boasts a photo of Finley... wrapped in the arms of a curvy black-haired beauty.

I recalled Lucy mentioning something about Finley having a past while she heavily researched him over the past few weeks after Hadley hinted that she would set Lucy up on a date with him, but I tuned out most of it because it didn't feel pertinent for me to know.

But now, as I click through picture after picture of Finley with different women, headlines of pop culture magazines deeming him the Prince of Hearts, I wish I would have listened to Lucy's droning.

She still wanted to go on a date with him even knowing that he's dated this much and has this reputation? I'm no longer certain she should. This version of Finley, though different from the one I met last night, is exactly the type of guy she'd be drawn to... and the type who would destroy her.

Which Finley is real?

The man I met last night was attentive, engaged, friendly, and well, I guess he was kind of flirty. Was our conversation regarding family, interests, and ambitions all a lie?

You lied to him, too, Lorelei. You pretended to be your twin...

I click to close the tabs I'd opened and end up shutting down my computer, wishing I could also shut down my brain.

Lucy has dated a myriad of men, so maybe that's why she was okay with his past. But does he plan to tell her? Will he come clean about who he is?

I rub my eyes and tug at my ponytail. In fact, the band is squeezing too tight, so I let my hair down and massage my scalp with my fingers.

At that moment, my phone rings. Hadley.

"Hello," I mumble.

"Well hello to you, too. What's wrong, Lor?" She's too peppy for my mood right now, but I clearly cannot tell her why I'm like this. I don't even know what I am. Sad? Grumpy? Disappointed? Frustrated?

I can't pinpoint the emotions. Nor the cause.

"Nothing. Just working through a complicated file at work." Which is true. The case on the other monitor has been a doozy. The mom is a recovering drug addict and is fighting to get her kids back from the foster care system. I couldn't promise her a win, but I pray every day that we will. Everyone deserves a second chance.

Even princes who've made the world their dating field...

"Ah, okay. Well, Lucy told me that you went on the date with Finley in her place last night. That was technically your first date, Lor. How did it go?"

Silence ensues for about thirty seconds as I think. How was the date? Aside from the rocky beginning, it was incredible, engrossing, and fun. So much so that I let the real me out too many times. It's odd he was more receptive to me as myself than when I was acting like my sister. Then again, that's probably just my bad acting chops. "It went well for Lucy."

"Hm. For Lucy?" Hadley pauses. "That's good, I guess. At least he's already asked her on another date."

"That's nice. It's what we wanted," I state. "How much do you know about Finley's dating history?"

Hadley doesn't skip a beat. "To be honest, he never dated anyone while we were in college. After college, however, I lost touch with him except for a brief reunion in New Orleans and then again in South Carolina." She takes a breath, her voice softening. "But yes, I've seen the stories, and I don't know what he's done to warrant them, but I do know Finley is a good man. We can't judge him because his dating life makes headlines while Lucy's only shakes up this little town."

"You're right," I relent. It's time to shake off this weird feeling and trust my best friend and sister. I saw for myself that Finley is a kind, intelligent, albeit flirty gentleman. Yes, his dating life is public, which means my sister may get dragged into the spotlight.

But we all know she'll love that. Maybe it would help launch her authoring career.

I grin, thinking of the happiness that would bring her.

After chatting with Hadley a little longer, I hang up the phone, toss my hair back into a ponytail, and get back to work on the case file in front of me, feeling more at ease over the situation.

I'll continue to ship the two of them… for now.

Chapter Four

Finley

"You sure about this? I'm all for surprises, but don't forget you sometimes learn things you don't want to when you try to surprise someone." Mason, my roommate, gathers his Bible before patting his jean pockets. "Ah, here's my wallet."

"Do you know something that I don't? Is there some reason I shouldn't surprise Lucy at church this morning?"

I glance around the kitchen island until I find my cup of tea and my Bible. I open it and glance at the picture of my family printed on the inside cover. My mamma's neat handwriting dedicating the Bible to me upon my fifteenth birthday is underneath the photo. I should get an English Bible, but this one holds a special place in my heart. The fact that it's in Korsan makes it difficult to follow along sometimes as my brain short-circuits on which language I should be thinking in, but I love this Bible too much and enjoy having it with me.

"Not at all. I'm actually glad you're finally coming," Mason responds. He's dressed in jeans and a flannel while I wear a polo and khaki pants. Mamma would screech at me for showing up to church in anything less than a suit and tie, but here in Mississippi, I'd get mistaken for the pastor.

I snap my Bible closed and take a sip of green tea. "As am I. It was hectic with the move prior, and then I was gone to Korsa. Now feels like the perfect time."

Mason grins and waggles his brows. "It's always for a girl, am I right?"

"She's a benefit, I suppose." Yes, I am anxious to see Lucy Spence again. The more I let the date Friday night marinate in my mind, the more I realized just how grand of a time I had. I found myself daydreaming of the excited inflection in her voice as she rambled on about random facts. Her eyes starred in my sleeping dreams. The way she avoided my kiss at the end of the night...

"Dudes, y'all are going to stick out like a sore thumb," Mason says, and I follow his gaze to Gabriel and Anders sporting their typical all-black suits. Both men, about ten years older than me, reside in this cabin with me and Mason; Father insisted I keep PPOs around me at all times while I'm here for the next three months since my status and future shifted with one sentence out of my brother's mouth while I was home last month.

Needless to say, it's getting too crowded and stuffy here. My precious peaceful and carefree life has come to an abrupt end.

"You American men should dress nicer. Especially for church," Gabriel huffs in his French accent. His brawny figure does not pair with his higher, snooty voice. But the man can probably kill someone a thousand different ways.

Anders, a tall, lean Korsan man and long-term friend of my family, shrugs. "I do not typically like to agree with Gabriel, but he's right on the money." His accent is much thicker than mine, which has all but disappeared with all my time in the States and traveling to other parts of the world.

"Please only monitor from outside the church, and don't be suspicious. Do what you do best and hide well," I tell them both. The last thing I need is to give Lucy a reason to be suspicious over me. No, she needs to think I'm a plain guy who chose to study abroad and fell in love with the country. I want a woman to fall for me. Not my title. That's why so many of my relationships in the past have failed.

Mason laughs, and the two men glare at him. Gabriel and Anders bicker back and forth often, but they both agree that Mason Kane and his southern ways gets under their skin.

"Let's get going, man. Don't want to be late." Mason claps my back, then we exit our little cabin. He climbs into his lifted Tundra while I slide into my 1969 Mustang, and I momentarily miss my collector cars back in Korsa. I had this one shipped to me back when I was in South Carolina, but it doesn't need any work.

I miss working on cars. Will I have time to regale in my hobby once I'm king?

Gabriel and Anders trail me in the blacked-out sedan. Glancing past my PPOs in my rear view, I watch the cabin grow smaller. This place was once Braxton's, but he let Mason and I stay in it after he married and moved in with Hadley. Mason's house is almost finished, so he will be moving out soon. I have less than three months before I'm summoned back to Korsa for good...

The drive to the church isn't long. Spring has made its way to the little town, and flowers are blooming on the sides of the road. Once we arrive, we park in the little lot and enter the red brick building. I say a small prayer that my PPOs go unnoticed. I don't want to have to explain why two men in black suits are following me around.

I'm given a brief tour from Mason, who started attending the church alongside his fiancée after they got engaged last month. The layout is simple: a sanctuary, a gym-slash-fellowship area out behind the sanctuary, and a side wing for Sunday school classes. That's the entirety of the place. It isn't much to look at, and it still retains old-fashioned pews and carpeted floors, but based on the warm greetings, hugs, and bright smiles, the people seem to be what make it an important and sacred building within this community.

But there's no sign of Lucy yet.

"Where're you from, Finley? You gotta little accent," an older lady who introduced herself as Netty asks as she sips her coffee from a small styrofoam cup. Mason and I stand around in a group of older men and women, all of them tuning into me.

"A tiny island country called Korsa tucked between England and Norway."

"Huh. What brought'cha here to Juniper Grove?"

As if invited by my very thoughts of her, though she isn't the reason I came to this area—Hadley did say she wanted me to meet Lucy, but I had no clue how that would turn out at the time—Lucy enters the fellowship room followed by a woman whose appearance is just like her but with bangs. Though identical in their faces and builds, the two present a stark contrast to one another in countenance. Lucy is taking my breath away in a dark gray pencil skirt with a white buttoned blouse tucked in, a pair of white sneakers on her feet. Though her clothing is business and plain, she looks like she should be on the cover of *Time* magazine. Her low, curly ponytail hardly swishes as she walks, her gait regal all in itself. Mamma would be remiss to not approve of her mannerism.

Her twin, Lorelei, on the other hand, is wearing a baby blue peplum dress (thanks, Astrid, for educating me on women's style) with white block heels, her curls and bangs bouncing with every step. She's beautiful, no doubt, but she doesn't carry that same refined air that her sister does. Maybe it's the swollen black eye throwing her off. *Ouch, that actually looks painful.*

The ladies wave and greet people on the other side of the fellowship hall, and I impatiently wait for Lucy's eyes to fall on me. I even scooch myself out of the group to be more noticeable.

Karoline pops up and swoops Mason into a hug beside me, saying something about being in their Sunday school room and organizing literature.

I, however, still go unnoticed, so I answer Mrs. Netty's question while flicking my gaze between her and Lucy. "I went to college at Ole Miss, and I decided I liked this area enough to stick around after some years of travel."

"Hi, Finley! Glad you made it this morning," Karoline interrupts, her arm looped through Mason's. I glance at Mason who has a sheepish look on his face. I specifically remember telling him *not* to tell people I was coming, but I guess fiancées are excluded from secrecy.

"Good to see you, Karoline." I turn my attention back to Lucy.

"Don't worry, I didn't tell her," she whispers, a hint of mischievousness in her voice, and I chuckle with a shake of my head.

Lucy finally turns in my direction, and we lock eyes. A look akin to horror flashes across her face, and my heart shatters.

"Oh, Lucy, Lorelei," Mrs. Netty hollers from the other side of me. "Come meet this here young man. He's from a different country."

I swallow the utter fear building in my throat as the twins exchange glances. Lucy's eyes are saucers, her lips pressed taut, while Lorelei's hand flies to cover her eye and her jaw drops open.

They simultaneously wave to the older woman and then make a bee-line for the restroom off to the right of them.

And to make matters worse, it's at that time Gabriel and Anders are ushered through the door by an older gentleman. "Found two lost souls wandering around outside. Figured they'd like some coffee and fellowship," he drawls.

"Three new visitors in one day? Color me shocked," Mrs. Netty says, then she saddles up to my PPOs who look like they want to make like a snake and shed their skins right about now. "Handsome young things. You should meet my granddaughters, Lorelei and Lucy Spence."

Granddaughters?

I snap my attention back to the old lady. "You're Lucy's grandmother?" The question slips through without my permission.

"Why yes I am, Finley." She ditches Gabriel and Anders, walking with her cane back over to me. The two misplaced men shift closer and closer towards Mason. Mrs. Netty places a frail, wrinkled hand on my shoulder and looks up at me with shining blue eyes, very similar to Lucy's. "Do you have a thing for my granddaughter?"

One could hear a feather brush across the floor; all eyes in the fellowship room cut to me.

The answer is obviously yes, but will she be comfortable with me proclaiming my intentions to date her to the entire congregation? Will that scare her away? The frown at the end of the night didn't have to mean that she had a bad time. It could have meant a million things, and I've tried to convince myself of that.

Saving me from answering, a man in a suit with gray hair and a kind smile—Pastor Rawls, Braxton's father—opens the door to the fellowship hall and says, "Time for Sunday school. Everyone get to your classes."

I sneak a glance at Mrs. Netty who now narrows her eyes, watching me like a hawk. Since she is Lucy's grandmother, I want to make a good impression. I paste a grin to my face, lean in, and whisper, "I'm very interested in Lucy, but I still have to find out if she's interested in me."

Mrs. Netty guffaws, a tear springing free at the corner of her eye. "Oh, darlin' boy. If that girl ain't interested in you, then I'd keel over dead. The men she's dated in the past..." She grumbles the last part. Something stirs in my stomach at her mention of Lucy's dating history, but I'm sure it's nothing compared to mine. I can't hold anything against her when my private life has been on full display for anyone interested in an obscure country's royal gossip.

While everyone shuffles off to various classrooms, the twins finally emerge from the restroom.

"Go say hey to the lady." Mrs. Netty nudges me with the tip of her cane.

I smile and nod, say a quick thank you and goodbye, inhale a steadying breath, straighten my back, and walk with false bravado towards the twins.

Everyone seems to have dispersed by now, except for Mrs. Netty, whose eyes I can *feel* burning a hole into my back. I might have shaken everyone else as an audience, but that lady isn't going anywhere.

I wave to Lucy, and by default, her sister. Both girls wave back and make no motion to meet me halfway. After a few more strides, I'm standing in front of them.

"Hi, Lucy." I step forward to embrace her, but her arms stay at her side as her eyes dart between me and her sister. Right as I'm about to drop my arms, Lorelei gives Lucy a little shove, sending her tripping into my open span, her hands flattening across my chest for stability.

Can she feel the intensity of my heartbeat?

I make quick work of steadying Lucy by snaking my arms around her tightly, and I cling onto her until her soft hands travel apprehensively up my chest and across my shoulders, like she's unsure if it's okay to touch me like this, before wrapping loosely around my neck.

Somebody call the fire department because this flame ripping through my veins is about to cause internal combustion.

To thank her for her service, I wink at Lorelei over Lucy's shoulder. She smiles, shifting her eyes away. Or, er, eye. The black one is pretty swollen, and I don't think she could open it all the way if she tried.

Though rigid in my arms, Lucy finally relents and closes the last few inches between us. Just like that, I'm wrapped in her essence. She smells of cottonwood and tea tree and summer rain. My long fingers stretch across her back as I hold her against me, her soft curves conforming to my sharp angles.

Is this legal in the house of the Lord?

"It's good to see you," I whisper shakily in her ear. My heart is beating erratically at this contact. *Attans,* this woman has already done a number on me.

"You smell nice. Like a winter forest," she says after a deep inhale.

I laugh, wondering why I was ever concerned that the woman didn't have a good time. She's just nervous about affection; I picked up on that Friday night. I'll be extra careful in the future to make sure she's open to my touches and hugs.

Hopefully.

I like physical touch.

A lot.

"You smell like spring, Lucy."

She stiffens again, then rips herself from my arms. She's going to give herself whiplash if she keeps snapping her head between me and her sister. "We can talk later! Time for class!"

Dragging Lorelei behind her, she darts off towards her classroom. I'm left alone in the hall.

Almost alone.

Mrs. Netty still stands in the corner by the coffeepot, staring at me with pursed lips and narrowed, wrinkling eyes.

I shrug and smile, trying to act as casual as possible, but I might get whiplash, too, if Lucy keeps this hot and cold act up.

Mrs. Netty meets me at the head of the short hallway that leads to the different class. She places her wrinkled hand on my shoulder once more. "Well, Finley. I might have been wrong. You might not be Lucy's type, but from where I stood, it sure looked like you are Lorelei's type."

"Excuse me?" I tilt my head at the woman, who only clicks her tongue. She drops her hand.

"Just a word of advice, son. Make sure you court the right twin." She hobbles off, and I'm left contemplating her cryptic words.

Hadley would have told me if Lorelei was a better fit, right? But she set me up with Lucy.

I have to trust her, and I have to trust my gut.

Lucy Spence felt like home in my arms, and regardless of Lorelei being her twin, there is no way she could replicate that feeling.

After Sunday School, which was a riveting discussion surrounding creationism and the fall of mankind, we are ushered into the small sanctuary. The moss green carpet matches the material on the pews perfectly, and though you can tell it's old, it's clean and inviting. Scanning the room of mostly elderly people with a handful of young adults, mostly Hadley and Braxton's crowd, I spot Lucy and Lorelei sitting next to their grandmother. The twins notice me and begin fidgeting in a similar way until Mrs. Netty whacks Lucy's leg with her Bible and motions for Lorelei to scoot down. They exhale dramatically, again, at the same time, but do as they are instructed.

The entire time, I haven't moved from my post leaning against the corner wall where I now appreciate the womens' similarities while amusement at their close relationship with their grandmother plays at the edges of my thoughts.

Plucking myself from my wallflower position as Mason passes by, I follow him across the front and then down the aisle a few rows until I arrive at the row with my Lucy. Mason slides into the row behind me where Karoline, Hadley, and Braxton sit. Behind them is Braxton's brother-in-law, Michael, and his wife, Brandi, whom I've gotten to know briefly while they work on Mason's house. I wave hello to everyone, specifically to Braxton, Hadley, Michael, and Brandi, who must have just come for the service this morning, and then I sit in the empty spot between the twins.

"How was your class?" I ask Lucy. When she doesn't immediately answer, but instead looks past me to her sister, I add, "We discussed how creationism can be proven scientifically and from a Biblical perspective due to the fact that the earth can't possibly be millions of years old because, if you're a Christian and believe scripture, then an old earth wouldn't be comprehensible. Sin would have had to enter the earth *before* the fall in order for us to have the evidence of disease from fossils that we have. That moves the timeline of creation up by millions of years."

By the end of my statement, I have gathered Lucy's complete attention. That spark of knowledge pursuit gleams in her hazel-blue eyes. "Fascinating," she comments. "I would like to explore that more. I've never thought of creationism from that perspective. We discussed how to use our emotions for the glory of Christ, but if I'm being honest, I don't know what emotions I'm experiencing half the time. I should have gone into your class today." She chuckles, and I smile, but on the inside, I'm realizing Lucy is more black and white than I once thought. I caught the feeling on our date, but with her outwardly saying that, it makes sense.

"That's why you journal and write so much, right, Lucy?" Her twin asks, looking around me. Lucy grimaces for a fraction of second then adheres a plastic smile to her face. She nods swiftly in agreement before looking away from both of us and focusing on the front of the room where Pastor Rawls approaches the small wooden podium with a cross etched into the front of it.

Is she embarrassed or ashamed that she's not that in touch with her emotions? It's perfectly normal. Not every human can be an overly anxious, sensitive worry wart like I am. In fact, I don't want her to be that way. We would be a disaster. I've dated that type before; we do not blend well despite what people would assume.

I lean over to whisper in Lucy's ear just as the pastor begins to welcome everyone. "I think you're quite perfect. Emotions suck, anyway."

The smile on her face pulls higher for a millisecond before she trains it back to plastic. I take it as a win and open my palm towards her. She cocks her head, and I raise an eyebrow.

It's yours if you want it, baby girl.

As my fingers intertwine with hers and the world explodes with new vibrant colors around me, her sister clears her throat. Lucy rips her hand from mine and folds hers together on top of her crossed legs.

Maybe there is a no-hand holding rule I'm unaware of?

Either way, my skin immediately misses the soft feel of hers.

And I kind of want to elbow her sister who seems to keep interrupting every potential good moment I have with Lucy.

After the end of the service, one where I honestly gave it my all to focus on Pastor Rawls but ended up too consumed by the static electricity between me and Lucy, I ask, "Let me take you out to lunch." I'm leaning against my car, trying to conjure all the charm that has worked countless times before in order to persuade Lucy to hop in my vehicle and go to lunch with me. She's been insistent that she can't, though her sister keeps saying otherwise. The warm, sticky air sits heavy around us as clouds begin to block out the sun.

"I have lunch scheduled with my sister and Grandma Netty. I can't cancel at the last minute."

"Sure ya can, *Lucy*," Mrs. Netty appears behind me. I gesture in the elderly woman's direction.

"See. You have permission."

"Yeah, *Lucy*. We will be fine to have lunch on our own. Go!" Lorelei bumps her hip against her sister, and I'm reminded of Lucy's behavior from the wedding. That is how she acted—girly, extroverted, and flirty. What happened between then and now that Lorelei seems to have adopted Lucy's behavior while Lucy has... matured?

No, that's not the right word for it. It's not that Lucy's behavior at the wedding was immature; it was flowery. Energetic and flirty. Whereas now she's demure, though when you nudge her to talk about her passions—plants, law, history, cats, random facts—she's as lively and animated as can be.

Whatever happened, I like it. I like this refined, intelligent side of her. Though I do miss the flirty banter. Regardless, she will fit in perfectly with my family. I don't *need* my family to approve, but it would make things much easier if they did. Especially Mamma.

Remember you have less than three months left, Finley.

Right.

"The people have spoken. You're mine for the afternoon." I grin devilishly, rubbing my hands together. Her cheeks and nose pinken.

"Fine," she bites, and the victory I was lavishing in vanishes.

"Unless you truly don't want to." My pride hurts even saying those words, but I don't want to force her.

Lorelei grabs her arm and yanks her close, whispering something in her ear. Beside me, Mrs. Netty snorts. Thunder echoes from a distance. Whereas I wanted to scold Lorelei for interrupting my attempts at physical contact earlier, now I want to kiss her cheek in gratitude for prompting Lucy to go on this impromptu date with me.

"I truly want to go," Lucy says after a moment. "Take me away, *Your Highness.*" And then *she* smirks, sweeping into a curtsey.

My heart hammers against my chest. "I, uh... You don't have to call me that." I can't tell her because I'm not a prince. That's an outright lie. I promised I wouldn't outright lie about who I am, but I did lie by omission because I have to protect myself and the crown.

A smug, angry look flicks across her face. "Don't I?"

"Lucy!" her sister snaps. Mrs. Netty snorts again, followed by a boisterous laugh.

Lucy ignores them both and walks around to the passenger side. Breaking free of my stupor, I rush around to open her door. She stands with her arms crossed, waiting. At least she let me exercise chivalry this time.

"Much obliged, *Your Highness*," she snarks, dipping into another curtsey before getting into the car and yanking the door closed, my body becoming one with the car door.

But don't mind my chest flat against the window. Something else is much more concerning. I glance over the top of my car at her sister.

One glance at Lorelei's horrified expression tells me everything I need to know. "She knows."

Lorelei nods her head, her bangs blowing gently in the light breeze revealing sympathy in her one good eye.

A Korsan curse slips through my lips.

CHAPTER FIVE

LORELEI

I'm done with the lies.

At least the ones I *can* be done with. I won't rat my sister out because it isn't her fault he showed up in my safe space and went in for a hug. It *is* her fault, however, for shoving me into his arms then shipping me off onto yet another date I don't belong on with *Prince* Finley Andersson. Like I'm a puppet on her crazy strings. But I will have that conversation with her later and tell her I'm finished with the switch and help her make a plan to be truthful with him.

Finley isn't family, though, and I have zero qualms about untangling his little web of lies. If he really wants *Lucy,* then he will have to be honest with her. The same way I'm going to make her be honest with him.

"Where would you like to go for lunch?" Finley's voice is scratchy and nervous; his long fingers are paler than usual as they clutch his steering wheel. I look longingly back out the window as we merge onto the highway.

"Books and Beans," I reply. At least he has the decency to ask where I wanted to go since he practically kidnapped me this afternoon.

Okay, I know that's not true, but I'm a little frustrated at the moment. I wanted to spend my afternoon with a murder mystery, tea, and Frizzle while Grandma Netty and Lucy gossiped about the town's latest happenings.

If we go to Books and Beans, I can sip tea. Salvage a fragment of this day.

He doesn't respond, so I sneak another glance. He keeps side-eyeing me, our glances awkwardly catching.

I sigh. "What? Is that not acceptable for you?"

"No, it's—" he clears his throat. "What I mean to say is yes, it's very acceptable, and two, I've never had a woman actually tell me where she would like to go. You are something else, Lucy."

I cringe at his use of my sister's name. I want to shout, "I am not Lucy! I am Lorelei! Free me from this madness!"

But instead, I flip the script. "Just checking, *Your Highness*."

His grip on the wheel is further secured as he presses his lips into a tight line. I celebrate my small victory with a suppressed smile and the crossing of my arms.

It feels *good* to allow myself to be frustrated without making excuses for someone... and to show it for once. A lot better than bottling it in and shoving it down to keep the peace. Hopefully I'll get it all out before confronting Lucy (whom I find it hard to be mad at because she's such a sensitive soul) and Finley will assume it's because he didn't tell me about his status. Then in a few days,

Lucy can reach out and apologize for overreacting and they can be on their merry way.

Happily ever afters and all that romantic mumbo jumbo.

"I guess you want to talk about it now," Finley says, though it sounds more like a question.

Not really. I just want to go home and let you have this conversation with my sister. "It would be better to talk in a private vehicle than in a coffee shop where ears can overhear." *Duh.*

"Right." Silence envelops us, only the quiet rumble of the engine and tires on asphalt. I angle myself towards him as much as I can while buckled in.

"So start talking, *His Royal Highness,* Prince Finley Andersson of Korsa." I can't even attempt to hide the contempt in my voice. Not because he's a prince or that he withheld the information, but because I. Am. Not. Lucy. My emotions are becoming a cloudy haze that's getting harder to wade through. The switch labeled "functioning human" is in mid-flick. So much for becoming unstuck. The messy situation has been like quicksand to my sanity.

He inhales, and I swear I can see a glisten of sweat coating his forehead. Then again, he has unnaturally great skin. Lucy's probably jealous of his fair, glassy complexion.

"My name is Finley Folke Andersson, and I am the second-born son to King Erik and Queen Sylvia Andersson, the ruling monarchs of Korsa."

Tell me something I don't know...

"And what is a prince doing galavanting around Juniper Grove, Mississippi, anyway?"

Hadley said because he wanted to carve his own path and life. He also said he was interested in Lucy when she told him about her before he moved down here.

"Please do not panic, and please do not presume that I'm asking your hand in marriage," he begins, and my breath hitches. He doesn't give me time to react. "While I'm the second-born, my brother Johan, the crown prince, is sick, and he will formally abdicate his position in three months, which means I will become the crown prince of Korsa."

I don't realize we have parked in front of the coffee shop, but Finley doesn't turn the car off. He does, however, unbuckle his seatbelt and pivot, pegging me with intense, pleading blue eyes. I'm still stuck on *crown prince.* Chills run down my spine as a wave of lightheadedness washes over me.

Lucy! Dang it.

The knot in his throat bobs up and down. "Furthermore, my father's reign will come to an end in less than a year. I was home celebrating his fifty-ninth birthday, which was the day before I left to come back here over a week ago. Our Laws of Succession state the monarch must retire from his position on his sixtieth birthday."

What does this have to do with marriage? And again, why is a crown prince, who will be a *king* in less than a year, wasting time in Mississippi?

My stomach continues to rumble like tea coming to a boil, and now I think I'm the one sweating. He opens his mouth, but I interrupt. I need him to get to the point. "I don't understand why you're here trying to date my—er, me, when you are about to become king."

Shifting eyes and nervous swallows churn my stomach like thick butter. He closes his eyes, his shoulders rise and fall. Then the future king fixes me with a crystal blue stare as if he is analyzing my soul. "I cannot take the throne as a single man. The Laws of Succession state the ascending monarch must be married."

"You want to marry my—" I cut myself off before I finish the sentence.

His brows furrow, but then his expression smooths. "Remember what I said at the beginning: I am not asking for your hand in marriage, Lucy. I am, however, asking to date you for the next three months because I think I *could* ask you to marry me."

My stomach lurches. "I'm going to vomit."

I fight to unbuckle my seatbelt, swinging open the car door and stumbling out of the low-riding vehicle. I hightail it into the coffee shop, barely making it into the restroom before tossing my breakfast protein shake into the sink.

A few minutes later, I rinse the sink and use the disinfectant stashed in the cabinet under the sink to clean. There is absolutely no sense in making an employee clean after me because I can't stomach the news that a crown prince and future king potentially wants to ask for my sister's hand in marriage... and he thinks I'm her!

And I've done an atrocious job at impersonating Lucy...

The thought sends another wave of nausea rolling through me, but I swallow it down this time. Pressing my hands flat against the counter, I stare at my reflection in the mirror. My hair is frizzing around the edges due to the sheen of sweat coating my face, my typically pale complexion an extra shade of ghost with splatters of freckles. I look like I've been through the ringer, but I guess that's what holding onto lies does to a person. Lucy WILL come clean this week.

"But for now," I scold my reflection, "you will go back out there and will be the best version of your sister that you can possibly be." *Because if Finley truly thinks he wants to ask for her hand, who am I to take that dream from her?*

She's going to flip out when I tell her...

Smoothing down my hair, tightening my ponytail, and rinsing my mouth out, I scan the restroom one last time to make sure it's adequately cleaned then contort my features to resemble what I believe would be my sister's shocked yet sorrowful expression. Unintentionally masking those around me has always been a speciality of mine. Time to really put it to use and be intentional. Very, very intentional.

When I open the door, Finley is standing a few feet away with an astute posture, his feet shoulder length apart, stable, and his hands clasped in front of him. His shaggy blond hair falls in front of his face, making him look like the rogue prince that's captured headline after headline.

Right.

I should talk to him about that. Lucy may not mind, but I do. And now I am on a mission: Make Sure This Man Will Thoroughly Love and Adore My Sister.

It's a working title. I should leave the titling of things to Lucy May, the romance writer.

"I didn't think the thought of a future marriage with me would be *that* revolting to you." His voice quivers, causing him to sound genuinely hurt. Maybe he's standing so confidently to mask it?

"No—it's not revolting. Just... unexpected," I say through a small smile, trying to keep my hand on the string in my brain that is labeled "Lucy."

He physically relaxes, his shoulders dropping a notch and his hands unclasping, falling to his side. "You spew history facts in uncomfortable situations and you vomit when taken by surprise." He laughs. *Laughs!* "Noted."

Lucy would never... "No, that was a one-off thing. A rather big surprise, wouldn't you agree?" I attempt another soft smile, but I think it comes off more like a grimace because Finley's thin lips turn downward.

"You're right," he says simply. He fixes a smile on his face. "Can I treat you to tea and something to settle your stomach?" He holds out a hand, and I know that if I take it at this moment, it means I am solidifying Lucy's intentions to allow him to date her.

I still have many questions, especially regarding his dating history. But I do trust Hadley, and I don't believe she would try to drive my sister into the arms of a man who would hurt her.

I slip my hand into Finley's warm one, our fingers interlacing. A perfect fit, as Lucy's hands will be. Other than the hot, star-exploding heat burning my hand, a new feeling stirs in my stomach, something I've never felt before.

Probably a queasy remnant from earlier. No big deal. A cup of tea and a sandwich will help it pass.

We make our way to the counter to order, and I silently panic when I notice Emma Jane's bright ash-white hair from behind as she fulfills the order before us. *Shoot.* I tuck myself behind Finley, still clutching his hand, in the hopes that she won't—

"Oh, hey, Lorelei! Who is this?" Her voice is one of shock. Rightfully so because I have never brought a man here. I've never brought a man *anywhere.*

I cough, wishing I could disappear. *Lucy Spence... You owe me so much.*

I peek my head out from behind Finley's shoulder. I'm just short enough that I actually look around his shoulder instead of over it. Or maybe he's just that tall...

"Not Lorelei. Lucy," I gently correct.

Emma Jane's perplexed expression has me doubling down. I try to mask my mellow voice into something more bubbly. I tilt my head and grin. "This is my... *friend.* Finley." Would Lucy have called him a friend? Would she have said date? Boyfriend?

She totally would have.

Finley's grip tightens as I attempt to pull away.

The younger barista, who graduates from Juniper Grove University this May, has always been perceptive. Lucy and I frequent this place enough that she would of course be able to tell us apart at a glance. It doesn't help that Lucy has bangs now while I don't. *Why in the world did I decide to come here of all places?*

"I am Lucy's *boyfriend,*" Finley boldly states. *We haven't defined anything, Finley Andersson! Plus you're stating your intentions with the wrong sister!*

"Hm, I could have sworn..." Emma Jane stops, a slow smile spreading across her face. Then... she winks at me. "My apologies, *Lucy*. You two just look so much alike."

Great. Just great. Now the barista is in on my lies. How much broader will I weave this web?

"No worries. Happens all the time," I say with a shrug, trying to be Lucy on the outside while inside I am two seconds away from splintering and breaking.

"What can I get for you two?" she asks, still eyeing my hand in Finley's.

We order, wait for our teas, and then Finley leads us to the dimmest corner of the room, which I'm thankful for because I'm scared my darkening whirlwind of emotions might break through my stoic expression.

The entire front side of the coffee-shop-slash-bookstore has floor-to-ceiling windows. Sunlight filters in without restraint on most days, but today, the clouds obscure the rays. Indoor strand lights are fixed to the ceiling, and there are lamps stationed throughout the shop. This is how they get around having those harsh ceiling lights, and it creates a calming vibe. It's why I come here often, though now, this safe space of mine is also tainted.

"It must be tiring, always getting mistaken for your twin," Finley states as he sips on the chai tea he ordered.

You have no idea how tiring it is... "We're used to it."

I close my eyes, bringing my mug to my nose, and inhale the lavender chamomile tea as if it will transport me away to my bed, tucking me into cozy blankets with an Agatha Christie book. But when I open my eyes, there's only a prince staring at me like I'm the most interesting woman on this planet. I tap my feet, grounding my thoughts with each miniscule movement.

"Excuse my forwardness, but Lucy, you are exquisite."

I clutch my plump, olive green mug, the heat burning my palms. I set it down, my hands reddened. Does my face match?

I've never been called exquisite before...

Lucy! My brain reminds me. *He's talking about Lucy. Isn't he?*

"Thank you," I whisper. And then an idea hits me, a way to figure out if he enjoys Lucy's look over mine. "I've been contemplating cutting my bangs like my sister. Do you think I should?"

Finley tilts his head, evaluating my face. My fire-hot face. The corners of his lips lift, then he stands; he's at my side in one step, his tall frame lingering over me. He kneels on one knee, and I think I might die of a stroke at twenty-five. *He said he wouldn't ask for marriage!*

"Finley, what are you—" but my words are cut short when his fingers pinch my hair tie and gently pull, careful to stop at snags and lightly tug, as if he's done this before. A wavy, frizzy mess of hair springs free from its constraint. He drops his hand and gazes up at me.

Instinctively I scrunch my fingers in my hair to fluff it out, though that's the last thing I need to do since it's already a captive of the humidity.

"While the bangs are cute, and they look nice on your sister, you should keep your hair just as it is. It's the perfect color." He slides his thumb and index finger over the ends of my hair, "The perfect texture." He stands but bends towards me, reaching out that very hand to cup my face.

Why am I not backing up? Why am I not slapping his hand away? Why do I feel like I might implode if he inches any closer?

Because I'm Lucy right now. Right.

"The perfect cut to frame your lovely face," he finishes. Though still a bent arms length away from me, his lips are way too close to mine, sending all the warning signals blaring in my mind.

Finley Andersson cannot be my first kiss. Even if by mistake.

I clear my throat and lean back. He takes the hint and straightens, smirking before returning to his chair across from me. "Don't get bangs, Lucy."

Not knowing what to do or say, I reach for my mug and scorch my tongue with hot liquid.

"Careful," Finley says, sipping his own tea with an amused expression.

At that time, Emma Jane brings our sandwiches out, placing the turkey BLT in front of me and the ham croissant in front of Finley. "Enjoy," she says with a wink, and the tone in her voice implies so much more.

I think.

To be honest, I don't know which way is up and which way is down right now. I feel out of control, and I want to go home. But I have to try and stick through this meal. For my sister. And then, I will spend the rest of the evening decompressing and blocking the chaotic world out. I've got to be focused at work tomorrow. For my clients.

"Would you mind if I prayed over this meal for us?" Finley offers his hand to me, but I don't think I can touch him anymore. It's getting to be too much.

"Yes," I answer, but I keep my hands in my lap under the table and bow my head. After a moment, Finley leads us in a simple prayer of gratitude for the food, the time together, and... *for me.* Finley thanks God for bringing me into his life...

When he says amen, I shove my sandwich into my mouth to keep from word vomiting that I am Lorelei Raine Spence, not Lucy. With every passing second, I feel sick to my stomach over these lies. I can't even bring myself to ask him about his past. Lucy will have to shoulder that herself. I just want to eat and go home and tell my twin that she needs to tough it up and tell this man the truth.

Because I can't touch him again. It's like touching the sun.

I can't continue hearing him praise me. Compliment me. Because I know I've done a horrible job at being my sister.

And for the love of all things, I can't have Finley falling for *me* instead of Lucy. The poor man probably thinks he found a woman who is somewhere between the two of us, and that's not who we are.

Lucy will make an excellent princess and queen. She will compliment Finley's flirty, outgoing personality and will elevate his liveliness. If Finley was with me, I would choke off his buoyant attitude with a thick rope of rigid structure. It would be a slow death for Finley Andersson.

"Is there anything you would like to know about life as a royal? I swear to be an open book for you, Lucy. I want you to continue to get to know me just as Finley, but I also promise to give you all the information you need, the good, bad, and ugly, to make an informed decision if we continue down this path."

I take a bite of my sandwich to give myself time to think. Lucy needs to have this conversation with him, not me. But I also have to be her right now. "Thank you, Finley. I appreciate your consideration and understanding. I think I am processing everything right now, but I promise I want to come back to this conversation in a few days on our next scheduled date."

Lucy informed me that their next date will be driving a few hours east to Alabama to tour Bellina Gardens. Not going to lie, I'm a bit jealous of that. Why couldn't that be the date I subbed in on? He apparently picked that date, though, because he remembered *my* love of flora from date one. More like an obsession, but love will suffice.

"I understand," Finley says. He takes a bite of his sandwich, and the rest of the meal progresses as we talk through various topics such as collectivism versus individualism (we both fall somewhere in between), constitutional monarchy versus rule by republic (we both agree that both types of government are effective; it simply depends on the size, population, and diverse nature of the country), and we even talk about our favorite philosophy books. It's an easy, stimulating conversation that reminds me of how smart and capable Finley is. He will make a great king.

And Lucy will look amazing by his side.

The rain begins to pour outside, and I swear a shadow darts past the window, but maybe it's only a passing cloud.

Finley's blond eyebrows knit together, then he says, "We should go."

CHAPTER SIX

FINLEY

"This is hopeless." I groan as I place the book I'm reading over my face to create the ambience I'm feeling: utter darkness. Mason isn't too impressed based on the way he throws an aztec-patterned pillow at me from across the room.

I confided in him about my situation, and he had a heyday making a mockery of my turmoil, much like I did when he confessed his situation with Karoline before they kissed and made up from years of hurt. *You get what you dish out,* he had said.

"What did you tell me back in January when I came to you for advice on how to get Karoline to talk to me?" Mason's tone is chastising like he's a condoning parent.

I sit up, the book falling from my face. "I've lived an entire life in the couple of months I was away. All I can remember these days is that I need to get married and I desperately only want to for love. Not because the crown demands it."

Mason makes a show of swooning, flinging his hand to his forehead and leaning back in the reclining chair. It tilts too far, and

Mason reaches for the ground with one arm and foot to prevent a crashing fall, pushing himself and the chair back upright. "Close one." He laughs through heavy breaths. Anders scoffs. I roll my eyes but grin. Thankfully, Gabriel is in the shower for this show of idiocrasy. Mason's great and has swiftly become a close friend, which I honestly don't have outside of my brother and sister, PPOs, and a few titled friends that I haven't been super close with since I became a globetrotter. I'm one of those people who gets along with everyone but only keep a few people close.

"Ahem." He clears his throat and settles back into the chair. "You told me to establish a friendship, back up my words with actions, and be patient. I know Karoline and I had history and you and Lor—sorry, I mean Lucy—don't." He glances away for a second before looking at me again and continuing. "But the rules still apply. Be patient with her. You just dumped a five-course meal onto her table. Let her pick and nibble and taste test until she's ready to commit to something."

I arch a brow. "Good. Yes, I should take my own advice. But Mason, should we eat dinner now?" As if right on cue, his stomach growls.

"Nah, sorry, man. I'm grabbing dinner with Karoline." He gets up and eyes Anders. "But you and Anders here can cozy up and make Gabriel whip up some French dish or something when he's fresh and clean from the shower."

"They're my PPOs, not my chefs."

"He's right, Your Highness. Gabriel *can* cook," Anders says.

"Your Highness." Mason laughs as he walks to his room. "Don't ever expect me to call you that. I'm too American."

"I would expect nothing less from you, redneck," I say just loud enough so he can hear me down the hall.

"I'll send you back to Korsa as a redneck. You can be their redneck king," Mason hollers.

"Am I stuck between a royal and a redneck?" I look at Anders for an answer, but he only shrugs. A hint of a smile glosses his lips, and there's my answer. I've been in the South too long. "Fancy that."

Mason leaves not long after, and Anders and I convince Gabriel to cook. After an admittedly delicious dinner (chicken alfredo for the win), I text Lucy.

> Thank you for lunch today. I had a wonderful time discussing philosophy with you. I'm honored to know a woman who can challenge me intellectually like you can.

Three dots appear. Then disappear. Then reappear again.

But a message never comes through.

Johan, however, calls.

"Hey, Fins. How is everything going?" he asks in Korsan. I switch back to my native tongue.

"I told her who I was and she threw up."

"*Attaans!* How was your delivery? Did you use your royal tone or were you just Finley?"

Recalling that moment in the car, I definitely slipped into using my state official tone. "I was nervous! I'm into this woman, Jojo."

"You've dated so many women. How is she different? What makes her special?"

I lie in bed, images of Lucy's beautiful face, intelligent eyes, and kind gestures filling my vision. "She's smart, Jojo. *Really* smart. She may know more than I do. And she's intentional and kind to and with those around her. You should have seen how she treated the wait staff on our first date. At church, she flitted around the room, making everyone feel seen and heard. Well, except me. It took her a minute to notice I was there. She's beautiful, of course. Put together, clean, professional. Jojo... I can already tell she'd make an amazing queen."

Johan breathes heavily through the phone. "Ah, Fins. You sound like you are in love."

My heart quickens though rational thought rebukes his statement. "*Pft.* I can't be in love. I've only known her for two days. The wedding back in December doesn't count. Whoever that version of her was, she's long gone. People don't fall in love over a weekend."

"Don't they?" Johan asks, and I can hear the wonder in his tone. Because that's exactly what happened when he met his wife, Marie. It was instant love and connection between the two of them, and it's only grown more fortified over their seven years together.

Could that be Lucy and me seven years down the road...?

No. She obviously isn't smitten like I am. Most women would be excited for an impromptu date if they liked a man.

"No, they don't. You and Marie are a rare story."

There is a crash on the other end of the line. "Johan! Is everything okay?"

A second passes before he answers. "Yes, sorry. A tremor got the best of me and I dropped the phone."

My heart sinks. "Is it becoming more frequent?"

"No. Just at random. It's the fatigue getting to me most days." He laughs mirthlessly. "Who would have thought a man could be diagnosed with Parkinson's disease at thirty-two?"

"Not me. But it's okay. You will have the best care in the world. I will make sure of it."

Johan sighs. "I'm so sorry you're being thrust into my role, Finley. I know you didn't want it. And I want to reiterate what I said when you were home last week: I am with *you* every step of the way. We will share duties for as long as I can."

As long as he can... Because there will come a day when he can no longer function without assistance. I try hard to believe that God has a reason for everything, but sometimes it's hard to remember that when life-altering news knocks on your door and uproots your known, thriving life. My brother has Parkinson's, and I will be King of Korsa in a year.

We chat for a little longer about the brief stalker encounter before Marie calls him off for lunch. (I momentarily forgot about the time difference.) Once I'm off the phone, my thoughts instantly drift back to Lucy. She still hasn't messaged back.

To distract myself, I grab my laptop and respond to correspondences with different ministries within our *Riiksdaag*. I pour over financial reports. Around midnight, Mason comes home, but I stay tucked in my room and continue analyzing different laws up for vote.

That's also the time my phone lights up with a message from Lucy. Grabbing the phone at warp speed, I also end up hoisting the forest green blanket on the bed to my face. When I drop the blanket, I accidentally drop the phone. I scramble again, finally securing just the phone in my hand, huffing a breath through my nose over my unreasonable reaction to a little text.

> Sorry it took me so long to respond. I was writing. I look forward to the Gardens with you on Thursday. And just so you're aware… I cut my bangs. I hope you'll like them even though you said I shouldn't.

I can hear the sadness in her text. At least, I perceive and read it in a crestfallen tone in my head, and that's when I realize a huge error on my end.

Never tell a woman what she should do with her hair.

I wanted to flirt. To touch her. To run my hands through her hair. She looks more sophisticated without bangs, and I wanted her to be confident in her smart appearance.

Talk about a backfire...

I do the only thing I can and quickly fire off a message saying that she's pretty regardless of her hairstyle and that I'm sure I'll love it. She doesn't respond, and I eventually drift off to sleep thinking about how big of a bugger I am.

Lucy's Journal

Sunday, March 14th * 10:01pm * Criss-cross applesauce on my bed with my facemask on

This is NOT GOOD. Lor came home in a fit because she's stressed over the lies. In typical Lorelei fashion, she presented her frustrations directly and without much emotion, but I could tell it's eating her on the inside. I promised I would clear everything up on my date with Finley in four days, and that seemed to help her focus enough to relay the details of the impromptu date. And man... I wish she hadn't. For starters, Finley is the CROWN PRINCE of Korsa now. He will be KING in less than a year. The kicker? He has to be MARRIED to be king. I love fairytales, but this feels too unbelievable. It's one thing to dream about being a princess and a queen, but it's another thing to have that opportunity presented in front of you through a handsome, royal, golden platter such as Finley himself. Queen Lucy... I can't wrap my brain around it for some reason. A prince wants to marry <u>me.</u>

Well, I think it's me he wants to marry. According to the other things Lor told me, and the text I received from Finley stating he loved talking philosophy with me, he might want to marry my sister right now. And I'd be lying if I said I was okay with that. It's my fault, ultimately, because I sent her in my place not once but twice. But everything will be fine! I'll go on my first date with him Thursday evening, be my charming self, and everything will be fine. Just fine! Can you imagine? Me? In a palace? With an actual title... whoa. That's a lot to take in. It's the kind of fantastical madness I write about. Speaking of, I should get back to my merman prince x female pirate story...

Chapter Seven

Lorelei

"It's nice to finally meet you, Lorelei." *Finley is standing underneath an arch of chrysanthemums; it's a collage of color and warmth as the sun shines like a beaming spotlight on the crown prince. He wears an all-white tux, his blond hair shimmering like a crown of gold.*

It's then I realize I'm walking closer without thought, as if he's holding a string connected to me and is reeling me into him. Step by step, his eyes come into view. His beautiful, sparkling, ice blue eyes that I'd love to take a dive in on a hot summer day.

I drop my head, his eyes too intense to stare into. Suddenly, our toes have infinitesimal space between them. Slowly, I raise my head until I'm tilting my chin up to reacquaint myself with Finley's eyes. But instead of landing on his eyes, my gaze locks with his lips. They are light pink, his upper lip a smidge thinner than his bottom.

He parts those precious lips and sighs, leaning down.

I close my eyes...

My eyes fly open, and I gasp for breath. My heart is pounding like a jackhammer in my chest. Hard enough to break my rib cage.

Probably. *I think.*

Frantically examining my surroundings, I find myself in my bed, tangled in my beige sheets and coffee-colored quilt, in a darkened room with a hint of sunlight peeking through my blinds.

No Finley Andersson in a tux standing under my favorite flowers about to...

Did I just vividly dream about kissing Finley?

Weird.

Well, that's something I will *never* tell my sister about. I must have dreamt that because of his coquettish behavior four days ago at Books and Beans.

I shake my head clear and glance at the analog clock sitting on my nightstand. 5:29 a.m. in sage green coloring.

Beep. Beep. Beep.

5:30 a.m.

With a yawn and stretch, I untangle myself, switch on my salt lamp light, and roll out of bed. After brushing my teeth, I struggle to put on my black workout leggings, as always. Then I wrestle a bear in order to get my extra-support sports bra on. I should really invest in one of those front-zip styles. After sliding on my socks, I do deep lunges towards the kitchen and grab my water bottle from the fridge. At the door, I tie my Brooks tightly to my feet and quietly slip out of the apartment to embark on my morning jog.

The air has a crisp bite to it, but by noon, it'll be warm enough to go for a swim if I wanted to. This is my favorite time of the day; it provides ample time to set my mind on things above and get my body moving, and I love the way the sun rises, kissing my skin good morning with its warmth.

Almost like how Finley kissed you in your dream...

I stop abruptly, my face heating to a degree that's probably hotter than the sun at the moment. Why am I giving any thought to a dream? A dream is simply an involuntary adhesion of real life and fantasy, a mixture of images, sounds, feelings, and perceptions experienced throughout the day.

I set my water bottle down on the trunk of my car so my hands are free for an effective workout. I begin my jog down my usual route, shoving the graphic image of Finley's lips advancing towards mine off a cliff to die. Regardless of if I wanted to, which I don't, I can't entertain such an outlandish notion. He belongs to Lucy, as it should be. A dream is nothing to get bent out of shape and blush in solitude over.

I round the corner of Maple Street, jogging by a long line of suburban houses that are similar yet unique. Some are bricked in various reds while others are a mixture of composite siding and stone veneer. One day. I will own a house here, settle down with my plants and cats, and possibly a nice man with a stable job who treats me well. I think I'll fall in love one day, but I don't like the idea of falling; that is more terrifying than when I thought I failed the LSAT because I read the email wrong. I want to float into love, to drift into it bit by bit. Conversation by conversation. Day by day. With surety, peace, and confidence.

Sweat builds on my forehead, and I wipe it with the back of my hand as I begin the jaunt back home. My runs aren't miles and minutes long. It's a quick fifteen-minute mile jog around the area simply to wake me up and get my blood flowing. I'll stretch when I get home, blend a breakfast protein smoothie, then get ready to be at the office at eight.

This is the life I live; it's simplistic, scheduled, and beautiful. And I'm finally basking in getting back to normalcy after a weekend of deceit, too many touches from the male species, and barely staying afloat outside my comfort zone.

"I've changed my ways, Attorney Spence. Do you think the judge will see that? Do you think I will get my babies back? Not having them home for Christmas was the darkest moment of my existence, and you know better than anyone at this point that I've had some pretty dark lows..." Ms. Gretta Hanes continues sobbing into the wad of tissues she's consistently pulled from the beige box situated on the corner of my desk. The image of her sunken, dark eyes and puffy nose tug at my heartstrings. I wish I could give her all the answers, but that's one rule I can't break. I can't promise a client something that may not happen.

"I hear you, Ms. Gretta." I stand and walk around my desk, sitting next to her in the empty chair. I've learned she calms with physical touch, so I take her hands between mine, forcing myself to ignore the bugs crawling under my skin, and look her in the eyes. "You know I can't promise you results because I am not the judge. But I can promise you that I am doing everything I possibly can to present the best case for you. I do know you've changed, and I do know that you will mother your three children well and with your whole heart. You do not have to convince me, Ms. Gretta. I see your goodness."

She wails again, yanking her hands from mine and slinging her arms around me in a wet, very personal embrace. Her faded pink hair invades my space, tickling my nose. I let her cry on my shoulder, patting her back gently, trying not to think about the way her touch sends signals in my brain to flee for safety.

But my client comes first, and I know she needs this.

Several moments tick by, my insides crawling and itching to have my big, beautiful bubble of personal space back.

I clear my throat and begin to break the hug once I can no longer mentally withstand the sensations invading me. "Let's go over your personal statement one more time, okay? Then you can leave the rest of the evidence gathering up to me. We have two weeks before the ruling, so let's get to work."

Ms. Gretta remains in my office for another hour and a half as we work on her testimonial for reunification. This case has stolen my time and attention, taking precedence over others. While we process and litigate many family disputes, a myriad of situations tearing families apart, it's unfortunately rare that we get to work on a case to bring a family back together. CPS makes it nearly impossible for the birth parents at times, even when they've shown over a year of hard-fought change.

As a girl who grew up with two loving parents, I've never known the pain of separation. But I watched Hadley suffer at the hands of her mother who was drunk and on drugs for most of her life.

Thankfully, Hadley was able to grow up under the care of her grandmother, but not all kids are that lucky. Hadley's mom is sober and clean, and their constant work towards reconciliation is heart-warming to watch.

I want the same for Ms. Gretta and her children. Every child deserves a mom who loves and cares for them. Even if the mother shows up late to the job. Even if the father isn't in the picture.

Which reminds me...

I should call my mom. She and Dad have been traveling around the United States over the past six months. They both can work from anywhere as Dad is a freelance writer and Mama is in marketing. They finally decided to make the most of that.

She picks up on the first ring. "Hey, Mom. How is the Grand Canyon?"

"Hot." She laughs, already transitioning the phone call to a video call. Her smooth, tanned face and large brown eyes fill the screen, and then behind her, Dad's freckled, pale skin and red, curly hair come into view. He smiles broadly and waves, his hazel eyes narrowed as sunlight pours directly over him. It's not rocket science to figure out who Lucy and I take after the most.

"I might finally tan like your mother in this sun," Dad says, wrapping his arm around her and gazing adoringly at his wife. My stomach flutters; I've always loved watching the two of them interact. There is a depth of love and understanding and respect for each other that I rarely see in couples. I'm holding out for that.

Mom playfully hip checks him. "Oh, Richard. You'd turn into a lobster. Which reminds me, we should apply more sunscreen."

I pipe up. "Make sure you are using all natural sunscreen if you have to use it. Dad, it's better for your skin just to wear light, linen layers."

"You got it, beautiful." My dad has never been one to shy away from showering the three women in his life with praise and compliments.

"How's work going, sweetie? Any big plans for the upcoming weekend?" Mom busies herself by applying sunscreen to Dad's face and exposed neck.

"Work is going well. I have a client that I'm growing a bit attached to, but I think it will help me work hard for her." I glance at the stack of papers I need to sort through. "As for weekend plans, I think I'm going to catch up with filing."

Mom frowns as she caps the sunscreen. "No fun plans?"

"You know me, Mom. Work is fun."

Dad takes the phone from the stand Mom had propped it on. "But there's so much more to life than your career, Lorelei. Don't forget to be *you*, not just Attorney Spence."

"Well, I—" I snap my mouth closed, realizing I was about to tell my parents that I went on not one but two dates this past weekend. But I don't think Lucy has told them about Finley, and once again, I have a secret that's not quite mine to tell.

"What, honey?" Dad asks.

"Nothing. Lucy has a date tonight, so I'll watch a documentary or something."

"Well," Dad says, and then Mom grabs the phone.

"We know you love those, so do that! Just don't touch work tonight while you watch the show. Take a break, sweetie."

I grin at my doting, child-like parents. They amaze me with their bubbly attitude (which Lucy totally inherited. I'm more like Dad's mom, Grandma Netty.) I know they love me and are looking out for me, so I vow to myself that I *will* watch a documentary tonight while I have the apartment to myself.

We chat for a moment longer before hanging up so that they can call Lucy and question her over not telling them about her date. (Yes, we tell our parents everything.)

Oops. Sorry, my little by-a-minute sister. I grin to myself, thinking this feels like slight payback for everything she's put me through.

I submerge myself back into work while checking out the streaming platforms for a good documentary to watch tonight. What am I in the mood for…?

"Ted Bundy? That's what you want to watch while you're all alone? Jeez, Lor. I sometimes wonder how we are twins."

I roll my eyes. *Me too, Lucy. Me too.*

"How do I look?"

My sister spins, her pastel yellow sundress billowing around her. She's tamed her natural curls, and they cascade in waves over her shoulders. Her straight bangs add just the right amount of girlish flare, perfectly suiting her personality. Her bruise is light enough to effectively cover with makeup.

I smile thinking about how she's kind of like the female version of Finley. "He's going to love the real you."

Her shoulders droop. "Do you really think so? Because from what I've heard so far, it seems like he likes the real *you*, Lor."

Something stirs in my stomach at her words, but I dismiss the uncomfortable feeling. Instead, I stand and give my sister a hug that she looks like she's in need of. Lucy is the one person I can freely hug without getting the *icks*. I even feel icky sometimes hugging Mom and Dad and Hadley.

Though when Finley hugged you at church, you sank into his arms, my brain decides to vividly remind me as I wrap Lucy in my arms.

But that was because I had to pretend to be my sister, I argue back like a deranged lunatic.

"Sure, he likes some things about me. But that's not going to hold a candle to what he will discover about you tonight."

Lucy relaxes a little, but she pulls away. "Will you go over everything y'all have talked about with me one more time? I need to know a little more regarding the philosophical and historical talk. Also, do you think I should dress a little more like you?"

I sigh, not wanting to rehash everything I've tried hard to distract myself from. But my sister needs this, and I want her to have the best date in the world with Finley tonight. That way, when she comes home tonight, all smiles and high on insta-love, I can officially discard Finley Andersson from my head the same way I toss out a rot-rooted plant.

That man has been taking up way too much space lately.

"You don't need to look like me. Remember? I went on that first date dressed like *you.*"

"True," she says. "But I still need to go over everything again. Make me book-smart like you." She beams, a little life flowing back into her energy.

"Sit," I tell her, pointing to the couch before I walk to my room to grab a book, preparing to give the highlights of this classical work to Lucy.

Once I return and sit next to her, I crack open the book and begin. "This is my favorite book. It's called *Common Sense* by Thomas Paine. Paine was a Founding Father and a revolutionary. He wrote this book in 1776, and it speaks to the need for independence from Britain. But the deeper meaning..." I trail off as Lucy's eyes glaze over.

Snapping in front of her face, she startles and focuses back on me. "Sorry," she says sheepishly. "Please continue."

I do, and as I inform her of the ideological gem that is *Common Sense,* she nods her head and asks questions, very much proving my sister *is* smart. She would just rather gain knowledge of other things and apply it in different manners than I do. She'd rather read *Pride and Prejudice* whereas I prefer books like the one I'm discussing. She wants to learn how to craft worlds and characters and explore the nuances between emotions and reason whereas I'd rather learn historical facts. Both are valuable skills, one not to be honored higher than the other.

A knock at the door rips us from our talk, which has turned more into a delightful and informative conversation. We both shoot to our feet, and my heart does a strange stutter like it can't determine if it wants to stop completely or flutter away.

"He's here!" Lucy squeaks.

"Might I recommend not squeaking or squealing tonight? Remember who you are and remember who he is. He's a crown prince, Lucy. He's looking for a queen."

"Right," she says, smoothing her dress down and fluffing out her hair. "I can do this."

"That's the spirit, Your Highness." I curtsey to her, winning a giggle out of her nervous expression.

The knock comes again.

I shove Lucy forward as I linger on the opposite end of the living room near the kitchen. She takes a breath and flicks an anxious glance back at me one last time. I give her two thumbs up and motion for her to open the door. She slowly relents, and then Finley stands in the doorway looking like someone who truly did step out of the royal world. He wears a navy blue tux that is perfectly tailored to his slim but fit body. His usually shaggy blond hair is styled back, creating a refined air around the crown prince. In his hands, he holds a bouquet of red, yellow, and white chrysanthemums.

"I love the bangs, Lucy. I'm glad you made that decision. You are," he leisurely peruses her, and that knotting feeling is back in my gut, "absolutely stunning. These are for you."

She receives the flowers with one hand while placing the other on his forearm. He beams at the contact like he's a golden retriever puppy who's just been told "good boy."

"Thank you, Finley. You look beyond handsome."

He quirks his head to the side, but then he seems to let whatever it was go.

"Here, Lor. Will you put these in the vase on the kitchen table?"

Finley's eyes follow Lucy's stare and land on me like lightning striking a metal rod in the sand. Even from across the well-lit room, I see something flash across his eyes. He shakes his head as if to shake off a thought.

On unsteady legs, I close the distance between me and the couple. "Hi, Finley. It's good to see you again." Even my voice is trembling. What is wrong with me? Am I getting sick?

"You as well, Lorelei. What are your plans while I whisk your sister away?"

I'm stuck on the way he says my name to my face, addressing me for who I am for the first time. It does something funny to my brain.

"Er, thank you," I say without thinking.

"Thank you?"

Wait. What did he say?

Lucy nudges me, and I snap out of whatever the mess that was.

"She's going to watch a documentary on Ted Bundy," Lucy answers what must have been a question Finley asked.

He nods with a smile, those twinkling blue eyes focusing on me. "Fascinating. American serial killers are a different breed. I should introduce you to a few that we've had in Korsa."

I choke.

"Not in person!" he corrects himself, though that's not what I thought he meant. I'm just over here dying under his intense eyes and the offer to discover new serial killers to dissect their brains. "Just the records and how we dealt out justice through our system."

"Our system is messed up. We could probably learn from your process. Do you realize how many innocents we have jailed over the years? It's been—"

Lucy clears her throat, interrupting me.

"Right," I say, flicking my eyes between the two of them. Finley looks engrossed and slightly perplexed while Lucy is frowning. Is it me or is it getting too warm in here? "Well, you two should probably be on your way!"

"Yes, let's get going," she chimes in, her gaze shifting between me and Finley, who still hasn't taken his eyes off me.

Finley takes my hand and applies a gentle kiss to my knuckles as I stand there like an ice sculpture teetering on the edge of melting under the presence of a burning star.

"A pleasure, Lorelei. Thanks for entrusting me with your lovely twin."

"Mhmm," is all I manage to get out before finally gaining mobility and ripping my hand out from his. Not because of an ick, but because of the lack thereof.

Lucy guides Finley out the door, taking one last look at me. She smiles, but it doesn't reach her eyes.

The door clicks shut, and their footsteps rescind down the stairs.

My head spins, my heart races, and judging by the sudden spike of heat in my body, I think I have a fever.

I've got to stay far away from Finley Andersson.

That man is carrying some sort of eternal sickness, and he's spreading it to me every time I'm in his presence.

CHAPTER EIGHT

FINLEY

Lucy Spence is acting strange tonight.

She looks the same, despite the bangs, which are admittedly cute. Though I do miss that certain sophistication she had without them. Her sister looked more like the Lucy I knew with pinned-back bangs that I can only surmise weren't styled tonight like last time.

I glance at the pretty woman beside me in the passenger seat, who is elbows deep in her big, white purse that looks more like a carry-on bag one might bring on a plane.

She notices my stare, peeks up at me through a cascade of strawberry blonde hair, smiles gently, and says, "One second. It's in here somewhere."

"Take your time." We are parked in the lot of Bellina Gardens, and Lucy is on the hunt for her lipstick. I don't have an issue waiting for her to find it, but it is a bit odd that she suddenly wants to make sure her lipstick is perfect before getting out of the car when it was getting smeared across her face on our first date. She ended up wiping it off during one of her several bathroom trips.

She's also been super chatty and touchy-feely, which hasn't been the case the past two dates.

Does this mean she's getting comfortable with me? She's definitely more like the woman I met at Hadley's wedding. Maybe it's because I cleared the air about my title. Maybe she thought she had to act differently since I wasn't being truthful with her right off the bat.

Who knows?

I need to enjoy this date without overthinking things and comparing each date we go on. I like this woman, no doubt, and I should focus on that. Learn to love and accept all sides of who she is—even the kind of annoying, overly girly side of her.

"Aha!" She plucks a small, black tube out of the massive bag and flips the visor down to apply the soft pink color. Watching the stick sweep across her bottom lip stirs desire in my gut.

I'm going to kiss the girl by the end of the night. *Got that, Sebastian?* I think as the tune to the red crab's song flickers to life in my head.

Hopefully... If she lets me. She has touched me a lot tonight. Plus, we held hands almost the entire two hour drive. I didn't feel that special zing I've grown accustomed to and felt when I touched her sister's hand back in Juniper Grove. I chalked that up to the fact that they are twins. But that's okay. At least my desperate need for physical touch is now getting met even if it's a comfortable touch over a passionate touch.

"I'm ready," she says with a grin, tossing the tube that took her three minutes to find back into the bag with a careless flick of the wrist. "Can't leave without freshening up with my beloved Rarest Beauty lipstick. Do you like the color?"

She purses her newly-mauve lips, and the desire to kiss her dissipates. I miss the natural look on her already, though the color is pretty against her skin.

Lucy frowns, and I realize my own lips are sagging. *Get it together, man.*

I shake my head with a forced laugh. "You look great. Let's get going. But please wait for me to get to your door. I don't want any repeats of the last time I attempted chivalry on your behalf." I take my first chance of the night and cup her face. She doesn't move, her cheeks warming under my touch. Her face continues to warm; she's red all over.

"Are you okay?" I ask. "Your face..."

She pulls back and my hand falls. "Yeah, sorry. I blush with my whole face."

Hm. I vividly remember a dusting of pink across her nose and her cheeks. Not her chin or her forehead.

Stop overthinking things, Finley. You always do that. Roll with it.

I get out of the car, walk around to open her door, and take her hand as I guide her out of the old, low-riding, blue mustang. I catch sight of Gabriel and Anders a few paces away, dressed in their black suits. I nod to them and interlace my fingers with Lucy's.

Still no zing, but she doesn't rip her hand from mine.

Instead, she squeezes my hand and leans into me with a broad, dazzling smile.

Something definitely changed over the past four days...

But thank goodness she's letting me touch her now. I'm sure the zing will come once we find ourselves amidst the flowers and sweet smells and underneath the romantic lights as the sun continues to set.

We shuffle through the line and have our hands stamped to indicate we paid our entrance fee, then we exit through double doors that open up to a magnificent row of magnolia trees that create the path to the opening of the gardens. The floral smell at sunset is captivating.

"Wow, it's beautiful," Lucy remarks. She's looking up the tall trees, her eyes bright with excitement. Today, I noticed earlier, they are more on the green side like I remember from the wedding. There's no trace of the hazel-blue I've come to know recently.

"Yes, you are." I squeeze her hand as she snaps her gaze to me, her smile somehow widening. She stands on her tiptoes and plants a quick kiss on my cheek, taking me by surprise.

"Sorry if that was forward of me." She's still smiling, but there's a caution to it now, mostly likely due to my stunned expression. "I don't tend to hold back when I want something." I swear she mumbles "or someone" under her breath.

"No, no. Don't be. I was just surprised, that's all." I rub the back of my neck with the hand not holding Lucy's. "You would hardly let me touch you on our past couple of dates, and you avoided my kiss. What changed, if you don't mind me asking?"

Her smile diminishes, and she looks perplexed with her nose scrunching and eyebrows pinching together. Yet another expression of hers that I don't remember seeing over our time together.

I must have a lot to learn about the multi-faceted Lucy Spence. I feel like I'm in an alternate universe.

And I really need to turn off my scrutinizing brain.

"Oh, um. I just, uh..." she trails off, looking anywhere but at me now. She snaps her fingers as if she just remembered. "That's right. I needed time to warm up to you, that's all. I feel more comfortable with you now that you've told me about your *position*."

Ah, so I was right. "So, you're saying I have free reign to touch you now, maybe even kiss you, since we are officially dating?" I smirk as her face reddens. But then she schools her expression and turns to face me, her free hand trailing up my arm.

I fully expect shivers to erupt through me, but there's... nothing.

"Yes, Finley Andersson. You have free reign to touch me." She stares into my eyes, a smoldering emerald. "And kiss me."

She steps closer and drops my hand, opting instead to run her hand up my other arm.

Do I want this?

Right now?

Her arms loop around my neck, and every fiber of my body screams at me to back up.

So I listen, and I take a giant step back as Lucy's arms remain outstretched towards me.

The woman I've fallen for sinks into a puddle of utter sadness and confusion, her arms finally collapsing to her side, her chin drooping.

I don't know what came over me, but I have to fix this.

"Lucy." I step towards her, but she still doesn't look at me. I place two fingers underneath her tucked chin and lift her head until she's meeting my eyes, a thousand questions rushing through her own. "I *will* kiss you. But please allow me to initiate our very first one."

Though even as I make the promise, I'm still unsure if I'll be able to. It doesn't make a lick of sense. I was craving her lips on mine by the end of our first date.

She swallows, the bottom of her chin moving with the motion. I drop my hand and grin, trying to work through this unease.

"Okay," is all she says. I lace my fingers through hers once more, and I guide us out of the treeline and into the first part of the gardens. Hundreds of various flowers and shrubs and trees sprout colorful and tall around the fountains and white fences and butterfly decor. The smell is intoxicating, a blend of sweet and stark spice, and I make a mental note to spruce up our royal garden when I return to Korsa for good. It could use a section devoted to chrysanthemums alone...

We walk in silence, Lucy only speaking up to compliment a flower on its beauty. Instead of calling them by their names, she simply uses the term "flower." I try to engage her in conversation surrounding the history of Bellina Gardens (I spent a few hours doing a thorough search, mind you), but she only nods along and doesn't add in any of her knowledge. Did she not look into this place, supposedly a place she's been wanting to go to for a while? Weird.

Come to think of it, she didn't engage me in conversation regarding history, philosophy, or law. She spoke up when I brought up Thomas Paine, but she went radio silent other than a few vague statements when I spoke about Aristotle, John Locke, and William Blackstone.

"Oh, look, Finley!" I follow her point to a bevy of swans in the nearby lake. "Swans are beautiful birds, aren't they?"

"Yes, they are. But do you hear their song? The term 'swan song' comes from the ancient Greeks. They believed that if you heard a certain song coming from a swan, it was about to die. Do you think their song is one of death?"□

Lucy's still gazing out on the white fowl, her eyes mesmerized. "I don't know about death or the Greeks, but swans represent purity. Something I'll never—" She cuts herself off, a certain despondency seeping into her expression as her eyes fall to the ground. After a fleeting second, she meets my eyes and smiles softly. "Do you want to go down to the lake?"

"That would be lovely."

As we begin our walk down the stoned pathway, Lucy lightens and begins to talk about her books. She's going on about fantasy creatures and a genre called urban romantasy and different plot lines and how she plans to make every book she ever writes tie together in some way. It's truly fascinating to get a glimpse into her brain like this as I know a writer's stories are highly personal, but I can't keep up because it's a lot of information thrown at me at once at high speed.

"What do you think about that idea?" she asks, and I redden in the face because I have no clue what she's referring to. Was it a pirate? A vampire? Maybe something about a ghost...

"I, uh..." I drift sheepishly as I watch her physically deflate. My heart pinches, and I decide honesty is the best policy. "I'm sorry.

I was trying to keep up but it was a lot and I kind of got lost in thinking about how it was a lot. I'm not huge into fiction. I prefer nonfiction."

She tilts her head and narrows her eyes, her nose scrunching up as she evaluates me. Yes, she looks me up and down like she's making a judgment call at this very moment. Then, she chuckles as she fiddles with her hair, leading us down to the lake in silence.

What's going on with her today? It's as if she's reverted back to the woman I met in December, but I had already started falling for and entertaining the differences I've noticed in her—the stimulating conversation, her muted character (and I don't mean that in a derogatory way by any means), and her soft but straightforward speech. During those few moments back at her apartment, when I made eye contact with her sister, all those feelings surfaced, and—

Wait.

Have I been...? Can I ask that question?

Am I on a date with the wrong twin?

The question bounces around my brain like a racquetball, and I find myself auditing everything about this woman I'm out with—the bangs, the bounce in her step, the full-face blush. She didn't engage in conversation about the history of this place or about the random swan facts. Granted, she could have truly not known, but I don't necessarily believe that Lucy wouldn't have at least shown piqued interest.

Suddenly, it's clear. I think I'm on a date with Lorelei, but I can't fathom why Lucy would send her in her place. Maybe to test me? But that seems out of character for Lucy. I hope she wouldn't do that to me. The twin I spoke with before I left started on a tangent about how the American judicial system was off-kilter due to many people being falsely accused. That was a very Lucy thing to say.

Oh no.

I think I'm on a date with the wrong twin. *Unless they are both that way...*

We walk around in silence for a few minutes, winding down the path to the lakes before we come across a splatter of chrysanthemums. Here's a good chance. The real Lucy would know all about and would want to talk about her favorite flowers. "Look, Lucy. Your favorite."

She follows my gaze and smiles. "Yep. Sure is." Her voice isn't as animated as I thought it would be. In fact, she sounds agitated. But I press on.

"Could you remind me of the history of the meanings behind each of the colors and how different cultures perceive them?" That should get her talking if it is the real Lucy.

She releases my hand and nears the flowers, lightly touching the stem, tracing her finger to the red petals. "They symbolize... love."

The inflection in her voice indicates a question, but she said it as a statement. *Strange.* "And?" I prompt, attempting to get her swept away into her element. *Please don't let my assumption be correct...*

"And..." she tapers off, still gently caressing the flowers. Suddenly, a dumbfounded look flashes across her face. "And..."

Lucy drops her hand, balling it into a fist at her side. She squares her shoulders as she turns to face me. Her lips are pressed into a tight line, an expression I am all too familiar with when it comes to her. This *is* Lucy.

Oh, no. This is the real Lucy, and she's going to break up with me because I'm pushing too far and acting too weird in my apprehensions.

I'm going to have to start this search all over, and quite frankly, I don't want to. I want Lucy, even if she has this alternate side to her. I want her brain. I want her zing. I want her heart. I want her lips... *I should have let her kiss me.*

"We need to talk."

Those dreaded four words pierce through my soul like the legendary *Svaard aav Dood*, a mystical sword in Korsan mythology that never left a soul it pierced still breathing. It was instant death.

"I'm sorry!" I blurt. "Kiss me."

As soon as I lean in, she steps away, her hand splaying across my chest as she strikes her arm out to keep distance.

Then she laughs...

Laughs!

"Seriously, Finley. We need to chat first."

Left feeling confused and unsure of what in the world is going on, I do all I can right now, and that's follow her lead down the remainder of the stone path until we are seated on a white bench overlooking the lakes with the swans, singing a song of what I'm sure is *my* impending death.

After a treacherous moment, she looks at me with a sad smile and says, "My name is Lucy May Spence."

"I know. I—"

She places a hand on my thigh like it's the most familiar, comforting touch she can muster. "Hold on. Yes, I am Lucy May

Spence, but the woman you went out with that first night, and again after church, was my twin, Lorelei Raine Spence."

She pauses, gauging my reaction I presume. But her words are still tumbling over me, and I'm trying to make sense of it. So this whole time, I've been falling for Lorelei, not Lucy? And I actually am on a date with Lucy? Not Lorelei like I briefly surmised? I'm definitely in some alternate universe...

After a deep breath, she spews everything out. "I sent her that first night in my place because I had received a black eye from a kid bouncing a tennis ball off a wall while I was at work. I am the event coordinator and stand-in assistant director at Juniper Grove Community Center, a job I only work because I'm a small-scale independent romance author. I haven't made it big yet, which is my goal, so I work odd jobs. I thankfully landed this one, a bit more long-term, but it's not what I want to be doing. I'm not as successful as my sister, I'm not as booksmart as she is, and I'm not as put together. I'm kind of a mess, a hopeless romantic, and well, not who you think I am."

I don't respond, mostly because I'm processing everything she's telling me. The woman I'm sitting next to *is* Lucy, but the woman I've fallen for is her *sister,* Lorelei. Logically, piecing together all the discrepancies, it makes sense. Even their names correlate to their personalities. Lucy is a fun, flirty name while Lorelei is structured and calm. There are so many differences between the two, but I let the fact that they look the same distract me. I can't even be mad... If I had a twin, it's a prank I would pull.

But then again, this wasn't some prank, I *do* need a wife, and the one thing that tops it all, I'm enamored with Lorelei.

The woman I've been eyeing and desiring this whole time might not even be into me. Because that's the feeling I gathered from Lorelei.

Now *that's* laughable.

And I do. I laugh, which prompts Lucy to do the same. We laugh until we are both doubled over with tears pulling from our eyes. Every time we attempt to stop, we glance at each other, and laugh again.

"I can't believe it took me as long as it did to figure it out."

She laughs some more. "Really? You think less than a week is a long time? We've tricked people who have grown up with us for much longer. You're perceptive, Finley."

As if that sobered her, she straightens and pegs me with a stern expression. "I've already caught the vibe of this date, and it was geared towards my sister. And to be honest, I think you are more into her than you are me. Plus, I don't think I'm as into you as much as I was into the idea of Queen Lucy May Spence. I don't want to talk about history and random facts. I want someone who can keep up with my book rambles and preferably enjoys fiction. Heck, I want to be free to initiate contact with a man without feeling like I'm some harlot attempting to steal your virtue." She gives me a sly glance.

I cringe. She's right, but I don't want to hurt Lucy. "I've gotten to know her, yes. And I have geared this date towards her because I thought that was who I would be with. I don't know you that well yet, Lucy. I could, though..." Even as I say the words, I know they aren't true. I want Lorelei.

Lucy must recognize that. "As much as I want to be a queen—RIP to my ultimate fantasy—I desire my sister's happiness more. I already had the feeling that you were into who she truly is as she recapped your dates to me, but today verified it. You keep wanting me to be her, and I keep trying, but I'm not. And I'm okay with that."

I place my hand over hers. Still no zing, which oddly enough, is everything I need to know. "As you should be. You are a lovely woman. I was instantly captivated by you at the wedding, but that was before I realized I would need to marry and that I was ascending the throne."

"Oof. So I'm not wifey material. I get that."

I backtrack. "No, Lucy. That's not what I meant, it's just that—"

She cuts me off, and I still feel awful for making that statement. "It's okay. Truly. Personally, and it pains me to admit, but if one of us has to be a queen and rule over a country, she is much better equipped than I am. I like the glamor of the idea, but she has the functionality to be a wonderful head of state."

While Lucy does sound confident in her decision, there is the undertone of sadness that is hard to miss. Whereas Lorelei hides her emotions, Lucy wears them on her sleeve. I understand why people are more drawn to Lucy, though. Lorelei's difficult to read, which scares people.

But not me.

She's going to become my favorite book. One that I read over and over.

"Lucy, you are wifey material, just not *my* wife. Don't ever let someone make you believe that you aren't." I squeeze her hand then remove mine. She follows suit, our touch effectively ending. "Being queen is hard. It involves a lot of wordplay, decisions, and a special touch of kindness and consideration."

"Which my sister has," Lucy says with a firm smile.

"She does. I think she'd make an excellent queen, but furthermore, I think she balances me out." I chuckle. "If you and I were a couple, we'd end up vacationing and gallivanting the world in pursuit of the next great thing. But Lorelei? She will ground me."

That elicits a genuine smile from Lucy. "You're right. I did catch the vibe that we could be good friends."

"Maybe even closer. Let's see... You could be my sister-in-law?"

She hops to her feet, a new energy radiating through her. She's like the sun whereas Lorelei is like the moon. Two suns would burn the world, but a sun balanced with a moon will create a beautiful peace that sets the world into perfect time.

"I accept my position as sister-in-law to the future king of Korsa. You are my future king-in-law." She waggles her brows. "Now, let's finish this date while I give you the rundown on all things Lorelei Raine Spence. If you truly want her, prepare yourself for the hardest chase of your life."

A shutter sound echoes from somewhere behind us, followed by a hissed curse. I snap my head around and notice a hooded figure already on the run with my PPOs in pursuit.

Grasping Lucy's forearm and peering into her eyes, I command in my royal voice, "Lucy, stay here. I've got to catch this man."

I hear her calling after me as I bolt, using every inch of my long legs to stride up the stone path after the stalker. My PPOs come into view; they are gaining on the figure. But right as Gabriel reaches to grab him, the perp cuts left and hurdles over a bush line. Anders cuts after him as Gabriel catches his balance and curses.

"Finley, halt pursuit!" Gabriel yells even as I clear the bush Anders and the stalker did moments ago. Suddenly, arms are wrapping around my torso as I'm thrown to the ground. Instead of landing on the dirt and grass, I land in a tangle on Gabriel, who groans curses underneath me.

"Respectfully, Your Highness. Get off of me," Gabriel grunts.

I stand on wobbling legs, my chest still aching from where I connected with Gabriel's shoulder and my breath heavy. I run and lift every morning, but the sudden burst of energy without a warm-up is taking its toll.

Gabriel's on his feet quicker than I was and is scanning the area, muttering into his earpiece how he lost the chase due to me getting in the way. Grass is speckled throughout his dark blond hair, his suit disheveled.

"I could have helped, Gabriel. Why did you stop me?"

He sighs. "In case you have forgotten, my top priority is *you*. I can't have *you* chasing after potentially dangerous stalkers."

"What in the—" Lucy's voice raises to new heights as she comes to a breathy stop in front of me and Gabriel. "What happened? Why was I forced to run?"

"I told you to stay put," I bark in concerned frustration, but then I bring my voice down. It's better she's here with me and the guys. "The stalker showed up."

Her dropped jaw and breathless "what?" remind me that I've never told her sister about this, much less her. "He's been sniping pictures of me and sending them to my mother since the first date with you, or, Lorelei, I should say. He showed up when we were at Books and Beans, too." I briefly recall the shadowed figure who passed outside our window as the rain began to pour.

Lucy runs her fingers through frizzed waves. "That's something we should talk about on our way back to Juniper Grove. I'd like for my twin to be safe when she's with you. Is your other PPO okay going to search alone? Should we help find him?"

"He's on his way back. Stalker got away again," Gabriel says and curses in French.

Guilt pricks at the edges of my thought, but I shove it down. "I wanted to protect Lucy. Make sure nothing happened to her because of me," I clarify to Gabriel before I turn to Lucy. "And I swear on my title that I will never let anyone so much as touch a flyaway hair on your sister's head."

"Literal swoon." Lucy makes the motion of fainting and laughs. "At least I know my sister is in good hands. You run fast, future king-in-law."

"I understand, Your Highness. And we all admire your protective nature. But we are here to protect you." Gabriel plucks grass from my hair. "Are you injured?"

"No," I sigh. "But let's wait for Anders. I want to finish this evening. I have things to discuss with Lucy."

Though I know it will be hard to focus after this. I make a mental note to call my father on the way home and discuss this situation with him. Until then, I need to learn how to win the right twin to my heart.

And probably take my PPOs out to a nice dinner on the way home.

Lucy tugs on my shirt, pulling me close. She whispers, "Can you set me up with him?" I follow her gaze to Gabriel, who is stalking away towards Anders. "I kind of like them grumpy."

Chapter Nine

Lorelei

Even Ted Bundy couldn't hold my attention tonight.

I find myself pacing around the room, eyes glued to my phone as my sister's location continuously moves closer to the house. She's still an hour away, and it's already midnight.

Between checking her location and trying to reorient myself into the murderous world of Bundy, I also have a few searches pulled up on my phone.

What does it mean when a man touches you and it makes you burn? (Don't search that, friends.)

Does it mean something if you can't stop thinking about his eyes? (Gag.)

Prince Finley Andersson. (Why is he so unbearably handsome?)

I don't like the answers.

They all point to the idea that I have feelings for my sister's man, which is simply NOT okay.

But that's just what the internet says, and we all know the internet lies. It doesn't *have* to mean anything. It can simply be a different reaction to being touched.

I'm not touched often because it gives me the ick, and though the reaction to Finley's touch wasn't icky, I'm not sure I'd categorize it as something pleasant.

Who wants to feel electrocuted when they touch someone, even with contact as simple as a brushing of fingers or lips pressed to knuckles?

And for the record, I only searched for Finley because he's currently out with Lucy. I figured I'd use the time to see if there is anything I need to look out for to help protect her. I already know he's a bit of a player, apparently, but I think Lucy can handle that at this point. But other than that fact, I can't see any red flags. He is a humanitarian, wicked smart, and the people of his country seem to adore him even though he has an international reputation.

Again, that's what the internet says. I can't take it too seriously.

I close out all the open screens on my phone and collapse onto the couch. The moment my bum lands on the cushion, Frizzle and Frannie jump onto my lap and curl up against each other. Frannie must be missing Lucy, whom she usually naps with at night.

"Hey, girls," I coo while I busy both my hands running through their short fur coats. As I'm petting them, a weird feeling settles over me.

Everything is about to change.

My sister will marry a prince and move to another country. Hadley is married now. Karoline, though I'm not super close with her like Lucy and Hadley are, will move to Nashville this summer.

My job will stay the same, and I will stay here for now with my two cats and slew of plants.

Or, cat. Lucy will probably take Frannie with her.

Am I okay with that direction of life for me?

For now, yes.

I won't rush my life. I will focus on my career; it is a fulfilling one. I love getting to help reunite families, or at the very least, settle disputes and bring about some semblance of reconciliation. In fact, I could work on case files until Lucy makes it home safe and sound. But then I remember that I left them at work this evening due to promising my parents that I would do something fun.

But how do I have fun when I'm worried about my sister?

And why am I so worried about her?

I trust Finley well enough. He will take care of her.

Resolved not to waste the last fifty-two minutes that I have left before she's supposed to be home, I open my phone again and click on my e-reader app. I flick through the many unread books I've accumulated and settle on trying out a political dystopian Lucy recommended to me. I don't read fiction much, but Lucy is usually spot-on when she recommends one to me.

She knows not to recommend the fluffy stuff, at least.

Slipping the blanket from over the couch, I tug it around me while the cats flee from the constraints and snuggle in.

You will relax, I chastise myself. *This is fun to you, and you will enjoy it.*

Thoroughly scolded, I open the book and immerse myself into a post-Soviet Union dystopian where the woman is apparently set to become the next ruler, but her plans fall through when she falls in love with the royal prince-slash-spy from the warring country. The romance thread doesn't bother me because the characters are already set up in such a way that I actually find myself cheering them on. My vision gets a little blurry and my head gets a little fuzzy, but I'm too immersed in the book to toss it to the side in favor of sleep, no matter how many times my cats nudge me and meow for me to bring them to bed. I can wait a little longer. An hour later, when Lucy opens the door, I'm startled and yanked from the world of premiers and sectors and deception. Lies are permitted when in fallen societies, after all. I glance over my shoulder as she walks in, but then I turn my attention back to the book.

"Welcome home," I say, a big, fat yawn hijacking my words and a shiver rippling through me. "Ugh, sorry. I'm glad you made it back safely. I'm enjoying this book you told me about."

"Did you doubt I'd keep my promise?" a decidedly male voice asks, and I turn my head quick enough my neck could have possibly snapped if I executed the motion any harder. Finley leans casually against the doorframe with crossed arms, a smirk painted across his face.

They must have had a good night.

Why does that thought sink my stomach and cause my head to spin?

"Not at all," I finally respond, not meeting his gaze and resuming reading my book.

Trying to, at least.

"I took tons of pictures for you, Lor," Lucy says, appearing in front of me.

I smile. "Lovely."

Lucy plucks my phone from my hand.

"Hey!" I fumble out of the hole I've put into the couch from nestling in for an hour. As the blanket falls around me, I remember that I'm in old gray joggers and a white shirt that has exactly three holes in it—one in the armpit, one on the belly, and one on the shoulder. My hair is a frizzy mess, and I'm basically a living troll.

This is what I get for taking people's stupid advice to have fun. I should have worked, gone to bed at a reasonable hour, and trusted my sister would be fine. Another prickly shiver overcomes me.

"Whoa," Finley says, his eyes widening. He captures my attention instantly, and I watch in horror as he looks me up and down... something I've seen happen a million and ten times to Lucy, but never to me. This is scarier than Ted Bundy.

Lucy appears at his side as his eyes freely roam over me. He must be astonished that the put-together Lorelei Spence actually dresses like a homebody teenager when she's alone and turned in for the night.

Yeah, that's it.

Finley takes *my* phone from Lucy, and I watch in a new wave of horror as Lucy unlocks it. Because we have the same stupid face.

I march over to the two of them, ignoring the weakness in my steps, and reach to grab my phone from him, but he holds it up over his head while Lucy steps back with her arms crossed. I reach and jump, but I'm still not able to reach my phone. I try again, but this time, I jump forward, knocking into Finley like we are two boys celebrating a sports victory with a chest bump.

Except Finley is a man, and I am a woman. I am immensely grateful I am wearing a sports bra.

The arm not holding my phone in the air braces around me, preventing me from stepping away from him. My head is tilted up as he lowers his. Finley's eyes twinkle like sunlight reflecting off the ocean. The smirk he was wearing slips away, in its place parted, light pink lips. Just like my dream...

He's so close I can feel his warm breath, and that feeling of being electrocuted alive radiates through every molecule of my person. It's painful and weakening.

Without another moment of hesitation, I throw myself backward, stumbling a few times as I catch my balance from the momentum of exiting his arms. My vision blacks out for a second before coming back to.

As I catch my breath from the sheer racing of my heart, I blurt, "What in the world is going on?" I glance between Finley and Lucy. Finley has lowered my phone, but the heat in his eyes as he gazes upon me is like a campfire in the middle of a snowy forest. Lucy is still standing with her arms crossed, boasting the biggest smile I've seen out of her in a while.

"I told him," she finally says. "About the switch."

Internally, I sigh with relief. I was praying she would tell him. "But what does that have to do with stealing my phone?"

Finley doesn't answer because he's still heating this apartment to a thousand degrees with that stare. It's so hot, yet shivers are becoming my constant companion at the moment. Finally, Lucy elbows him, shaking him loose of whatever trance that was.

"Should you tell her, or should I?"

At that moment, Finley Andersson, Crown Prince of Korsa, future king, types something in my phone before passing it off to

Lucy, picks up a crown of flowers that I apparently missed him setting on the stand by the door, and takes two large steps in my direction.

My cats flank my side and mew, clawing at my legs. I kick them away but almost fall, so I stop. Finley pauses directly in front of me, bends to one knee, and reveals a flower crown woven of white and pink Chrysanthemums.

My heart stutters, immediately recognizing the symbolism of those colors—white for loyalty and innocence and pink for new love and affection. Why is he kneeling before me with this wondrous crown of my favorite flowers?

Finley gazes at me through his long, black lashes from his lowered position, and says, "Please keep in mind that I have your sister's support and blessing." Then he clears his throat as I fight not to pass out. "I added my number with my first and last name, as Lucy says you prefer, to your contact list. Lucy has already given me yours. Lorelei Raine Spence, will you do me the immense honor of dating me with the goal of marriage and queenship in mind?"

My vision blurs in a more permanent capacity, and at the moment, I realize what's happening as a familiar numbness settles into my limbs. I hear my cats screeching before they claw at my legs. "Lucy, I need juice. Now!"

As I collapse, I lean towards Finley who is still on one knee. He tosses the crown and bravely catches me, tugging me tightly against his chest as he cages me in strong arms. The momentum of my fall rocks him backwards; my eyes flutter close to the pounding of his heartbeat in my ear as I lie wrapped in the fallen prince's arms.

CHAPTER TEN

FINLEY

"Chew, Lorelei," I instruct as I prepare another sugar tablet in my hand. We've already given her two cups of apple juice, and this will be her second sugar tablet in the span of thirty minutes as we sit on the floor in her living room.

Turns out Lorelei is hypoglycemic, and I'm not the cause of her weak knees and racing heart and sweaty palms.□

"I'm chewing as fast as I can," she mumbles between jaw movements. Then she sips on her third glass of juice. She's no longer sweating or shivering. Instead, she's barely making eye contact with me and is careful not to touch me when she accepts the sugar tablet from my hand.

"Why did you let your sugar drop like that, Lor? That's not like you. What happened?" Lucy asks as the cats who have been glued to Lorelei's side continue to lick their paws.

Lorelei flicks her eyes to me before looking back towards her sister who sits beside me with her legs tucked underneath her holding the rag we were using to dab Lorelei's sweaty forehead.

"I got sucked into that book you recommended."

"Still. You are always on top of your game. You take care of yourself."

Lorelei sips the rest of the juice down and whispers, "I'm not perfect. I have bad days, too."

Lucy immediately takes her hand. "What happened?"□

Lorelei fidgets with her pant legs, rubbing the fabric between her fingers. She looks at me then back to her sister. "Can we talk later?"

I receive the memo and stand. "Well, ladies. It's getting late and it appears like everything is under control here. Lucy, thank you for a great evening. Lorelei, I hope we can talk soon. *Kryaa paa diig.* Feel better." She nods, and Lucy smiles softly, mouthing "thank you" as she continues to rub the back of Lorelei's hand.

I spot the flower crown on the floor where I tossed it as Lorelei fell, so I pick it up and give it to her before leaving. Her cats nuzzle against my hand as Lorelei takes the crown from me, and she gawks at them like it's odd behavior. It grants me a tinge of joy as it seems her felines approve of me.

As I'm walking down the steps, I verbally pray, "Lord, please work this out. I don't understand why this happened, why the girls switched, but I know You arrange all things for a purpose, and if You laid it on their hearts to switch places, it must have been for Your purpose. All I know is that I don't think any other woman would satisfy me the way Lorelei does. I don't even know why she does, but I can't deny the feelings I have coupled with what I do know about her. She's got to be it. Please, God. Work this out for Your—and my—good."

Gabriel and Anders are standing outside the black SUV when I get to the bottom of the stairs.

Anders smirks. "You have it bad, Your Highness."

I shrug, unable and unwilling to deny it. Gabriel chuckles and shakes his head.

"Let's go home," I say, already opening the door to my beloved sports car. The men follow suit and tail me all the way back to the cabin.

Once we are back, I close myself in my room to contemplate everything I've discovered today:

1. I was falling for Lorelei, not Lucy.

2. Lucy and Lorelei are truly very different women.

3. According to Lucy, Lorelei has never dated nor kissed a man.

4. Also according to Lucy, Lorelei is not great with emotions.

5. It was probably a really stupid move to put her on the spot tonight.

6. I will do anything to make Lorelei my queen. Not because she's a good candidate but because I have never felt this way about another woman before.

7. My father is adamantly looking for a lead on the stalker while Mamma is freaking out that I may choose an American girl over Her Royal Highness Karin of Vespen.□

Lucy gave me the rundown on all things Lorelei, and while some of it was intimidating, I also found Lorelei more and more intriguing. I'm excited to discover her for myself, to pry open the emotions of Lorelei Raine Spence… What a beautiful name she has.

Lorelei Raine Andersson…

Even more beautiful.

Her Highness the Queen of Korsa Lorelei Raine Anderson.

Perfection.

In the middle of my night time daydreams about the woman I pray and hope to woo, my phone buzzes with a video chat request from Astrid.

"*Haalaa.*" She waves, her bright blue eyes and shiny blonde hair reflecting the daylight. From the roses and peonies behind her, I gather she's in the Royal Gardens. "You're up late."

I grin an admittedly tired but hopeful smile as I talk in my native tongue. "You won't believe what happened…" I spill everything to Astrid. About how the twins switched, how I fell for Lorelei, how I have plans to win the heart of the woman who's never been in love.

"So, she threw up when you told her who you were, and then she almost fainted when you presented her with a handmade gift and knelt down to propose dating with marriage intentions in mind."

I brush off her words. "First off, she vomited because I was presenting the information to her as if I wanted Lucy. Secondly, her blood sugar was low tonight. And she has no idea about our customs and how we kneel and present a handmade gift to propose a serious relationship. I never got the chance to explain due to the almost fainting thing."

Astrid rolls her eyes. "I support you, *broor*, but I don't think this woman is going to go for you. She sounds like she doesn't match who you are. You're an outgoing, sociable man. You two might be too different for each other."

"That's why I like her, *systeer*. She balances me. You know, you and I—or even Father and I—get into trouble when we are together, but when I'm with Johan or Mamma, I'm balanced." I think about how grounded I feel when I'm with Lorelei. How she makes me feel like I can rest, relax, and breathe. "She's my *mysaa*."

Astrid stares at me through the screen, her eyes growing round before a smile creeps up her face, causing little wrinkles in the outside corners of her eyes. "I absolutely cannot wait to meet this woman. When are you bringing her to Korsa?"

"Whenever she actually agrees to date me. Did you forget the little fact that she hasn't yet?"

"Call me a hopeless romantic." She flips her luscious blonde hair. If Astrid were a male, she'd look like me. And if I were a female, well, you get the point. "I never thought there would be a woman who was able to captivate you and intrigue you long enough for you to actually consider marriage. Which means..." She frowns as she trails off, then she looks off in the distance. The sun shines brightly, and I find myself wishing it was morning already here. "Which means I need to ask... Are you pursuing this woman because you have to have a wife to take the throne, or do you truly love her? Or at least, think you can love her? Because if you're trying to protect the crown from passing to me..."

I cut her off. "I know you are perfectly capable of marrying any man. You have a long list of suitors who would love to tie you down and rule side by side with you. But I know you don't want that, Astrid. And you have so much life ahead of you. I've lived enough, and I'm ready to accept this responsibility."

She stares into my soul, her mouth twisting. "You didn't answer my original question."

I breathe, admitting to myself—and now to my sister. "I love her, Astrid. Don't ask me to explain it. I've rarely said those words to any woman I've dated, and usually when I did, it was because they said it first and I felt obligated. But with Lorelei," I can't help the smile that captures my expression, "I mean it. She's it for me. I feel it in my soul, in my bones. And she is the woman Korsa needs. More importantly, the woman I need."

My sister slowly smiles, hearts practically pounding out of her eyes. Then sternly, she says, "If you don't bring her here within a month, I'm coming to you. At that point, your usual charms haven't worked, and I need to step in."

We both laugh, but I fear she might have to. I have a habit of coming on too strong, and most ladies eat it up, but Lorelei? That is going to push her far, far away from me.

And that's not the kingdom I'm hoping she'll rule.

I continue to tell Astrid about how the stalker struck again. "It's frustrating because this feels personal. They aren't leaking photos to the press. They aren't giving the press my location. They are only sending photos to Mamma, apparently. We must know this person."

Astrid hums in agreement. "I've thought about it, and I have suspicions that Karin may have hired someone to interrupt your dates..."

I grimace and run a hand through my hair. "Yeah, that's what I was beginning to suspect, too. Father spoke with Anders, Gabriel, and me tonight. We told him that we thought Karin might be involved. He will speak with her father."

"I hope they don't get deadly like that one time Johan was stalked as a teenager," Astrid whispers, and I nod.

"Regardless, we are safe. Anders and Gabriel are great at what they do. We will get the guy."

My finger hovers over the send button.

I read the text over one more time, looking for any spelling errors, grammatical errors, or utter nonsense. While Lucy wouldn't have minded, Lorelei will. I have to present my best, smartest, most composed self moving forward.

Good morning, Lorelei. I pray you received plenty of rest last night and are feeling better. I would like to speak with you about my dating proposal last night. I meant every word of it, and I'm sure your sister has filled you in on everything by this point. When you're ready, please reach out and let's set up a time to talk in person. No rush.

It sounds good to me, but then again, am I being too formal for a man who is wishing to pursue a woman? I begin to delete the message.

"Are you requesting her presence at a state dinner or whatever it is you royals attend frequently?" Mason's deep timber startles me, and I do the unthinkable...

My finger hits the send button.

I had deleted all the way up to the "I meant every word of it, and" and apparently prior to the accidental send, autotext had typed the words "I want kids."

I stare at the screen with a dropped jaw and seething thoughts towards Mason Kane.

Good morning, Lorelei. I pray you got plenty of rest last night and are feeling better. I would like to speak with you about my dating proposal last night. I meant every word of it, and I want kids

How did this even happen? Is this from texting my brother the other day about how he wanted kids but couldn't have them because of his condition?

Stupid predictive text technology.

I didn't mean that last part. It was an accident.

I do want kids. One day. But not anytime soon.

I'm fumbling this. Big time.

Let's talk soon. In person. Not about kids.

Mason is roaring with laughter while I slowly die inside. I stare at the evidence of my overactive brain and then click the side button of my phone, watching the screen darken… just like my mood.

I shift my glare at Mason, who doesn't bother to do me the decency of ceasing his laughter. Instead, my glower elicits another round of howling laughter from Mason.

"She's going to find that absolutely charming or absolutely insane. There's no in between, my friend." Mason slaps me on the back before going to rummage through the refrigerator.

"I'm not one to typically play the blame game, but dude. You may have just ruined my life."

Mason chugs an energy drink, something he's been doing a lot lately as he bounces between here and Nashville. "You sent the message."

"You loomed over my shoulder and frightened me."

"And we are at an impasse. Should I call Braxton to settle this?" Mason plops down in his chair, and I take my usual position on the couch, placing my phone next to me. At that moment, it vibrates. I eye my phone as if it might bite me.

Finally, I pick it up.

Lorelei.

"I don't know if I can read this," I say.

Mason snickers. "I swear you can be such a woman sometimes."

I roll my eyes and toss my phone at him. "Emotional men exist, Mason. Maybe if you were one, you wouldn't have left Karoline alone for three years." After the words leave my mouth, I immediately regret them. "I'm so sorry, man." I can't say I don't mean them because I do.

He swipes my phone and grins. "You're not wrong. But God worked it all out in His timing. I was plenty emotional. Just didn't know what to do with them other than bleed into songs like a tortured country poet."

I nod as Mason reads whatever text is on my phone, his smile widening, which in turn causes my heart to beat a little faster. It must be a good message, right?

Mason clears his throat, then says, "Thank you for checking on me. I want kids in the future, too. Let's meet up at Books and Beans tomorrow for lunch."

"She really said that?" I rocket to my feet and am standing in front of Mason after two long strides. I hold out my hand, and he slaps his hand into mine. "Phone, Mason," I rumble in a commanding tone.

He laughs but obliges me.

I read the text, and sure enough, it's exactly what he told me she said.

But then I wonder if Lucy actually wrote it because I'm having a hard time believing that Lorelei would have responded that quickly and with that much ease. "Do you think she wrote it or her sister?"

Mason shrugs. "I don't know. I don't know the two of them well enough."

"Pft. Some help you are. Speaking of, did you know about the twin switch situation?"

Mason sheepishly grins, crossing his hands behind his head full of thick, dark brown hair. "Yes, I knew about it. But I was sworn to secrecy by Karoline. Braxton must have sworn secrecy to Hadley because I tried to get him to confess that he knew, but the man would give me nothing."

I click my tongue. "You both better sleep with one eye open. There will be revenge." But then I laugh because there is literally no point in getting worked up and angry. I understand why the girls did it, and Lucy has apologized. Lorelei made herself physically ill over the lie. I'm in love with her, and love excuses a lot of things apparently. I'm just ready to move on. With Lorelei, preferably.

"Do you think Lucy wrote this?" I question again.

"Just ask her." Anders shuffles into the room, already dressed in a suit while I still sport my sweaty workout clothes from my morning run.

"Want me to do it for you?" Gabriel follows Anders out. "You said Lucy was into me, right? I will happily talk to the pretty, bubbly redhead."

"This house is getting too crowded," I mumble loudly enough for everyone to hear me.

Mason pops to his feet and stretches. "Well, I'll be out of here in two and a half months and living it up with my wife in Nashville. Thank goodness Hadley decided to open a store there. I don't think I could have handled going between here and Nashville for much longer."

"Try going between here and Korsa."

Anders and Gabriel nod in agreement.

Mason claps me on the back again. *Why are American men like this?* "Go get Lorelei to fall in love with you and then whisk her away." His face grows solemn. "But promise me we will stay in touch."

The sincerity in his voice tugs at my heart. "Of course, Mason. In fact, I'll have you play at my coronation."

Anders audibly gasps.

"Country twang at your coronation?" Gabriel asks with a bewildered expression.

I grin at my PPOs. "Yep. I have to show the country just where half my heart now resides."

As the words leave my mouth, I know they're true. I've traveled the world, but no place has captured my soul like this little town.

Or the woman who calls it home.

Lucy's Journal

Friday, March 19th - 9:21 am – In my bed still rocking morning breath

I did it. I gave up my prince. God, is this what You wanted? To tease me with actual royalty and then rip it away from me? Ugh. I'm sorry. I can't blame You. Your plan is perfect and good and... Well, God. I'm struggling to actually believe that if I'm being honest. I'm so happy for my sister. Truly. She deserves everything that is good plus some. I'm happy I can help her for once. I'm happy I can serve her adequately for once. But I'm still hurting. I crave a happily ever after. I crave the comforting arms of a man—of a true love. I dream up these worlds and romances, but I don't have one for myself. When will it be my turn? Oh, God... I know I sound so selfish right now. My heart aches, though. The pain of loneliness runs so deep in my veins. I can't admit this out loud to anyone. I can only bring it to You. I can only ask You to fill me up. Please, God... fill me up. Make this hurt go away. Help me to look outward more. Oh! Gabriel just messaged me. THANK YOU, GOD.

Chapter Eleven

Lorelei

I almost became an only child this morning.

When Lucy snatched my phone out of my hand to reply to Finley, I croaked. *Stupid me for asking my bold, romance-loving, senseless twin for advice.*

As if I wasn't tired enough from waiting up for Lucy to return home, Finley just had to go and state his intentions (ahem—date for marriage!!!) towards me. He just had to present me with a perfect flower crown that I couldn't even enjoy because hypoglycemia had to attack. And finally, Crown Prince Finley Andersson just *had* to make not one, not two, but *three* appearances in the short few hours I actually got some shut-eye last night.

So when he messaged me this morning, I was groggy, confused, and experiencing a feeling I don't think I've ever known before, especially after reading he apparently wants kids. When I described the lightness in my bones and the cloudiness of my head and the irrational beating of my heart after reading his text, Lucy emphatically informed me that I was falling in love.

Love.

I told her people shouldn't fall in love. That love should be comfort and safety and peace. Not this... weak-in-the-bones, racing heart, cloudy head confusing mess.

She smirked and told me that people stumble into love in all sorts of ways. Sometimes it's calm, collected, and sure, but sometimes it's hot, messy, and leaves your head spinning.

I'd picked option number one, but she said I didn't get a choice.

But that's beside the point.

I'm *not* falling in love with Finley Andersson.

No matter what type of love it looks like.

I'm simply confused; the man who was supposed to date my twin popped into my home and *proposed* to me. What was with that? Who does that? He doesn't know me well enough to want to marry me. We've had two dates, and he believed I was my sister! Crazy man.

My sister preyed upon my confusion and told Finley that I'd love to have kids someday and that I would meet him tomorrow for lunch.

Which I most certainly did not agree to.

"Everything okay, Lorelei? You've been grimacing at your computer for the past thirty seconds."

I startle at the voice as Mr. Austen lightly closes my office door.

"Sorry, sir. I'm fine. Just..." What do I even tell him? I know I shouldn't talk about personal things with my boss, but I also don't like lying. And we've talked about plenty of other personal things like his past and my autism.

"Just what? You can talk to me." He sits down, tugging at the excess pant material on his thigh before crossing a leg.

"Well, um..." How do I even begin? "My sister's date asked me to date him with marriage in mind last night. And then I almost fainted." He blinks with long, light orange eyelashes. "Because I had a hypoglycemic episode. Not because of him," I quickly add. Though, I'm not sure if his proposal of sorts wouldn't have warranted the same reaction.

"That's..." Mr. Austen grins. "Something."

When he chuckles under his breath, I join him, the release of the pent-up worries and concerns washing away with every breathy laugh. Eventually, I say, "That's an understatement."

His eyebrows almost touch. "Did your sister know about this?"

I nod. "Oh, yeah. It seems she was in on it. At least, that's what she told me last night after he left. She said they were not compatible but she thought I would be. And that he liked me a lot."

Me.

"Hm. Tell me more."

So I do. I spill my guts to my boss in my office because there is no way I can talk to Hadley or Lucy or my parents about this. Maybe my parents, but they would let something slip when chatting to Lucy.

Because apparently there is something to slip, judging by Mr. Austen's next words...

"You like this man," he says plainly. As if it were the most obvious thing in the world. He leans back in the chair.

"Yes." I process, thinking over my next words, trying to be as accurate as possible. "I do *like* him. As a friend. He's intelligent, kind, and funny. But there are many people in this world with those same qualities. Why should I jump into a relationship with someone simply because they measure up to at least a quarter of the population?"

"Well," Mr. Austen drums his fingers on his bent knee, "I think that's what relationships are for, Lorelei. When I met my wife eleven years ago, I was instantly swept away in her beauty. As I began to talk with her, I realized she was kind, witty, smart, loving, and caring." He pauses and nods towards me. "Qualities many possess, as you've stated."

"So how did you know dating her was the right thing to do?"

Mr. Austen's eyes glaze over as if he's been transported back in time to the happiest of memories. A faint smile tugs at the corner of his lips. "I didn't. I took a shot. I asked her out on a date. I liked it and had fun. So I asked her for another one. We dated for three years while I was in college. Before I knew it, I was down on one knee asking to date her for the rest of my life. Those few days married to her were the best of my life."

The love in his voice for which he speaks of his deceased wife is nothing short of inspiring. But also... devastating. He spent a few short days married to that woman before God took her away from him. My stomach clenches at the thought of losing someone I love, especially after a short amount of time with them when I was expecting forever.

That's another thing that scares me... completely devoting myself to one man for the rest of my life, only to have his life end way before mine.

How does a woman crawl out of the dark depths that would be left in his absence? How did Mr. Austen do it? It must have been such a painful journey for him, one that he constantly revisits, I'm sure.

"I don't know if I have ever told you this, but you inspire me, Mr. Austen. Not only as my boss but also as someone I can faithfully look up to and trust."

He uncrosses his legs and leans forward. "Thanks, Lorelei. You are a wonderful employee. And as much as I would not want to lose you to a different country, I have the inkling you should give this Finley a chance. From what you've told me, he seems sincere. And you'll never know if you should date him unless you do. Unless you give him a chance. Unless you allow him the time to show you how set apart from the rest of the men of this world he is."

"Well, when you put it that way..." I joke, but in reality, my stomach is clenching for another reason: If... a huge IF... I was to get serious with Finley. *IF* I ended up marrying him, I would have to leave Donwell Law Firm. I would have to leave Juniper Grove and my friends and my...

No.

I can't leave Lucy alone here. She needs me.

I school a neutral expression and say, "Thank you so much for the advice and for listening, Mr. Austen. I'm going to take what you've said into consideration and pray over it."

Pray over it.

Will I end up praying for God to remove me from this whole situation or will I actually pray for His will to be done? My boss wasn't wrong. I like Finley Andersson. That much is perfectly clear now. But I think it's just as a friend. Sure, he's got wonderful qualities. And he's handsome.

But I can't date him.

I can't be taken away from my home and family.

The answer is absolutely not.

This is a quality I was *not* expecting from Crown Prince Finley Andersson...

"Lorelei! Will you kill it already?! Quit toying around."

I glance from the black dot on the floor up to the café chair where a crouching prince resides. Snickers float around us from our unintended audience as we stand on our unintended stage, but Finley pays them no mind. His rounded blue eyes are glued to the now-moving nickel-sized spider on the floor.

"It's a spider, Finley. A living creature made with a purpose. I am not going to kill it."

"My heart is going to detonate, Leilei. Get rid of it!"

I roll my lips into my mouth to hide the grin wanting to break free. For starters, why is this masculine, regal prince standing on a chair, his chest heaving with anxious breaths, over a little spider? It's not even big and furry. But secondly, he called me Leilei, pronounced "lay-lay", something he has taken to since he met me outside Books and Beans this afternoon and held the door open for me to walk through.

No one has ever given me a nickname other than "Lor." And that has almost felt like a lazy way to not say my whole name.

Maybe "Leilei" could be classified as the same, but to me, it feels like he softened the sharpness of my name. Almost as if I was given permission to simply breathe and exist without having to be in control.

Except now I am in control.

In control of getting Sir Spider out of Finley's keen sight so that both can live long, stress-free lives apart from each other.

Finally squatting down, I use the plastic cup the barista, Emma Jane, gave me (she, too, is not a fan of spiders) and a napkin to sweep the innocent little thing into its temporary trap. Walking the distance from our back corner table that Finley chose so as to not draw attention to us (he didn't anticipate a tiny friend lurking in the corner), I set Sir Spider loose outside and bid him farewell and best wishes.

When I turn around after closing the door, the few people within the bookstore-slash-cafe applaud me. My face heats, and I scamper to the back corner where Finley now sits in the chair with his legs crossed, hands folded lazily in his lap as if he wasn't just fearing for his life over a black moving dot on the floor moments ago. Sitting down, I meet his eyes, and he looks away with pink-tinged cheeks.

"If you didn't want to be embarrassed, then you should have simply avoided the spider."

He looks at me incredulously and huffs. "Easy for you to say. Do you not understand the way my heart races, brain fries, and veins run hot when I see such a creature?" Then, he smirks. "Come to think of it, I do believe it is a similar response to when I see you. Do I fear you, or do I love you, Leilei?"

Now *my* heart races, *my* brain fries, and *my* veins run blistering hot. And it's definitely fear, not love.

"You fear me," I state, drawing on my sensibilities instead of allowing the haze of confusing emotions to take over. "I am not Lucy, who is sweet and lovely and soft, and you have your wires crossed thinking you love me. I came here to tell you that. Furthermore, I will jump straight to the point. I do not wish to be a princess or a queen, and I do not wish to move to Korsa. Yes, I find myself liking you, but nothing more is plausible."

Finley blinks once. Unfolds his hands and rubs them on his navy pants. Then he blinks again.

Does he wear dress pants everywhere he goes? I don't think I've seen him in anything less than. What does he look like lounging around his house? Does he opt for holey shirts and baggy sweats like I do?

Not yours to think about, Lorelei.

"Let's talk about how you are finding yourself liking me. Can you elaborate?" Finley uncrosses his legs and places his folded hands on top of the table, leaning in.

"You are kind, intelligent, and... nice. I find your company enjoyable and your brain fascinating."

Finley doesn't respond, and I worry I spoke too honestly. But then, he smiles ear to ear and says, "So you do want to date me, but you are wholly committed to not leaving Juniper Grove. Therefore, you won't date me. Did I get that correct?"

My neck heats, and I sip the chai tea that has cooled from the amount of time it took me to make my spider rescue earlier. I appreciate the way Finley is verifying my words before making assumptions. "Can I speak honestly?"

"I'd have you speak no other way, Leilei."

I set the light blue, rounded mug down. After inhaling, I close my eyes and say, "I've never dated a man before. I am clueless about the process. I've watched my sister and our friends date, but I'm fearful. I don't want to mess up. I don't want to fall in love. I don't want to leave my home, family, friends, and job. I like you as a person, yes. I could see our brains connecting well. But I can't see you standing side by side with a woman like me. I am... inexperienced. You are not. I am a small town homebody. You are a traversing crown prince. I like peace and quiet and plants and cats. You like adventure and flirting and shenanigans. We do not make sense, simply put. But we could be friends while you're here."

My shoulders droop as if everything I've needed to say has weaseled its way out of me. Finley sits unmoving across from me as Emma Jane quietly and quickly sets our sandwiches down. Though the silence is suffocating me, I manage a whispered "thank you" to Emma Jane before she departs.

Finley's eyes roam from my bouncing leg, to my fidgeting hands, and finally, to my face. I believe he may be looking into the depths of my soul at this very moment, which causes the bounding leg to go double-time.

"Leilei, are you scared to date me because you are scared you will fall in love with me?" He tilts his head to the side and a wave of blond covers one of his mesmerizing blue eyes.

Yes. No? "And I don't want to move."

"So you are also scared you will *want* to move if you date me and fall in love with me?"

Dang this man. Dang him! He has no business taking my rambles and coherently presenting them back to me with such ease and clarity.

"Yes, Finley!" I recognize my rising voice and reel it back in. It's not anger… Is it disbelief? Confusion around how he is reading me so well? "I've never been in love, and I've never had the desire to *fall* in love. I don't want to be a tangle of emotions and passion only to fizzle to a painful, burnt end. I want safety, trust, security, and the feeling of home."

Finley clears his throat, and I look anywhere but at him. The cracks in the wooden floor, the teens in the bookshelves across the building, the way the light filters through the Dragon Tree by the windows…

"Lorelei."

How could I allow myself to say those things? Yes, he gave me permission to speak honestly, but did he really mean it? He must desire a whirlwind romance. Look at his past for crying out loud! I can't compete with those women…

And mercy! When have I ever even entertained the thought of competing with a woman? I am in no competition. A man will want me as I am, or he will not want me at all. It's perfectly okay that I don't want to fall in love. I'm like the Dragon Tree plant. Tall, sword-like, and easy to care for. A plant, er, woman like me doesn't need much. Too much would be overwhelming. Finley is...

"Leilei. Look at me."

Finley's pastel yellow shirt interrupts my admiration of the Dragon Tree.

"You're too much for me, Finley. I need simple. You aren't simple." My eyes plead for him to understand, but instead, the man crouches and holds my fumbling hands firmly between his own, the touch simultaneously soothing and shocking me. He sets his jaw and blue fire rages in his eyes.

"I'm not going to try and persuade you here and now, but I do have to ask you this: If you truly believe there is something between us, would you please do me the honor of taking a risk and exploring it and testing me against your perceived notions? I gave you the hand-made gift and asked you to date me with serious intentions as is the custom of our country. I am dedicated to this. To pursuing you."

Huh? That little show was a custom to ask someone out. Lucy must have loved helping him prepare that. It'll end up in one of her romance books. That knowledge settles my nerves, but only a little bit.

Back to the topic at hand, though. "You have less than three months. I wouldn't be ready to move anywhere in three months. You should focus on a girl who would... like my *sister!*"

"With all due respect, Lorelei, your sister is a lovely woman, but she is not the woman I desire. I desire you. I want you. I want your brain. I want your soul. I want your random facts. I want your shy glances. I want your individualism. I want your fears. I want your doubts. I want your weird."

My heartbeat thunders in my ears as I process his words. I search his body language for seedlings of error. He is crouched, grasping my hands, staring up at me as if I... as if I was already his world.

Too much, too much, too much, my mind echoes. The processor has reached its limit. If I were a cartoon, steam would be wafting upwards over my head.

"Can I have time to think it over?"

Finley smiles softly, though it doesn't reach his ears this time. "Of course. I know this is not an easy request being who I am. I know on paper we are opposite in every way. But I want you to get to know me as you. Not as Lucy. I want to get to know you as *you.*" He brightens. "Why don't we hang out tomorrow. We can go to the bookstore and go for a nature walk. Maybe we can visit an antebellum home."

"Oh, we could go to tour Adeline's Place. It's supposedly haunted, but I don't quite believe in that stuff." Then what he's doing hits me, and I narrow my eyes. "Hey. Unfair. Books, nature, and history..."

He waggles his brows, his lips turning upward. "I never said I would fight fair, Leilei."

"If I say yes to this, do you promise it's just as friends?" Darn man. Tugging on my weaknesses. This must be Lucy's doing. How can I say no to books, nature, and antebellum homes?

"No, Lorelei. For the sake of not lying to you, I can't tell you I will treat tomorrow as an outing of friends. But I can promise you that I will respect your boundaries. I want to get to know you better. I want you to get to know me better. Romance can come later."

As I process, I take a sip of my tea, which has cooled to a temperature I no longer enjoy. He was honest with me. That's respectable. And maybe if I go, he will realize that I'm not the right woman for him. *Romantically.*

Lucy's words flitter back into my mind.

Sometimes love is unexplainable.

But while this might not be love, maybe the same applies to friendships, too. Maybe some souls are simply meant to be acquainted and befriended.

I evaluate him even though my processor is done...processing. His blue eyes are wide and pleading as he leans over the table towards me on his elbows. Blond hair frames the edges of his face, and I want to feel if it's as silky as it looks. That's a sensation I thoroughly enjoy.

He wants this, and maybe this is my ticket to shaking him.

"Okay. I'll go. But I'm viewing this as an outing with a friend. Thank you for your honesty."

The biggest smile overcomes his face as he steeples his hands under his chin. He looks... calculating? Mischievous?

"I'm ecstatic to hear that answer from you, Leilei. I'll pick you up at five." He grows solemn. "I know we are supposed to have this meal, and I don't want to ask this question, but do you need some space to process everything alone?"

My heart stops. No one outside of my sister and Hadley has ever asked me that before... has never seen the need.

"Yes, please. If you don't mind. I would actually like that very much."

He closes his eyes slowly and nods, inhaling softly before opening his eyes. "I figured as much. I'll see you tomorrow evening."

As he grabs his sandwich from the plate and walks away, I shout, "Thank you, Finley! See you tomorrow."

He waves while wearing an expression that looks halfway despondent and halfway hopeful before turning on his heel and leaving. Two men in black suits follow at a distance, and I realize those must be his protection officers. Will they come with us tomorrow?

I'm going out on the town with a man I've known for two weeks. A man who wants to date me. I gulp. *Marry me.*

What have I gotten myself into? Why did I agree to this?

It's not a date. It's not a date. It's not a date. Just an outing among friends.

My brain conjures all the reasons I should text him and say nevermind. *He's a prince. A crown prince. He will be king within a year. He wants to date me with intentions. He will move me to Korsa. He will take me away from my comfort.*

And somewhere in the depths of the chaos and confusion of rivaling emotions and logic, a whisper. *He sees you. He wants you for you. He is giving you space and time. He believes you are good for him. He validates your fears. He is willing to prove himself. He knows you well enough already to reel you in with books, history, and nature walks.*

Lucy would have been putty in his hands had he said those words to her, but I'm not Lucy. I'm confused. I like him, but I can't leave this place. I'm a rooted plant. He seems so good and so honest, but those headlines about the Prince of Hearts stir suspicion. He's a flirt, and I'm not sure I completely understand the concept. He may love me, and I don't know if I fully comprehend what it truly means to love someone in such a romantic capacity...

"Is everything okay, Lor?" Emma Jane waves a hand in front of my face, which is still turned towards the door Finley walked out of while biting his sandwich moments ago. He saw I needed space and time, and he gave it to me.

Is being comfortable enough to say yes to an evening with him in town a sign that I do like him? Or that I could? Or that I could possibly...

"Yes, EJ. I think so." I fragilely smile at the waitress who is a couple of years younger than me. She called me Lucy when we first arrived, and I corrected her to Lorelei, and now she's positively beaming at the idea I'm here as myself with Finley. I wonder... Would it be weird to ask her...?

"What do you think love truly is? And how do you know if you have the potential for it?"

I slap my hand over my mouth, blaming Finley and his desire for me to be honest for the fact that I'm asking Emma Jane such a question.

But to my surprise, she smiles and sits down where Finley once resided. "Oh, Lorelei! This is my favorite subject. You know I want to be a matchmaker, right?" And then she launches into a spiel on how love *is* security and trust and safety, but she says it is also magic and connection and unknowns.

I leave forty-five minutes later with a lot of information to process, confusing emotions to sort through, completely people-d out, and...

And the tiniest seedling thought that maybe I should give Finley one date. Maybe I should state that tomorrow is a date.

After one real date with me, I'm sure he will change his mind and want to find someone more flirty, experienced, and fun. Then he goes on his merry way and I settle back into my routine.

No one's hurt. I get a fun evening. (Yes, an actual fun evening filled with things I enjoy.) He gets to see firsthand how wrong I am for him.

A win-win.

Though my heart silently cries that if he does walk away from me, I might not feel like the winner.

Chapter Twelve

Lorelei

"You are absolutely stunning, Lor," Lucy squeals, holding her fists to her mouth as she rocks back and forth on her feet.

The woman in the mirror is me, just... modern?

Not that I don't wear modern clothes, but I don't bother myself with wearing up-to-date fashion. I wear what *I* like. Like anyone should. Now, I'm wearing black leggings (I don't wear jeans as the material suffocates my soul) with a flowy white off-the-shoulder cotton shirt with my black sports bra strap poking through. Thankfully the fabric of the shirt is thick enough that the bra doesn't show through. My hair is in its typical ponytail, and I'll sport my white sneakers when I leave.

Athletic chic, Lucy called it.

If I wasn't actually beyond comfortable in this outfit, I would toss it and put on my work clothes. I'm not trying to impress Finley tonight. I'm trying to show him why I am not the woman he thinks I am. Not good for him. Not queen material.

Queen.

My breath hitches thinking about that.

That reason alone is enough to say that nothing can happen between me and Finley. Even if I wanted it to. Which I don't.

I look at my beige walls and plants in my window and my ordered desk holding my client files and laptop. Frizzle and Frannie lie on my bed. Lucy stands at my side in a cute little pink dress with a bow in her hair. I can't leave this. My place. My people. My home.

It's okay. After this evening, Finley will see that I am not the woman for him.

"Hmph," is my only response to my sister.

She rolls her eyes as we stand in the same place, looking into the same mirror, like we did a mere week ago. Seven days. I've known Finley for seven days.

"This is too much too soon, Lucy. I can't go on this outing. I—" My voice rises to a squeak, choking off my words. My nerves feel like livewire beneath my skin. The places where the ends of my hair meet my neck feel like needles. My brain fogs over as I desperately wish to strip my clothes off because everything feels like too much.

So I do.

I strip down to nothing and tie my hair into a bun. Lucy only gathers the clothing that I've thrown haphazardly around the room and folds them into a neat pile on the edge of my bed. I stand there, naked, shuddering. Not because of the cold but because the sensation of air on my skin is grating. I can't sit on my bed or wrap a blanket around me because the fabric would push me further into panic. I can only stand there, wishing I could levitate so that my feet weren't touching the hardwood floor.

"Lucy." I choke on a sob. "Help me."

It's a lost plea. There's nothing my twin can do. I have to wade through this on my own. I have no idea how long it will last. It's been years since I've had an episode like this. Patterns keep me safe, and my patterns are broken. Finley has tornado-ed into my life and misplaced everything. He was supposed to love my sister. He was supposed to laugh off our switch and date my sister. He wasn't supposed to want to date me.

"Breathe with me, Lorelei," Lucy says, launching into breathing exercises. I follow her lead, breathing in, holding, and slowly releasing. She encourages me to flex my toes. To feel the hardwood beneath my feet. To point out specific objects in my room such as my aloe vera plant, the one bulb that's out on my string of iridescent indoor lights, and the stuffed elephant that I clung to as a child. As she coaches me through breathing and grounding, she reminds me that I am safe within the confines of my room. That she is with me and everything is okay. She reminds me that even though I'm not well, I am okay. Safe. Secure.

Slowly, ever so slowly, my brain clears and my body relaxes. A chill definitely associated with the air conditioning wracks my body, and Lucy gestures to my clothes then turns around.

Heat floods my cheeks as I realize I am standing naked in my room with my twin. I'm not embarrassed that she sees my naked body, but I am embarrassed that I had that episode. But mostly, I'm unbelievably grateful for this woman who nestled me close in the womb at one point in our existence together.

"I love you, Lucy. Thank you," I say through tears as I get dressed. The sensations are still lingering, but they are not taking over me. I continue to remind myself that I am safe. Secure. In control. *Okay.*

"I love you, you amazing, beautiful, wonderful woman." Lucy opens her arms to ask for a hug, but I can't risk it right now. I shake my head, so she holds her pinky out. Where most people would view this as a pinky promise, as I interlace my pinky with hers, we view this as a hug. To me, it's just as meaningful as her real hug would be. "You can do this tonight. I know you can. You're scared; I see that. But I truly don't think you should let your fears stop you from what could be a lifetime of love and happiness. Finley really likes you, and I know it feels sudden. It is. The man is a male version of me—falling hard and fast. Sending you on that first date was my romance mistake, but it seems like God has His hand in this. Go on the outing, Lorelei."

"I'm sorry. But did you just see what happened?" I gesture around the room and then up and down myself. "What if I'm triggered by something while I'm out with him?"

"We should tell him that you have autism and that you just experienced sensory overload. We can encourage him to be gentle with you, and I can instruct him on grounding exercises to help you."

"But what if I strip again?"

"I doubt you would do that. You retain enough of your sense and are in control enough to wait until you are in private. You stripped so quickly just now because you were safe with me. Don't discredit all the years of work you've put into understanding yourself and learning how to live with your autism."

She's saying all the right things, and I want to believe her. She's right. I have done so much work, and I can still think even through the fog of sensory overload. I could at least make it to a restroom or the car or somewhere private. Finley's mustang does have tinted windows, after all.

"But what if he runs when we tell him?"

Lucy smirks. "As you tell me when I overthink a date, if he runs away because of something out of your control, we will wiggle our fingers as he leaves saying 'Bye, scared little boy.'"

I chuckle, and then I remember that I'm supposed to scare him away. That way my life will go back to normal and I can reestablish my routines. Maybe if he learns I'm autistic then he will go back to Korsa and find another woman to date with *intentions.*

"Deal. But please do not tell him I just stripped naked in front of you." Even if I am actively attempting to scare him away, that is too much to reveal about a person.

Lucy beams. "Deal!"

An hour later, the doorbell rings, and I open the door to let in a very handsome, very casual crown prince. He wears white sneakers that are like the male version of mine, dark wash bootcut jeans, and a white Henley quarter-sleeve shirt that pulls taut across his chest. For a slimmer man, he sure has muscle definition.

Which I should definitely not be noticing.

Nor should I be reeling over the fact that we match. Was this Lucy's doing?

My cheeks heat as he takes a seat on the couch like Lucy instructed once I gestured for him to come in. I follow him without saying a single word because, if I'm being completely honest, I haven't been able to rip my eyes away from him and his excited blue eyes and luscious blond hair, styled to where only the left side falls across his face.

He is objectively beautiful; I cannot allow that to cloud my mission.

"Hey, Finley," I finally say, taking a seat on my reclining chair, a safe distance from him. Lucy plops on the other side of the couch so that Finley is between us. "Would you like some tea?"

"I was thinking we could stop at Books and Beans for tea before going on the nature walk," he says. "If that's okay with you."

"That is fine with me." I nod my head then shift my eyes to Lucy. She mimics the nod I gave Finley, firm and decisive. "But we would like to talk to you about something important first."

Finley sits up and folds his hands in his lap. "I'm all ears." And an image of a small Finley with Dumbo ears pops into my brain. I fight to stifle a laugh, but at least it lightens my mood. Sometimes I enjoy the weirdness of my brain.

After taking a breath, I state, "I have autism."

Finley's engaged expression doesn't falter or change. After a moment of silence, he says, "Thanks for telling me about that. Could you explain more about how it impacts you specifically?"

My heart races at his affirming, receptive response. That is not what I was expecting. I don't make a habit of telling everyone because it's honestly none of their business. I also don't make a habit of beating people over the head to make them accommodate me. That's selfish, no matter what other people may say. But this response is a rare one. And it does something funny to my heart.

And apparently my brain because I have forgotten how to speak.

Lucy fills in the silence. "My sister is a socially awkward, intelligent, often overloaded with sensations, wonderful specimen of society."

I glare at her, but she laughs. It helped me find words, though. "Yes, I'm those things, but it's because I think and process a little differently than what others consider normal. One of my most showing and prominent quirks outside of blunt honesty and a desperate need for routine and pattern is sensory overload. That's why I've panicked when you've touched me in the past. Sometimes it's too much."

"Ah, that makes sense," is all he says. In a tone like everything has clicked and he's perfectly okay with it. "Thanks for letting me know. I will be extra cautious from now on with touch. What other things get under your skin?" He chuckles as I gape at him. "Bad pun. But I'm not sorry. Okay, can we talk more about this during our nature walk?"

"One more thing," Lucy pipes in while my brain struggles to catch up with the fact that Finley is not scared, shocked, or disturbed by this revelation. At least, if he is, he does a better job at masking than I do. He even nods along as Lucy instructs him on how to help me out of sensory overload and panic. Once she's done, he salutes her and promises to take care of me. Lucy giggles and turns heart-eyes on the two of us before she says, "I can't believe you are going to get married before me."

"Not happening," I quickly retort, and Finley doesn't even seem fazed by the comment. He stands, holds out a hand to me, which I politely decline because I'm still not feeling up to touching after the overload experience an hour ago, and then opens the door for me to walk through.

As he steps out behind me, Lucy hollers, "Have her back by ten, King-in-Law! That's her self-imposed bed time. Even on the weekends."

Finley yells back, "Roger that, boss."

And I laugh. Those two would probably be the best of friends if I married him.

Banishing the intrusive thought of *marrying him*, I make my way to his old Mustang and wait for him to open my door.

Well, darn.

The man already has me trained to accept his chivalry.

After we stop at Books and Beans for tea, Finley takes me to the nature center in Juniper Grove. I've been here plenty on my own, but this is the first time I've gone with someone. With a man, at that.

Well, three men if I'm being completely honest. His two PPOs, whose names I learned are Gabriel and Anders, trail behind us. Far enough to where they can't readily hear our conversation but still close enough to act if something was to happen. I don't mind as much as I thought I would when Finley introduced us earlier. They seem nice enough, and I think Lucy has been talking to Gabriel quite a bit.

Being here with Finley creates a different atmosphere than when I'm alone as we walk down the paved dirt path through labeled trees, plants, and the occasional informational sign noting the different wildlife in the area. I inhale the earthy smell. If I could have a cottage home out in the middle of the woods where I was given this smell every single day, I think I'd thrive. It's hard to detach or spiral when I'm surrounded by God's stellar creation. Every tree, animal, and plant is a fingerprint of His intelligent design, pulling me into a closer relationship with Him and worship of Him.

"You're a Christian, right? Judging by the fact you came to our church, ask for prayer before our meals, and have your own Bible. I know those things don't make a Christian, so I would like to know more about your faith if you are willing to share." I reach out to touch the smooth bark of a red maple tree.

"I was saved when I was fifteen years old. I grew up going to church as the church and state are hardly separate entities when it comes to our country. Though, my faith didn't become my own until I was fifteen, when I truly realized what sin was and recognized my need of a perfect Savior."

"I was nineteen," I say as I squat to play with the leaves of a young sweet shrub. "Though I always followed a Christian moral compass, I didn't actually surrender my life to Christ until I was nineteen. I had thought that I had proclaimed Christ as my Savior before, but I forgot to proclaim Him as my Lord. Conviction swept over me, and I decided that I couldn't navigate this life without His leadership and guidance."

He squats down beside me; heat radiates from his closeness as he reaches to touch the leaves of the shrub. "I think that's a common occurrence with people who have grown up in the church. That's what happened with my sister, Astrid."

"She's twenty-one, right?"

"Indeed. And my older brother, Johan, is—"

"Thirty-two," I finish for him, and then I realize what I did. I stand and offer a sheepish apology before stating, "I may have searched you after that first date. I wanted to make sure you were good enough for my sister."

He laughs, standing. "That's normal. So," he trails off for a moment, "you must have seen my title of Prince of Hearts."

"Yeah," I say with the scrunch of my nose as we continue to walk. "About that. I figured it was fine. People date, and they date often. My sister is one of those people, which is why I thought your dating history didn't matter. She probably has a list as long as yours. But me... I've never had a boyfriend as you already know."

"Does it bother you?"

We turn down a lesser-walked path, stepping over fallen branches as I lead us deeper into the woods. "A little? If I'm being honest. It's not that you've dated a lot; it's that I haven't. You're experienced, and I am... not."

"Are you worried that you won't measure up?"

The bluntness of the question catches me off-guard, and as I turn to look at him, my sneaker gets caught between two limbs. My ankle pops, and I tumble backwards towards the ground, closing my eyes to prepare for impact.

But the impact never comes.

Instead, I open my eyes to see Finley's perfect face mere inches from mine, his breath, which smells of peppermint tea, wafts over me as he releases a breath of relief and begins to lift me up from the dip he held me in. If we were on a dance floor, we would have received a ten out of ten for perfect execution.

Once I'm stable and on my feet, he drops his hands from my back.

"You okay?" he asks, his head tilted as he examines me.

"I'm fine," I lie. Okay, on the surface, I *am* fine. But on the inside, my heart has decided to compete with racehorses and my nerves buzz with a strange desire for more. More of Finley's hands on my back. More of his closeness.

S-T-R-A-N-G-E.

I don't ever desire those things. Ever.

"So, is that your worry? That you won't measure up?"

I shake my head clear, which he must assume is me saying no.

"Then what is it?" he asks.

"No, it is that. I think. Maybe also that I might be naive to dating norms and will embarrass you one day."

"Not a chance, Leilei." Finley's eyes are a blazing blue fire as he steps closer to me, lifting his hands as if he is going to place them on my biceps. "Is this okay?"

I nod, swallowing any hesitancy. I *do* want to feel his hands on me again. And the feeling of being set on fire overwhelms me as he plants his hands on my biceps and tugs me closer to him. Again... mere inches between us as I tilt my head up and he tilts his down. I stand like a statue. Waiting. Though I don't know what I'm waiting for. And I may crumble before long.

"You could never embarrass me. You are brave, kind, gentle, sweet, intelligent, cute," his gaze trails to my lips, "arresting." He bounces back to my eyes. "You could fall flat on your face in the middle of a ball, and I would help you to your feet, make sure you are okay, and kiss your cheek. You could become overstimulated while in the midst of a state dinner, and I would whisk you off to a private room where you could decompress however you need to. You could," he grins wickedly, "flatulate in the middle of a church service while everyone is bowing their heads in prayer, and I would rank it on a scale of one to ten with a sultry whisper in your ear."

At that, I shove him away and laugh, a blush warming my cheeks and a bit of anxiety creeping in at the thought of that. I shudder, dismissing the thought. "I would never!"

"Never say never, Leilei. Stomach problems hit everyone at the most inconvenient of times."

I laugh some more and he joins in, the sound echoing off the trees around us. "Has that happened to you or something?"

He grins. "Wouldn't you like to know?"

"Duh. That's why I'm asking."

Finley shakes his head, making me beg him to tell me the riveting tale of when he almost didn't make it to the restroom at a State dinner. The rest of the date is light-hearted and, well, fun. We finish the nature walk while bantering back and forth with the occasional topic change when he asks me to talk more about what it's like for me being autistic. We visit the local library where he shows me his favorite philosophy books and historian authors. Then, around eight, after a quick dinner at the hibachi restaurant where I got to know his PPOs a little more (I couldn't let them eat off by themselves; it felt rude, plus I wanted to vet Gabriel a little. He checks out.), he takes me on a private tour of the Adeline House.

Naturally, these tours always happen at night due to the haunting factor, but I didn't know he booked the entire place for us from eight to ten.

Of course, I find no evidence of a haunting, though I did find out that Finley kindly asked the staff not to initiate the usual jump scares that they do to toy with guests. My heart warmed at his consideration. *I didn't even have to ask for it...*

As he drops me back off at my apartment and walks me to the door, hugging me gently, I remember that I was supposed to scare him off.

But instead, I think I had one of the best nights of my life.

Chapter Thirteen

Finley

Humming the lyrics of "She's Got It All" by Kenny Chesney, I shut the door of the Mustang and walk down the little dirt path from the parking area and onto the dimly lit porch. My PPOs are still in the black sedan on a phone call with my father. I'm reaching for the door when laughter sounds from the side of the porch.

"Someone had a good night," Mason comments, Karoline snuggled up beside him on the wide porch swing. I didn't even see her car when I pulled in.

"I love that song," Karoline coos. "And your humming is quite melodic."

"Hey, now." Mason cuts a look at his fiance. "I'll get jealous. Don't go complimenting the crown prince's singing voice."

Karoline lifts her head so that her chin is resting on his chest. "Nobody sings better than my Peppermint." She kisses his cheek after using his strange nickname, and Mason beams with pride.

"I love you, Vroom."

Yeah, her nickname is even stranger.

"I love you." Mason cups her face for a kiss.

"Okay," I say, wrapping my hand around the door knob. "While you two snog, I'll be grabbing a late night snack."

"Bye, Finley!" Karoline waves.

I close the door behind me and continue my humming. Maybe one day that'll be me and Lorelei. I will have a swing installed by the chrysanthemum flower display that I will plant in the Royal Garden. Every morning or every evening, we can cuddle on the swing amidst her favorite flowers and kiss.

Kiss...

When Lorelei tripped and I caught her, those pink, plump lips were too close for comfort. It took every ounce of restraint I had to not carve a trail of kisses across her lips and neck. Images of kissing her rooted in my brain, and I had to spend the rest of the night trying to disregard them.

I grab a cup from the cupboard and fill it up with water from the spout on the refrigerator. It's cool going down my throat, and I guzzle the entire cup in one go.

After filling it up again, my thoughts return to the date.

Amazing. It was utterly amazing. Lorelei was herself, I restrained my desire to touch her, and we had so much fun learning about each other.

"Thank you, Jesus," I whisper with a slight victory fist pump. Then in Korsan, I continue. "Please continue to work on her heart and mind. We were created for each other; I know this in my bones. You have led me to her. Let me be patient while her feelings catch up to mine. Thank you for this lovely, captivating woman You have brought into my life."

"Talking to your people?" Mason's voice echoes through the house as he walks inside.

"No, just praying."

"Oops, sorry."

"You're good." I make my way into the living room where Mason has switched on the corner lamp. "I was just finishing."

Mason sits on the chair and I take the couch. Gabriel and Anders finally come inside with twisted looks on their faces. Gabriel says, "We were still in the car, Mason. Next time, make out with your girl behind closed doors."

"Agreed," Anders says with pursed lips as Mason roars with laughter. I can't help but smile. I want to be in a place where my girl and I are so in love that we freely make out on a porch swing.

But with Lorelei's autism, I know I have to take the physical things slow. Which is extremely hard for me because physical touch just so happens to be my top love language. The Lord is truly making me practice patience and restraint, which are both wonderful qualities for a husband and a king. Heck, for a man in general.

"Your Highness, please give His Royal Majesty the King a call before you go to sleep tonight," Anders says in Korsan, a perfect mask of blankness covering his face. "It's about the stalker."

I nod swiftly as the two men walk into their room down the hall and shut the door.

"Was he saying how much he hates me?" Mason asks, a trace of laughter still lingering in his voice.

"No, not at all," I vaguely reply. I cross one leg over the other as half my brain begins wondering what Gabriel and Anders spoke with my father about. The stalker didn't make an appearance tonight, at least, not that I'm aware of. Was he caught? Did Father find out who it was? "I hate to deprive you of the information you are surely chomping at the bit to know, but I have to call my father it seems. Lorelei and I had a wonderful night, and I am in love with her."

I stand as Mason does. He clasps my back in a tight hug. "Finley, I—I'm happy for you, man. That's great news. Are you two a thing now?"

"Not yet," I sigh. But then I smile as I recall the night we had. She was buoyant, happy, and open. She seemed to be completely herself, and I fell hard. "But hopefully soon."

Mason releases me. "I'm praying for you two."

"Thanks, brother. I should really call my father now."

Concern flickers across his dark brown eyes, so I place a hand on his shoulder. "Everything is okay. Just some important business to attend to."

He nods and walks into the kitchen as I disappear into my small, logged room.

Sitting on my wooden chair by the cheap fold-out desk I bought for work purposes (seriously, nothing bigger would fit into this room), I search for my father's personal contact and hit the call button.

Father picks up after two rings, his tone breathy. "Finley, *haalaa*. Thanks for calling promptly."

"Of course. What's going on? Anders and Gabriel said you needed to speak with me regarding the stalker. I don't believe he made an appearance tonight during my date with Lorelei."

"Ah." Father's voice lightens. "How is the young woman? Have you won her over to you yet?"

I chuckle, "Not quite, but tonight felt like I took massive leaps in the right direction. You're going to love her, Father. She's smart, organized, thoughtful, kind, and beautiful. She's going to make a lovely queen."

"I'm happy to hear that, Finley. You deserve someone capable of ruling by your side, especially since your kingship is coming out of the blue. Thank you, again, for stepping up. You will never understand how much it means to me, son. Our country will be in capable, honest hands."

I beam with pride; Father always knows the right things to say to encourage me. An ache spreads across my chest as I think of his old state, my brother's condition, my little sister in the palace without me, and my mother's overwhelming fear that I will not secure a wife in time. Maybe I should plan a visit soon? Would Lorelei go with me...?

Father is silent on the other end as I ponder within my mind, his heavy breaths the only noise. Then, he says, "I found out who hired the stalker. You were never in any danger, my son. I am taking necessary action as a husband, a king, and as your father to correct the matter, so please do not hold this against her. I am handling everything."

My stomach drops and my heart pounds wildly against my chest. My head spins with questions that come unbidden from my lips. "No... you can't be serious? Mamma hired the stalker? Why? For what purpose? How did she think that was a good idea? What was she thinking?"

"No! Goodness, no. It was Karin Nilsson of Vespen, not your mother. Though I think your mother may have given her the idea on accident. I'm still getting to the bottom of everything, but you should be okay moving forward. You were never in danger, but I know the thought of someone following you and snapping pictures, sending them back to your mother, is not a way to feel safe."

I regain composure knowing my mamma isn't at fault. That would have been detrimental to me. My mother isn't the kindest, most motherly woman, but she loves our family. Why did my brain jump to that conclusion? Maybe because Father said he was handling the situation as a husband.

Is Karin that desperate for my attention? Did she truly think this was the best route to take to win me over to her? The more I think about it, the stalker's actions were not merely observational. They were intentional, meant to interrupt and impede. Finally, I state, "I'm going to give her a call tomorrow. I trust you are handling everything, but she needs to hear from me, too."

"Of course, son. Be gentle. Be understanding. Be firm. Be cautious in your decisions. You will be king in under a year, and we do not need to burn our bridge with Vespen. I trust you. This is part of kingship—humbling yourself and attempting to understand things that do not add up or make sense. And when you do make a decision, stick with it and dole out corrections in a gentle but firm manner."

"Thanks, Father." Even in the wake of this news, which to be honest, I saw coming, I'm in awe of my father. He has been an excellent king, and he is going to leave me with some mighty large shoes to try and fill. If I can be half the king that he has been, then I think I will be okay.

After we say goodbye, I begin to write out what I plan to say to Karin. She's not getting off the hook for this.

Chapter Fourteen

Lorelei

"Tell. Us. *Everything.*" Hadley elbows me before taking a sip of sweet tea. I'm sitting around Hadley's table in her grandmother's old house that she inherited. Lucy is fixing her plate while Karoline is already shoving a bite of spaghetti into her mouth. Hadley demanded we all come over for dinner after work; she shipped Braxton off to Finley and Mason's place, which is his old cabin.

"We walked the nature trail, went to the library, ate hibachi, then toured the Adeline House," I say, shoving noodles in my mouth. The girls glare at me, and I find the garlic bread on my plate very interesting.

"More details, Lor. That's not *everything*. I was at Mason's when he came home last night. The man looked absolutely drunk in love." Karoline sings the last part off-key, matching Beyonce's song. Something I only know because Lucy once played it on repeat for days. "Plus you two sat next to each other in church this morning. *Close* to each other. What did you do to that man? And what did he do to you?"

Hadley tosses her hair into a platinum blonde ponytail before digging into her spaghetti. Lucy's green-hazel eyes warm as she mentally nudges me to speak from across the table.

"I don't know. It was a lovely evening. We talked. Laughed. Had fun."

"So do you have a boyfriend now?" Hadley asks, her fork paused at her mouth.

"No?" As I think about the night, the one that very much felt like a date by the end of it, I can't deny that the thought of actively dating Finley is intriguing. But I still know I can't move. I can't become a queen. So therefore I can't date Finley.

"That sounded like a question," Hadley says with a smirk.

"Maybe I find the idea appealing." I shove garlic bread into my mouth while the three women erupt in applause and excited squeals. The corner of my lips tugs upward as I chew.

"Please give us more information. I'm starved to know everything," Lucy exclaims, sweeping her braid to one side of her shoulder. "You went to bed when you got home and then we didn't get to talk much because I woke up late for church."

I recount the conversations, carefully including the way he made sure I was safe all night and how it feels like our brains were meant for each other as we challenged each other fact for fact in the library. But I was sure to leave out his personal admission of *stomach issues*. "But I can't date him. It wouldn't be right. I don't want to leave Juniper Grove. And I definitely do not want to become queen of an unknown country."

Lucy scoffs. "That's the coolest part!"

"To you, Little Miss Romance Writer." I shove a forkful of spaghetti into my mouth.

"I don't think you should write him off just yet, Lorelei," Karoline says, surprising me. She typically doesn't put her thoughts into conversations like this. I set my fork down to listen. She tucks a lock of brown waves behind her ear. "I didn't want to leave this area either, but in three months, I'll move to Nashville. And while I'm going to miss Juniper Grove and everything this place has given me, I know that I'm going to build a new life with the one my heart was meant for."

"But I've been here my entire life," I state.

"You're right," she says. "I moved here from Dallas, but this place quickly became home. And once you find a place that feels like home, you don't want to leave. But I've learned home is more than a place. It's the people."

"That's the—"

She cuts me off. "Before you say that's why you want to stay here, remember that you can build new relationships. And you won't lose the ones here in the process."

"Hear, hear." Hadley holds up her glass of sweet tea. "You couldn't get rid of us if you died. We'd just die with you."

Lucy clinks her glass with Hadley's. "Speaking truth, my dear friend."

I shove another bite of spaghetti into my mouth as I process their advice. I hear what they're saying, and I do trust that I wouldn't lose their friendship. I definitely wouldn't lose my twin. In fact, she'd probably move to Korsa with me to search for a duke or something.

Hm. I wouldn't mind that, actually. It would be nice to have her around.

But there is still the idea of being a queen. A whole queen to an entire country. One I'm not familiar with.

You'd have Finley to guide you through, my inner voice comments out of the blue. No. That wouldn't be enough. Would it?

"When are you seeing him again?" Lucy asks, taking a sip of her sweet tea and ripping me, thankfully, from my confusing thoughts.

We didn't make plans at the end of the night, nor did we do so today. The thought makes me sad, I notice. *Huh.* "Probably not until the weekend. I have a big case plus some smaller ones I'm preparing for at work, and I will need the evenings this week to work."

Karoline stands, placing her hands on the table. "Well, I do need everyone to make themselves free Saturday morning. I have a dress fitting booked for us."

We exchange glances as Karoline walks to the living room, quickly returning with an armful of olive green and white flannel shirts. She holds up the backside of the flannel where it reads "BRIDESMAID" in bolded, bubbled, black font. She hands one to Hadley, Lucy, and then me. "Will you all be my bridesmaids?"

"Thought you weren't going to ask!" Hadley jumps up and hugs Karoline.

"Yes! Yes! Yes!" Lucy shouts.

Me? You think of me *as someone worthy of standing beside you?*

"Of course," I say aloud, stunned.

We each take our flannels, and the fabric is scratchy beneath my fingers, causing my skin to feel like a bug is crawling beneath it. My heart drops. How will I tell her that I absolutely will not be able to wear this for any length of time? *Another time,* I think to myself as I watch her celebrate this moment with our friends. I'll ask Hadley the best way to approach it. For now, I paste a smile to my face and lay the flannel across the back of my chair.

We spend another hour eating and pinning boards on social media for Karoline's wedding. At least, they do. I sit as an outsider to the conversation as I truly have no opinion regarding colors, decorations, and dresses. Though, I do enjoy that Karoline is doing beige and olive green and white. Those colors are earthy and pretty. Plus, Lucy and I look great in green. *Finley will think so, too.*

Huh. That's a thought I've never had before. It's more of something my twin would think and voice. But I find it's true. I know Finley will think I'm pretty in that color.

And I want to look pretty for him.

"What will the fabric of the dresses be?" I interrupt. Three sets of shocked

eyes look at me while Lucy's jaw drops. I briefly wonder if I've asked the question in the wrong way, but as I recall the conversation around me prior to my interruption, I remember they had moved on from dresses and were talking about flowers. I smile sheepishly. "Sorry. I'm a bit late to the dress discussion."

"No, that's totally fine, Lor," Hadley says. Then her ivory white face turns to Karoline. "Did you have a specific fabric in mind?"

Karoline places a black-painted fingernail to her chin. "No. I want each of you to choose the style and fabric that works best for you. Just as long as our colors match, I'm perfectly fine with different styles and fabrics."

I smile. "Great."

Lucy tilts her head, an action that is my own when we are perplexed with one another. "Do you want to see the different styles that I think will look good on you?"

"Sure."

My twin's eyes sparkle as she rises from her seat on the reclining chair and moves to sit next to me on Hadley's worn couch. She pulls up an app on her phone and searches through pictures of dresses. As she shows me different styles and cuts, going into detail as to why each would look good on me, my mind is in awe of this moment. I'm not this girl. I don't talk about dresses and colors and styles. But they have easily allowed me into the conversation. I send a silent prayer of gratitude for my sister, my best friend, and Karoline. I truly have wonderful women around me who get me. Or at the very least, they don't complain all the time that they don't understand me like so many peers that I've tried to make friends with have done in the past.

"That's a strange way to file," my coworker, Hannah Thompson, says, her arms crossed and eyes squinted.

What a lovely Wednesday afternoon you're providing me with, Hannah.

I want to reply, "Then why are you hovering over me inside *my* office," but I don't. I grin a plastic smile and shrug.

"It makes perfect sense to me. Pictures register in the brain quicker than words. By using pictures to file my reports, I can easily identify them." I know I shouldn't explain. She will not understand, but I can't help but try to help her to understand.

"How do you immediately know that the pictures represent certain words?" She sounds skeptical, but at least she's considering my method rather than dismissing me offhand.

"I associate the pictures on the top of the file with each of my clients. For example," I hold up the file I've been working on but took a break from to organize my other files, "this image of a Christmas tree tells me I have Ms. Gretta's file in hand before I even register her last name on the side. I associate her with Christmas because it's an important part of her story."

Hannah snorts. "Weird. But okay. You do you." Then she walks out of my office in her clicking heels, her board-straight brown hair swishing behind her.

I have gained nothing but frustration from this interaction.

"Why are you so concerned with how I choose to organize and label my files? They are mine. You don't have to touch them," I grumble under my breath after my glass door clicks shut. Okay, she wasn't mean. I think? But it still frustrates me when people treat me like a child who isn't capable simply because I create my own systems instead of being "normal."

Once I stuff all the files away into the metal cabinet, I take a breather and boil water in my electric kettle for tea time. I send a quick email to Mr. Austen, inviting him to my office. He doesn't always come, but he definitely shows up a few times during the week for my 2:30 p.m. tea time. The clear kettle chimes, letting me know it's ready, and I pour a cup of steaming water into my oversized light brown mug that reads "BAE" in bold, black letters, and underneath it in a smaller black font, "Best Attorney Ever." It was a gift courtesy of Hadley when I passed the bar exam a couple of years ago.

I plop in a bag of ginger honey tea, then I reach into my mini fridge under my desk, hunting for my bag of sliced lemons. While I'm bent down and moving around lunch meats, cheeses, and a variety of fruits, my office door opens.

"Do you want lemon with your tea today, Mr. Austen?" I ask as I snag the bag from the back of the fridge. I really need to organize this next.

"Lemon sounds grand," a smooth and chipper voice that is decidedly not Mr. Austen retorts. As I jolt—because I *know* that voice—I slam the back of my head against the underside of the metal desk. Pain spreads and radiates down my neck.

A word that I don't recognize is hissed as footsteps draw near. My chair is lightly rolled away from the desk—with me on it and still hunched over my knees. Knowing I'm in the clear to sit up, I do, slowly, as one large, slender hand wraps around my shoulder, guiding me gently. The other hand rests right above my kneecap as Finley Andersson squats down in front of me, a look of pure worry creasing his blond brows as he asks if I'm all right.

"Uh-huh," I respond, pressing my hand against the backside of my head just to make sure there are no bumps or blood. "Just give me a second. I think I am more embarrassed than anything. I thought you were my boss."

He removes his hand from my shoulder, flashing the number "two" before asking, "How many fingers am I holding up?"

I laugh, the motion of my shoulders rising and falling sends another little wave of pain coursing through me. "Two," then I add, "You should choose an odd number next time. They are superior."

"Yep, you're all right," Finley breathes a laugh as the hand resting on my thigh squeezes. My gaze zeroes in on that hand, wondering how so much heat can be packed into one man's touch. It's too much. I shift away, and he releases me, letting me bend back down to pick up the bag of lemons I dropped. Though this time, I'm extra careful to swing my body away from the desk as I come back up.

I notice he has placed his hand over the edge of the desk where I would have hit if I hadn't swung my upper body around. That's... sweet? Or is he already making fun of me?

"I trust that you wouldn't repeat the incident, but I wanted to be extra careful," he says as he lowers his hand to his side and props himself on the side of my desk. I nod at the reassurance I didn't even need to ask for as my gaze trails from his hand to his light-wash jeans up to his tucked-in blush button-down shirt. Strands of golden hair frame his face, not quite obscuring his crystal blue eyes.

"You look like a sunrise today."

Finley crosses his arms and his feet as he semi-sits on my desk. "How so?"

"The light blue of your jeans fading into the blush shirt with a golden crown on your head. It's like a sunrise."

His lips turn upward, then he unleashes a brilliant smile. "I think that's the nicest, most poetic compliment I've ever received, Leilei. Thank you."

Something warms inside my chest at his praise. I am not the woman known for flowery words or—gag—poetry, but it was the first image to come to mind as I gazed upon him.

"Maybe I have a concussion," I joke, unzipping my lemon bag and squeezing a wedge into my tea. "Want some tea?"

Finley moves behind me. "One second. Stay still. I want to check your head now that you mention concussions."

I do as I'm told, mostly because a small part of me is excited his fingers will be on me again. I may not be able to withstand the contact for long, but mercy, I enjoy it before it gets to feel like too much. He lighty prods my scalp, and I applaud myself for wincing only a little before he moves his hand and returns to his propped position beside me. "No bumps or blood or caving in. You should be in the clear."

"Duh," I say, knowing good and well that I didn't hit my head hard enough for a concussion. "And what are you doing here?"

His face falls, and I realize that I might have sounded rude. "I mean, I'm glad you are here, don't get me wrong, but what prompted the visit?"

"I've missed you over these last few days while we've both been swamped with work," he says plainly, not a hint of sarcasm or flirtation in his voice. It is a fact. He missed me. That warm feeling in my chest from earlier expands.

"What kind of tea can I get you? I have peach ginger, honey ginger, elderberry green tea, black tea..." I pause from fiddling through my tea stash in my desk drawer to look over at him with a raised brow. "I have so many more, Finley. We could be here all night before I'd finish delivering your options."

He shakes his head, wearing that dazzling grin of his. "Black tea will suffice." Then he actually sits on my desk; his long legs allow the tips of his dark brown dress shoes to reach the hardwood floor. "Thank goodness you keep your desk space clean and clear. I do enjoy sitting in places I shouldn't." There's something about his tone as his voice trails off to a low rumble that fans the flame of heat within my chest. How much longer can my heart, my ribs, my skin withstand the increasing warmth?

"Oh, darn it. I don't have an extra mug. I typically take tea time alone, and when Mr. Austen joins me, he brings his own mug."

Finley shrugs. "No big deal. I'll sip whatever you're having..." he looks at my cup, a smirk flicking across his face as he glances back to me. "Bae."

"Hadley bought me that," I say, reaching for the mug and looking at the front of it. "Best attorney ever." I hold the mug up to my face and smile.

"You're adorable, bae. And yes, you are the best attorney ever. And you're my bae."

Huh?

"I'm your best attorney ever? Did you need an attorney for something? Is that why you're here?"

Finley cocks his head, perplexed. "What do you think bae means, Lorelei?"

"Best attorney ever?" I state this as a question because now I'm reconsidering the acronym.

He chuckles and looks down, running his hands down his jawline. Which, by the way, is sharp. It gives him that haughty, regal air that I once condemned him for. But now I think it's... Well, I think it's kind of hot.

Man.

I'm becoming my sister...

"Bae is an informal way to address your significant other. It's an acronym for Before Anything Else."

Oh.

Huh.

"That's interesting. I think I like 'best attorney ever,' though. Plus, we are not each other's significant person." I gesture between us and take a sip of my tea. The warm, spicy goodness slides down my throat. Tea is like an immediate sedative for me. Calming and relaxing.

"Not yet." He winks. "I like calling you Leilei, anyway." He holds out his hand. When I lift a brow, he motions towards my cup.

Oh.

I give it to him. I don't ever drink after people, so the tea is now his.

He takes a sip, placing his lips in the same spot mine were moments ago. A shudder runs through my body. "You aren't grossed out drinking after a person?"

He shrugs, setting the mug down between us. "Not when the person is you."

"I don't carry any less germs than the average human, Finley."

He stands then stretches out his hand towards me. I take it and he guides me to my feet, tugging me into a hug. "I'll happily consume all of your germs, *bae.*"

I move my hands to splay across his firm chest and shove at him lightly, but his chest rumbles with laughter underneath me as his arms snake around me tighter. My hands maneuver to his back, and I latch them together. This is hot and tingly and *good.* After a moment, he puts a small amount of distance between us, just enough that I can look up at him as he stares down at me. His eyes move from my own and down to my lips for a fraction of a second before he closes his eyes and presses his lips to my forehead.

The warmth in my chest finally explodes, rivaling any too-hot sip of tea I've ever taken in my life. It's unnatural heat. The chaotic need to be closer to him. The raw desire to press my face to his and become one. It's encompassing.

And that's a feeling I've never had before, but I know exactly what it is because my twin is a hopeless romantic, always feeding me her personal and fictional stories.

I want to kiss Finley Andersson.

I rip myself away from him and turn around, discreetly fanning my blistering hot face. We aren't dating. Right? Even though last Saturday felt like a date. Him showing up here feels like something a boyfriend would do. Hugging him feels like hugging the sun, but it's *oh so good.* But kissing? I wouldn't even know where to start. Do I initiate? Does he? Am I supposed to tilt my head? Yes, I've seen my parents do that. What will his lips on mine feel like? Will I be okay with it? Will it ick me? And what about...

Oh, heavens.

What about *tongue?*

I don't think I could do that. Just the thought of a thick piece of wet muscle invading my mouth...

I dry heave once. Twice. And then I take deep breaths and think of plants and my cats and tea and law reviews... Yes. That's better.

"Lorelei?" Finley's voice sounds like what I imagine a hurt puppy would sound like if they had human voices.

"I'm good, Finley. I'm okay," I hurriedly say, spinning around to see the concern in his glistening eyes.

He steps towards me, but I automatically take one step back. "I'm sorry," I quickly state. "I don't know what came over me, but there's a lot of internal and external feelings, and I don't think I can touch you right now."

"That's perfectly okay, Lorelei. Thanks for voicing that to me. I'm sorry if kissing your forehead was too much." And he genuinely looks sorry. The helplessness in his eyes breaks me, and I wish that for two seconds I could be a normal woman with normal sensory experiences.

"This is why you shouldn't choose me, Finley. I'm not normal." For the first time in a long time, I feel ashamed of my disabilities. Of who I am.

Finley, however, smiles and his eyes genuinely light up as he says, "Normal is so overrated, Leilei. I can wait for you. I will wait for you." Then his face darkens, and I imagine this is what he must look like when dealing in state affairs back in Korsa. "And if you dare start to berate yourself for the way you process different sensations, I will be there to remind you that you are absolutely perfect. God made you, and He doesn't make mistakes. You are whole. Loved. Adored. Desired. Just the way you are, Lorelei Raine."

My mouth opens and closes like a fish gasping for air on land. I have no intelligent words to speak back, but that doesn't seem to bother Finley. In fact, I believe it amuses him. As if he didn't just wrap me in a verbal hug and give me a verbal chastising all at the same time, he turns around and takes another sip of tea from my mug.

I have never been so jealous of an object before.

Lucy's Journal

Thursday, March 25th * 11:06 pm * Sitting in Bed Stewing in Anger

Stone Freaking Harper is the bane of my existence. The man has been asking me to do menial tasks around the office. And he apparently has the time to supervise every single one of them. Nitpicking everything I do. And then the man had the NERVE to ask me on a date. He's my boss for crying out loud. I would never date him. Sure, he looks like a Greek god. But he's not. He's Stone Harper, my playboy boss who is younger than me. By only like two years, but still. Uuughhhh. Whatever. He'll move on to some new woman in no time. He's only stuck on me because we danced together on Valentine's Day. He'll get over it. I do, however, need to change the looks of the merman prince in the story I'm working on. He resembles Stone a little too much.

Chapter Fifteen

Finley

"All this work just to move to Nashville," Braxton says, shaking his head, sawdust flying from the dark strands as he does.

"At least you got paid." Mason elbows the bear of a man. Mason is a built guy, but next to Braxton, he is dwarfed. Which means I look like a toothpick. I'm in the lean-but-cut camp, which isn't normal for these beef- and corn-fed Mississippi men. But I am tall. Taller than Braxton, in fact. At least that's going for me.

"I think it looks grand," I state as we all three gaze up at the two-story home built with logs and stone. The structure itself is of log, but the middle of the house is made of stone. It's aesthetically pleasing for the location it's in—the last house down a several-mile-long paved path. There are other homes down the road, Braxton's cabin included towards the beginning of it, but Mason's sits at the end with lots of trees surrounding it for his privacy.□

"I'm already excited to escape here," Mason says. "This is going to be the perfect getaway for Karoline and me when we need a break from the city and tours and the rat race of a life that is being a musician."

"Say, Braxton. Maybe you and your brother in law can build me a place like this? For when I need to escape being a king."

Both men look at me before Braxton says, "You can do that? Just run away from being a king?"

"Absolutely not," I reply with a grin. "But I am me. And if I decide I need a break, I will take a break. I trust my country and the people who are in positions of decision-making power."

Mason shakes his head through an exhaled laugh.

"Well, boys. Want to tour the house?" Braxton asks.

An hour later, we finish viewing Mason's new vacation home and head to eat lunch at Books and Beans.

"Just you five?" the black-haired barista asks. It's not Emma Jane, whom I've gotten to know as she is usually the one working here. The name tag reads Selene, and she looks to be around our age, though I think she might be bulkier in muscle than I am. Impressive.

"Hadley will be joining," Braxton says.

"Karoline, too," Mason says sheepishly, looking away from me.

"Well," I look behind me where Gabriel and Anders stand. "At least I have you two."

Both men grunt, which causes Mason to burst out laughing. "Dang, Fins. Even your PPOs don't want to date you."

"Sh," I hiss at Mason, elbowing him for good measure. There's not a lot of people in here, but yelling I have PPOs is bound to raise interest and questions. In fact, the barista cocks an eyebrow as she goes about her business opening her notepad.

"Just kidding," he says at an equally loud volume. "All a joke, my friend." He winks but mouths "I'm sorry."

"All's well that ends well," I whisper back.

"I'll go ahead and get you all started. What will it be for you?" the barista asks, directing her gaze at Braxton since he's closest to the counter, but she constantly bounces her eyes back to me with a hesitant expression.

Maybe she did overhear? *Great.*

We give our orders, and right as we finish and head to pull some tables together in the back corner, the ladies walk through the door.

With Lorelei and Lucy in tow.

Lorelei is here!

Confetti rains down in my head while a marching band plays a joyful rendition of that annoying song "Happy" by Pharrell Williams. All thoughts of possible exposure decimated.

"Could you possibly smile any wider, you lovesick dope?" Mason laughs, but I don't pay him any mind.

Because Lorelei is walking straight towards me.

I wave with one hand, feeling very much the dope Mason just called me. She waves back, a small smile painting her face. "Hi, Finley."

Her voice sends a thrill racing through me. "Hi, bae."

She grimaces and crosses her arms. "I thought I said not to call me your bae."

I grin even wider somehow. The way she narrows her eyes and purses her lips is beyond attractive. This is not a good thing. I shouldn't be turned on by the thought of making her irritated with me. That's what Mason does to Karoline.

I'm sweet. Gentle. Kind. The Prince of Hearts is a mere media image.

But Lorelei makes me want to live up to the reputation... only for her, though.

"Admit it. You like it." She blushes. "See," I place my finger close to her face, but I don't touch her. "Look at this lovely shade of pink coating your cheeks." I drag my finger across the bridge of her nose, still not touching her skin. But I can feel the heat radiating off her. "And your cute nose."

Her breath hitches, then she swats my hand away. She cocks her hip to the side, and it takes all of my willpower not to allow my eyes to linger on the prominent curve of that black, pencil skirt she wears. "So this is how you made the female population fall in love with you."

"Whatever do you mean?"

She gestures towards me with an open palm. "Prince of Hearts."

I place my hand over my heart and act appalled. "Me? No, no, baby girl. I am the Prince of one heart. Yours."

"Oh. My. Gosh," Lucy says. Both Lorelei and I snap our heads towards her proclamation.

She's staring at us, fanning her face while giving a toothy smile. "Baby girl? Are you two official now? Oh, I would *die* if a man called me that."

"No," Lorelei says, a little too quickly for my liking, then she looks back at me. "Finley is just being a rake and attempting to live up to his earned international nickname."

"But you like it." I wink. Lucy feigns a swooning motion.

"Lucy, let's go order," Lorelei says, turning her back to me and grabbing her twin's arm. Hadley and Karoline are already at the counter ordering. I join the guys at the table.

"Well, well, Mr. Andersson," Braxton says as I sit down. "Way to go. Looks like you're well on your way to Lorelei's heart. I've never seen her approach a person the way she walked right up to you."

My heart sings. "Really? I hope so. The woman has me smitten."

"We know," Mason, Gabriel, and Anders say at the same time. It's interesting to hear a phrase spoken in southern, French, and Korsan accents all at once. Mason laughs while the other two scowl.

My PPOs are some of the grumpiest men on the face of this earth, but hey, at least I know I'm safe with them. They won't have fun, so at least I know they are constantly aware.

"Hi, Lucy," Gabriel says as she slips into a seat beside him, placing a hand on his arm. Well, so much for observant PPOs. Gabriel's eyes are now hearts as he focuses solely on the twin I was supposed to date.

I glance at Anders as he rolls his eyes.

Hadley and Karoline join the group, sitting next to their men. Lastly, Lorelei joins, sitting in the last available seat. The one right next to me.

She scoots a little closer to me and away from Anders as she sits down. The action warms my heart because it tells me she feels safe enough to be closer to me than someone else.

"How'd the house look?" Karoline questions Mason as she throws her long hair into a ponytail holder.

Hadley begins talking with Braxton about something that happened in her store earlier. Lucy is distracting my PPO fully, but Anders remains on guard. Lorelei fiddles with the cuff of her white dress shirt.

I pull her ponytail to get her attention because I have apparently gone back in time to five years old.

"Yes?" she questions, her hand tugging her ponytail over the shoulder not beside me.

"You are adorable with your ponytail. That's all."

"Thanks?" she says just as Selene interrupts everyone while bringing us our drinks. I opted for lemon water while Lorelei got a chai.

"How has your Friday been?" I ask before sipping my water. Lorelei blows on her tea, and my insides light up like an electric fence. *Tone it down, Finley*, I demand myself.

Lorelei tests the temperature of her chai before answering. "It has been good. I have almost wrapped up my arguments for a big case I'm presenting on Thursday next week."

"Can you tell me about it?"

She smiles sadly. "Not all the details, but it involves a local woman who had been on and off drugs and alcohol for years. She lost her children last year, and that woke her up. She's been clean ever since, and we are trying to get her custody back."

"That must be hard on you," I say, itching to reach out and touch her because it's how I would want to be comforted. But she's not me, and it would only make her nervous, especially with everyone around.

She nods slowly. "It is, but cases like these are my favorite." Lorelei turns her pretty hazel eyes to me. "That moment when kids are reunited with their parents is a beautiful scene. It makes every hard thing I have to hear regarding their stories worth it. God works everything for His good. I see that over and over again in my field of work."

"You've got to be kidding me," Lucy hisses loud enough to stop all our conversations and turn to see what's got her worked up. I follow her death stare to a tall, bulky blond man dressed in light, fitted khakis and a pink dress shirt who just walked through the door. Hm. I like his style.

"Who's that? And why is Lucy murdering him with her eyes?" I ask Lorelei. She shrugs.

"That's Stone Harper, her boss. She hates him, though I'm not quite sure why. She won't talk to us about him. Every time we ask, we only receive grumbled insults attached to her cursing his name."

"Interesting." I note the way a certain passion burns behind her eyes, and I think I might see why she hates him even if Lorelei can't. Lucy Spence might have a thing for her boss. But that's not my story to intrude upon. I turn my attention back to Lorelei who is sipping her chai. "So, what are you doing tomorrow?"

"I have a dress fitting with the girls for Karoline's wedding in the morning. We are getting lunch together after. I really need to spend the evening finishing preparations for the case so that I can rehearse all next week."

Selene interrupts the table once again as she brings out our sandwiches. After she sets down my Reuben and Lorelei's BLT, I ask, "I don't want to intrude or take away from your preparation time, but would you happen to be able to spare some time to go on another date with me?"

Lorelei looks lost in space before she answers. "I really need to get work done, but I wouldn't be opposed to us watching a movie or something while I work if you want. You can come over anytime after three p. m. tomorrow."

An open invitation into her home? Yes, please! "Sounds like a plan, bae."

Lorelei bumps into my side, but instead of grimacing, she's hiding a smile.

I read over the script I've prepared for myself one more time before dialing Karin's number from my business cell phone. Which reminds me, I should make sure Lorelei has this number.

Once I'm satisfied with my plan of action, I hit the call button. She waits until the last ring to pick up the phone. "Hello, you are speaking with Her Royal Highness Princess Karin Nilsson of Vespen," she answers, speaking her country's native tongue in a prim, proper tone.

I respond in Vespen. "Princess Karin, this is Prince Finley Andersson. I believe we need to talk. Do you have a moment to video call?"

She swallows on the other end of the line, her voice subdued as she stutters, "Y-yes." I immediately hit the video call button and set my phone onto the holder attached to the table. I'm in a private meeting room in the town's library. I didn't want her seeing where I'm living right now. It felt too personal to call her from the cabin.

Her face appears, as pale as mine. We are both from Icelandic countries, after all. Her hair, however, is a rich chocolate color, her eyes just as brown. "Hi, Finley."

"Hey, Karin. I assume you know why I'm calling, so I'll jump straight to the point. You hired a stalker to capture photography of and interrupt my dates. I want to hear from you why you did this." My tone is cool and smooth. Practiced. I'd taken necessary time to calm down from the affirmation that it was indeed her, so now I need to allow her to speak before I take action.

She shifts her eyes away from the screen, rubbing the mustard-color fabric of the sleeves on her dress. "I'm sorry, Finley." She goes silent again, still not looking into the camera.

I release a breath. "Thank you, but it is hard for me to accept your apology without understanding your reasoning. So please, help me to understand so that we can salvage our working relationship."

Karin closes her eyes, her chest rising and falling. Then, she opens her eyes as she says hurriedly, "I thought if I had intel regarding your dates that I could somehow recreate what you desired when you came back to Korsa to try and win you over once and for all." Her voice is calm. Matter-of-fact. Like what she's saying was scripted, too. "Once I realized you were falling for the woman, I told the man I hired to interrupt the next date, which was the garden date. He intentionally turned on his shutter sound."

I'm processing her words, still conflicted. "But why, Karin? I've made it very clear that I only thought of you as a friend. Why would you hire someone to stalk my dates even after I've made that abundantly clear in the past?"

Tears prick in the corner of her eyes now, and my heart lurches. No matter what she's done, I don't want her bawling her eyes out. I hate seeing women cry. "I just had to, okay? I don't know what came over me. I was acting in jealousy. I'm sorry, Finley. I deeply regret my actions and I promise not to meddle any further. You can rest assured."

Though I'm not satisfied, that seems to be all I will get out of her. I sigh. "I understand. Thank you for your apology, and I accept. I will offer grace to you this once. If anything like this happens again, I will take immediate action against you and your country. I love this woman, and you are not to mess with her or us."

Her lips form an "o." "You—you love her?"

I pinch the bridge of my nose. "Yes. I do." Right as I say the words, my other phone buzzes on the table. I sneak a glance. Lorelei. "I should go now. Thank you for talking with me."

I hang up, knowing I went completely off script. I was supposed to tell her that I would be speaking with the king of Vespen and would demand a formal apology to the twins since both experienced the stalker, even if Lorelei wasn't completely aware of it like

I was that first night. Her tears moved me a little, though. I have a soft spot for crying women.

I check my text.

Have you read the U.S. Constitution through?

I shake my head with a laugh. Only Lorelei.

I have. It was a part of my studies and training growing up. Why do you ask?

She doesn't respond for another eight minutes.

Okay, so I was reading it for fun after I finished up my case load for the night, and I noticed the 27th Amendment stated...

I can't contain the amusement seeping out of me as I continue to read her text. This woman texts me at eight o'clock at night about not only reading the U.S. Constitution, but about an amendment regarding the salary of congress. Lorelei is a precious soul I will cherish and love and protect for all of my existence.

Now to get the woman to actually agree to dating me. Does she even realize she already is, even if it's not official? Over the past week and a half, we've hung out in the evenings, cooked dinners for one another, and sat in delightful silence as she worked on her big case that's tomorrow and I drowned in state paperwork. Her companionship is comfortable and inviting. And she must feel the same way about me because she keeps coming back for more.

Chapter Sixteen

Lorelei

The elder members of Juniper Grove Church's congregation are bright eyed and bushy tailed while the younger members yawn and slouch in their fold out metal chairs. The air is hot and sticky for six-thirty in the morning, and I notice that many of the ladies don dressy hats today.

That was a no for me, so of course, my hair is tied back in its usual low ponytail, even if it's Easter Sunday.

"You are magnificent to behold in a flowy skirt. Be careful, Leilei, you may take down kingdoms looking like that." Finley sits down on the chair to my right, a dazzling white smile highlighting his sparkly blue eyes. His blond hair is styled back, and paired with his dark gray slacks, sage green dress shirt, and the sharpest of jawlines, the man looks ready to take down kingdoms himself.

But of course I'm not brave enough to say those words out loud. Not yet.

Instead, I tune into my girly nature and preen under his praise. I wiggle my shoulders and tilt my head with a soft smile. "I'm feeling rather exuberant after Thursday's big court win."

"As you should." He folds his hands together in his lap as he stares straight into my soul.

At least that's what it seems like he's doing.

He continues when I remain silent, startled by his intense expression. "I know I said it Friday evening at our celebratory dinner with our friends, but I truly am proud of you. You worked so hard on that case, put so much of your heart into it. And it paid off. You're quite amazing, Lorelei Raine."

The spring heat has nothing on the flush burning through my face at the moment. "Thank you," I state, turning away from his attention and trying to find my twin somewhere in the small crowd that's gathered for the sunrise service. I finally spot her in her pink floral dress that sits right above her knees, her white heels sinking into the damp morning grass. She's chatting with Hadley, Braxton, and Pastor Rawls, and she's wearing a plastic smile that only I can tell is falsified. Lucy's been down for about a week, and when I ask her about her melancholy, she only replies that she's PMSing.

Though I have doubts because I'm fairly certain she menstruated a week and a half ago, but I could be wrong.

"Hello, future love birds." Karoline Wright stands on the outside of our row in a pretty sunset orange dress. Mason Kane stands next to her, his arm looped around her waist, tugging her close.

"Future? There's no time like the present." Mason sticks out a hand to Finley, who stands and gives it a shake before pulling him into one of those hugs all men do, complete with a few hearty pats on the back. Karoline waves at me from around the embracing men, and then she scoots past them to sit to my left where I was hoping Lucy would be.

"Hey, Lorelei. Having a good morning?" Karoline's yawn breaks off the last word so she sounds like she's saying "mawnin." She shakes her head. "Oops. Sorry about that. It's a wee bit early."

I smile at her as if I understand, though I'm wired and awake like the elderly folks of the congregation. "My morning has been typical. Went for my run, drank my smoothie. Made a fruit dish for our breakfast this morning."

Her eyes glaze over as I talk. "You are a different type of human species, my friend." And as she nears the end of the sentence, she yawns again.

Mason excuses himself as he walks in front of me to sit on the other side of Karoline, then I finally catch Lucy's eye. Her smile falls as her face softens; she makes her way to sit in the chair in front of me, Hadley and Braxton in tow.

We all exchange greetings as Pastor Rawls goes to stand on the long utility trailer where the sound system has been set up and the pulpit stand with a cross embedded on it now resides. "Good morning, Juniper Grove Church. And welcome to our sunrise service. What a blessing it is to wake up, gather together, and offer praise and worship to our resurrected savior, Jesus Christ."

Music begins to play through the sound system, and I find I miss the gentle tones of the piano that we usually sing to. Grandma Netty arrives during the second song we sing and shuffles through the row in front of me to sit to the left of Lucy. She turns around, bounces her eyes between me and Finley, then nods her head once as if approving something.

"I think your grandmother likes me," Finley, leaning down, whispers into my ear.

"She likes everyone," I whisper back. But Finley must not hear me because when I glance up at him, his brows are knitted and he mouths "what?"

I stand on my tiptoes to get closer to his ear as he leans to meet me, but as I cup my hands around his ear, my balance wavers. Falling into his chest is like colliding with a rock, and when his arms hook around my waist to steady me, I'm fairly certain this is what standing in the middle of a bonfire would equate to.

"Careful, Leilei," Finley whispers against my ear again, except this time, my head is pressed firmly against his chest alongside one hand that is perfectly splayed over a pectoral. My other hand is clutching his shirt in a fist.

I gasp in flustered shock and jump backwards, slamming into Karoline, causing her to fall backwards into Mason, who, judging by the fact I'm still standing, is the sturdy domino that doesn't collapse. Though, Mason and I are making a Karoline Sandwich.

Finley wraps his large hands around my elbows and assists me to a straight position just as the music comes to an end.

But the melodies playing and the voices lifting didn't seem to stop the entirety of the church rubbernecking to see what the commotion was towards the back of the rows of metal chairs.

"You all good back there? Don't make me split y'all up," Pastor Rawls says into the microphone in what I am taking to be a joking manner.

I casually smooth down my skirt and look down because my head is currently whirling faster than a fidget spinner in the hands of a child. In fact, I can feel every eye on me despite not actually seeing them. Panic begins to rise in my chest, but I close my eyes and focus on deep breathing while someone reads scripture from the makeshift altar. Guilt tugs at my conscience for disrupting the service and for not focusing on the passages.

Another song begins to play.

Suddenly, Finley's low voice is in my ear. "This one time while I was attending a wedding for a prince of a neighboring country, the priest was in the middle of reading scripture when I sneezed eight times nonstop. The echo through the cathedral was insane, and by the time I stopped, over five hundred people were gawking at me in disbelief as if I could control the monster exiting my body through those sneezes."

I slap a hand over my mouth to keep from laughing because all I can picture is eight little dark figures spewing out of the sunshine man's mouth as he sneezed. I envision women clutching their pearls and men shaking their heads in disapproval at the human prince.

Human.

We are all human, and we all do embarrassing, weird things at times. Even in the middle of church services.

With that thought, I lift my head to find everyone has gone about their business, singing the next song. Moving my gaze to Finley, I flash a quick smile and mouth, "Thank you."

The returning smile I receive is nothing short of heart-stopping. How did this man that I barely know understand exactly how to distract me from my spiraling thoughts?

"And I thought, 'This is my moment. I can be the hero for once.'" Mason continues to recount what has now become known as MKL sandwich—Mason Karoline Lorelei—among our friend group. We all sit at a rounded table, plates full of gravy, biscuits, grits, and other various southern comfort foods. I opted for a slice of the breakfast casserole with a side of fruit since I had my smoothie earlier.

"Ha, ha. You're such a stud," Braxton remarks, unimpressed, before shoveling sausage gravy into his mouth.

Hadley elbows him before taking a bite of bacon.

Karoline rolls her eyes.

And I sit there, using my fork to play with my fruit, placing the melon, pineapple, and strawberries into a smiley face.

"Okay, that's enough. Change of topic," Finley says. I offer him a grateful smile.

Lucy speaks up. "What's everyone's plans for this upcoming week?"

"Imma have Roy come over and help me with some plumbing issues," Grandma Netty says as she joins us at our table. She sets her plate down to the right of Finley though there is no spot there. Finley looks at me with a nervous glance, and then I chuckle when I notice he turns to his PPOs who have been captured in conversation with a couple of the older men. "They aren't going to help you," I tease.

Finley swallows but then moves his seat closer to me as Grandma Netty squeezes in with her long, floral dress that looks exactly like something a grandmother would wear.

"I wasn't wrong earlier, right? She likes me?" This side of Finley, a little worried and anxious over an old lady's opinion, is beyond adorable. He runs his hand through his hair and releases a breath.

"So, Finley, I see you took my advice and started to court the right twin." Grandma Netty spoons grits into her mouth as she awaits a response. The table's chatter about weekly plans has been suspended.

Everyone, myself included, focuses on Finley.

I want to offer him a funny out like he did me earlier, but also, I am curious as to what my grandmother means by her cryptic statement.

After a few seconds, Finley squares his shoulders and smiles. He meets every eye at the table—Hadley, Braxton, Lucy, Karoline, Mason, and lastly, me—before addressing Grandma Netty.

"Yes, ma'am. Turns out I was falling for Lorelei this entire time. Lucy graciously helped me to see that."

"And are you dating my granddaughter officially?"

Finley laughs and then holds my eye contact. "If she will ever accept my intentions. That's been the hard part. I'm mad about this woman, yet she's giving me the race of my life to prove myself to her."

The table erupts.

"Lorelei! Say yes to the handsome prince," Hadley says.

"Dude. You're not doing something right. Try writing her a song," Mason says.

"Be patient," Braxton says.

"I'm trying to talk you up to her," Lucy says. I kill her with a glare.

Karoline, surprisingly, remains silent.

While Finley bickers back and forth with everyone, defending his efforts while also defending my reluctance, my phone buzzes in my lap. I pick it up and see a text from Karoline.

Are you okay? Do you want to escape to the bathroom with me?

That's... oddly kind of her to offer.

I think I'm okay for now. But the offer is kind of you, and I appreciate it.

Though I am thankful, I have to ride this out. If I leave, it will look suspicious. I'm stable enough right now, and I trust everyone at this table has my best interests at heart.

"She will say yes to me if and when she pleases. There is no rush. She is in charge of her timeline, and I will not disrespect her needs." Finley claps his hands together to end the discussion, and while I had tuned most of it out, I caught that last part, and...

Huh?

Did he just...?

What?

I stare at him, my jaw open and head tilted as I analyze the man sitting next to me. How in the history of this world does he read me so easily? And the pure respect and intentionality rolling in waves off his speech and actions...

Be still my heart.

Is this what security is supposed to feel like?

"How about a camping trip this weekend?" Mason says, yanking me from my thoughts. Immediately I want to shout that I'm in, but I have to contain myself. See who all is on board first.

"Oh, yes. Let's do it!" Karoline says.

"I'm a no," Lucy replies. "But my sister loves camping. Especially when there is a hike involved."

"I'm down to go," Finley casually says, his thigh rubbing against mine. I can feel the heat through his slacks, and though I should want to shy away from the feeling, though it should feel icky...

I don't move.

In fact, I forget we are talking about a hiking trip.

I'm so tuned into this feeling—heat mixed with tingling pleasure—that I startle when everyone begins to stand from the table.

"Great. Finley and I will pick you two up from your apartments Friday morning. Sound good?" Mason looks at Karoline and then me.

"Huh?" I respond. "Erm, yes?"

"See you then! We are about to head out. Traveling to Nashville this evening for a show tomorrow." Mason wraps his arm around Karoline as she gathers their empty paper plates. "Happy Easter, everyone."

We all say our goodbyes to the couple, then minutes later, Lucy, wearing an enigmatic expression, decides to leave. Without even giving a reason.

What is going on with her? She's acting all out of sorts lately.

But then I watch as Gabriel excuses himself from the table of old men and follows Lucy out.

Huh?

Maybe she's got something going on with him.

Hadley and Braxton leave the table to go and socialize with his sister and brother-in-law, leaving me, Grandma Netty, and Finley at the table. And then it hits me: I'm going camping this weekend with Finley. My legs immediately vibrate at the thought of stretching them out, touching dirt, surrounding myself with trees and plants, and soaking in the mid-March sunlight. But I'll be with Karoline and Mason and Finley. None of whom I am super close with. Will I be able to handle that?

I think I could...

But what if something happens and I'm triggered?

Oh, why did I say yes to this stupid idea?

Because you're desperate for the outdoors and you have someone you feel safe going with sitting in front of you asking...

Safe. Despite not knowing Finley for very long, I do feel safe with him. Though the idea of it seems irrational, I can't deny the logical fact that it's true.

But what does that mean?

Lucy's words flitter back into my mind unbidden.

Sometimes love is unexplainable.

No. This isn't love. Safety does not automatically equal love. But while this might not be love, maybe the same applies to friendships, too. Maybe some souls are simply meant to be acquainted and befriended.

Maybe, at the very least, I'm meant to be really good friends with Finley.

Grandma Netty clears her throat, pulling me from my mental sparring. "You two behave yourselves while camping."

I look aghast, especially because of the thoughts I was just having, but Finley laughs. "Don't worry, ma'am. I'll be a perfect gentleman towards your beloved granddaughter."

Grandma Netty clicks her tongue. "I said behave. I didn't say don't ruffle her feathers up a bit. She needs it, right, Lorelei?"

My grandmother's hazel eyes glisten with mischief, giving her a youthful glow to counter the wrinkles on her face. I swallow, heat brushing my face. "My feathers are just fine, thank you."

Finley and my grandmother laugh as if they are in on some joke that I'm not privy to, so I decide it's time to leave.

Mostly because the idea of Finley ruffling me up in any way does something funny to my nervous system. And by funny, I mean... *desired.*

"Wait! Lorelei," Finley says as he trails after me to dump my plate into the trash can.

"Yes?" I ask, looking him in the eyes as I shove the paper plate down into the black bag.

He follows suit, not bothered by my challenging scowl. Which is good because I'm more agitated with myself than him at the moment. "Are you sure you're okay going on a hike and camping trip this weekend with me? If it's too much, tell me."

"Let's talk outside." I walk out the backdoors and out under the overhang. The temperature has risen alongside the humidity, but I bask in the feel of spring. Finley stands beside me, close, but not touching me. He waits for me to speak.

"For some reason, I'm okay. In the name of honesty, I feel safe with you." Okay, that's enough confession. After puffing out a breath, I smirk. "You aren't going to mind camping? Sleeping on the ground won't be an issue for *Your Highness?* There will be spiders."

I can't imagine this prim and proper man who jumps on chairs when he sees spiders laying underneath the stars with bugs and birds singing around us.

He chuckles and places a hand on my shoulder.

I don't fidget away, though I'm totally aware of every inch of skin where his fingers heat through my shirt. It's uncomfortable...

But not in a bad way?

I tap my feet, trying to distract myself from the feeling.

"I'll have you by my side to kill the creepy crawlies. What is there to be afraid of?"

I glare at him, which only causes him to laugh harder. He gently squeezes my shoulder before growing solemn. "I'm still vested in going at your pace, but don't be surprised when my antics ramp up. I meant every word when I said I see my future with you and you alone."

His declaration is one of war.

And suddenly, I find myself wanting to lose the battle for once in my life.□

Chapter Seventeen

Finley

God, send blessings upon Mason and Karoline for bailing at the last minute and giving me this weekend with Lorelei...

"Are you sure this is where you'd like to set up camp?"

Lorelei gives me a look that says *Yes, Finley. Now will you please stop questioning my guidance?*

I toss my hands up and divert my attention back to setting up the tent meant to sleep four comfortably that I had purchased from Walmart after leaving Lorelei at her office Thursday evening. My heart skipped a beat at the thought of camping with her, and now that we are doing this out here alone, I might die from the anxious tension. We've built a good friendship, and she's obviously grown comfortable with me, but that's not what I'm after. I'm after a lifetime of loving this woman. I'm after the opportunity to tell her I love her without her freaking out on me.

I've learned the woman is just as anxious as me, just in a different capacity. She gets upset with herself for not being able to process events and emotions quickly whereas I process at lightning speed, leaving me to daydream a million and ten different scenarios before whatever it is I'm distressed over actually happens.

Which I have done since I walked out of her office. There are thousands of ways I can mess this epic date—she isn't calling it that, but I am—up.

"There. All done," Lorelei clasps her hands together, and my jaw drops at the record time it took her to pitch her small, single-person tent. I drop the poles I was finagling around with and move to stand by Lorelei.

"Leilei, I am impressed. Your brain and skill continues to stun me. Could you possibly help me with my tent?" I look her over. Her hair is in a high, curly ponytail, little curls and flyways spinning around her face in the light breeze. She wears black joggers and a light gray athletic t-shirt, the hints of a black sports bra peeking through the wide neck of the shirt. Sweat glistens on her face, but she's not drenched...

Like me.

Whose white t-shirt might turn yellow.

I run a hand through my hair, and it doesn't flop back in front of my face as usual, the dampness keeping it slicked back.

Lorelei's accomplished grin widens as she crosses her arms. "No, Finley. If you're going to sleep in a tent, then you put your tent up. Every man for himself."

"And if I don't put my tent up? That means I can sleep in yours?" I waggle my brows. It's hard to see the butterfly blush blooming on her face due to the fact the sun and seven hours of hiking have turned her pale face pink.

She turns her face away and huffs. "No. You may not sleep in my tent. You will sleep on the ground with the bugs." She begins to march away, waving a hand and stating that she's going to go scavenge for mushrooms and other plants.

I chuckle, thinking over the day we've had. While actually hiking, conversation was limited. When we stopped for snacks, hydration, or to simply rest, however, we talked.

Conversation was natural, flowing easier than the river we are currently stationed on the bank of for the rest of the evening and night. We talked about her childhood, how she's always wanted to be a lawyer, how she misses her parents who are off gallivanting around the states, how she wishes to do that one day, how she's never had a romantic relationship, and how she spent her high school years in cognitive behavioral therapy because she thought something was wrong with her.

That one boiled my blood a little. It was at the nudging of her parents, who seem like really great people and I hope to meet them one day, but why do people assume something is wrong with someone simply because they are shyer, quieter, have "abnormal interests and obsessions," and do not date-slash-attempt to befriend the entire world in order to be liked and accepted? Autistic or not, Lorelei is still Lorelei. And there are plenty of people who struggle with the same things she does even if they aren't autistic.

If you ask me, Lorelei is more normal than the lot of us in this world. She knows who she is, accepts it, and is happy. Sure, she trips up on emotions, but she works through them. She does know how to identify them in the long run. She proved that today. When I've gotten tired, she plainly asked me if I was because of how my body began to droop, and then she recommended we rest. She's caught on to most of my flirting attempts because she can read me better now, which has flustered her because she doesn't know what to do with it. (She openly admitted that to me, and I told her I'd be her teacher on how to flirt. She threw leaves in my hair.)

Overall, Lorelei is underestimated. And I think she does it to herself at this point. She's not just book smart. She is emotionally smart. She simply operates slower, which, if you ask me, is a grand thing. It proves she thinks through her thoughts and feelings and decisions. She isn't rash, like me.

Lorelei is my *mysaa*. My comfort. My grounding. My home.

And I know all those things because my brain and heart leap and jump to latch onto the idea of love. And then I hyperfocus on it...

Enter: I am already in love with her.

Yes, it's chemicals in my brain.

But also, I choose her. And I'll choose her when the chemicals fade.

I've never met a woman like her, and well, when you know, you know.

Shaking my head clear, I set to work on my tent. The sun is well on its way to setting; the rustling of the river settles a peaceful feeling into my soul. Ten minutes later, my tent is up and I unpack my hiking bag, rolling out my sleeping bag and setting out clothes to change into later.

The forecast said it is supposed to rain later, so I walk over to Lorelei's tent and check to make sure it's sturdy and secure and completely covered so that there will be no leaks. After that, I begin to build a fire spot.

Eventually, Lorelei hollers out, "I found several different mushrooms, but they aren't quite ready for harvest. We should start a fire, though. And start preparing dinner. Oh, and make tea!" She appears from a trail off in the woods, a small twig sticking out of her hair.

I laugh and meet her by the wood pile I gathered earlier. She begins to bend down, but I grab her wrist and take a step nearer. She sucks in a breath as I move closer, my lips quite capable of touching her forehead. She tilts her chin up and closes her eyes, and I bite my lip to resist the urge to kiss her. I pluck the twig from her hair, but it pulls a chunk of her hair with it. She winces and her eyes fly open as her hand wraps around mine, hovering an inch above her scalp.

"What was that for?" she bites, then her fingers move to feel the twig. "Oh."

"Sorry. I forget your hair captures anything that nears it like a Venus flytrap." I smirk, thinking I'm teasing her, but she laughs.

"People used to stick pencils in our hair when they sat behind us in school," she says nonchalantly. "It made Lucy mad, but I just kept their pencils. I never had to purchase a pencil throughout my entire high school career."

"Resourceful," I hum, noticing the blue-gold color of her hazel eyes. Her nose comes to a cute point, her cheeks resting high. The desire to trace the delicate bone structure of her face with my nose is overwhelming. I clutch my fists by my side and step back. "Let's get this fire going. Looks like there are rain clouds on the horizon."

Lorelei looks up. "Huh. I didn't realize it was supposed to rain. Yeah, we should get dinner out of the way so that we can tuck ourselves in before the rain."

An hour later, we are sitting on the ground, drinking tea and eating ramen. No, not the packaged kind. Lorelei brought gluten-free noodles and spices to use. We cooked it over the fire, and now my mouth is aflame with the heat of the Korean chili pepper she brought. She licks her lips, and the desire to kiss her settles deep in my chest. We haven't talked about that yet, and while I don't want to necessarily plan our first kiss, I know she hasn't been kissed yet. I do want to verify that it is something she wants. I'm already aware of her difficulties with sensory overload, and I don't ever want to make it worse or catch her off-guard.

Will she ever be able to kiss me? Touch me for long lengths of time? Make love to me?

The thoughts sucker punch my stomach. That would be something to heavily consider moving forward. I love physical touch, and quite frankly, I like kissing. Will I be able to be with Lorelei romantically if she can't give me those things?

I want to shout yes and be the man who doesn't care, but that wouldn't be true of me. *God, please help us find a way,* I plead silently as I slurp noodles.

"Leilei, can I ask you something personal?"

"That's why we're doing this, right? So that I can scare you away from liking me?" She takes another bite of ramen as I roll my eyes. She's been attempting to sabotage this date by saying I'm not supposed to like her, but I keep reminding her that I like her weirdness. I had thought we were over the whole self-sabotage after our date on the nature trail and Adeline's House, but apparently she was wholly distracted with her court case. Now that it's over, she has time to ponder us.

But hey. She *is* pondering us. That's a good sign.

"You've never dated anyone, so I will assume that you've never been kissed. Is that something you are saving for marriage, or are you open to kissing a man if you're dating him?"

The ramen slides from her fork, which rests at the edges of her lips as she stares at me. Rounded hazel eyes bore into mine, surprise flickering across her face. "I, uh," she continues to stutter, her mouth opening and closing like a fish in the nearby river. "Yes?"

I set my bowl down and rest my forearms on my knees, leaning closer to Lorelei. "That sounded like a question more than a confident answer."

"I've never given it much thought," she whispers, then twists her fork until she slurps noodles. Liquid dribbles down the corner of her mouth, and I reach forward, catching it with my finger. Then, I bring my finger to my lips and lick the liquid. Lorelei tilts her head, as if she's analyzing my actions, and then she coughs, whipping her head away from me.

Rolling my lips into my mouth, I fight the urge to smirk. Instead, I finally respond. "Would you be opposed to kissing me..." I let the question hang in the air with the sound of the cicadas singing, "if we were dating, that is?"

She wipes her mouth with the back of her hand as she meets my gaze. "*If*," she says, "and that's a big *if*, then no. I would not be opposed to kissing you. *If* we were dating. I am, however, not practiced in the art of kissing. No idea what I'm doing in that department."

A smile that could probably rival the rising moon breaks across my face. "I would happily teach you, my bae."

"*If,* Finley! I said 'if.'"

"Right," I say, picking my bowl back up and twisting ramen around my fork. At that moment, rain drops begin to fall, and the wind starts picking up.

I curse internally, wanting more time with her. Seems the weather report had the wrong time, but what's new?

To make matters worse, thunder rumbles. It wasn't supposed to be a storm, just rain.

"Um, Finley…" Hands grasp my forearm.

I tear my eyes from the sky to find Lorelei has scooted closer to me and is sitting on her knees. She's slightly shaking, her breaths ragged. "I'm scared of only a handful of things. Thunderstorms happen to be on that list."

Lightning flashes in the sky, followed by another crack of thunder. "Let's go."

I grab her by the waist and hoist her up as her nails bite into my skin. Keeping one arm snugly around her, I usher her into my tent.

"My stuff." She pops her head out of the zipper door just as another flash of lightning brightens the darkened sky. Then like a turtle, her head retreats inside. I dash in several long strides over to her tent, grab her bag and the already unpacked sleeping bag and small pillow, and bolt back to my tent, zipping the door behind me.

Lorelei is curled in a ball with her hands over her ears, tears pricking at her eyes as her breaths come heavy and labored. Just as she starts what looks to be a soothing rocking mechanism, I crawl over to her and sit behind her, wrapping my arms tightly around her. As I pull her into my chest, her legs sprawl out and I hook mine around her. Astrid taught me this strategy for helping someone who is experiencing a panic attack, which it seems is happening to Lorelei.

After several minutes, she begins to breathe easier, and I feel her muscles relax in her arms and legs. She leans her head back on my shoulder, closing her eyes, but she doesn't move her hands away from her ears. I touch my lips to one of her hands and whisper, "You're safe. I've got you." I remember what Lucy said about grounding techniques when Lorelei experiences overload, and I briefly wonder if the thunder is too loud for her to handle. "You're safe, sweetheart. Feel my hands around you. Feel the soft fabric of the blanket on your feet. Notice the lamp hanging in the middle of the tent. Hear my voice. You are safe with me."

"Safe," she repeats in an exhale. Another round of thunder echoes around us and I hold her tighter. She doesn't shake, but she scoots closer to me, as if we could possibly become one in the moment. "I'm sorry, Finley. Just... Please don't let me go."

Chapter Eighteen

Lorelei

Well, this is embarrassing.

Probably my top most-embarrassing moment ever. Stripping in front of my sister doesn't even compare to this. Because she's my sister. I probably have some embarrassing moments as a child that I've deliberately chosen to forget about, but in my adult, functioning life... this is the most embarrassing.

It's a little past ten, the storm has passed, and only a light drizzle remains. Finley still has his arms around me as we lay on top of his sleeping bag, but judging by the light snores and the loosened grip, he's fast asleep. Slowly, I wiggle out of his arms; the heat of his touch is overwhelming now that I'm in my right mind. He groans, but turns to the other side of the tent. I stand, tiptoe over to my backpack, shove my own sleeping bag and pillow underneath my arm, and quietly unzip the tent. I poke my head out, allowing my eyes to adjust to the darkness. When my vision comes to, thanks to the battery-powered lamp Finley has hanging in his tent, I gasp at the gruesome sight of my beloved tent lying in a pile of shambles.

"Lorelei?" I snap my attention to Finley, who is in the process of sitting up and rubbing his eye with the back of his hand. A shiver ripples down my spine, and I curl my toes at the energy zinging through me as he says my name again in that husky, tired voice.

So that's why Lucy "screams, cries, and throws up" (her words, not mine) over a man's sleepy voice.

I think I get it now.

"Hm?" is my only intelligible response.

"Everything okay?" He's fully sitting up now, his hair a golden mop of waves sticking up in different directions.

"My–uh... My tent is demolished."

His lips tilt upward for a fraction of second before he schools his expression into a slight frown. "Guess you're stuck with me tonight."

I blink, trying to remember if I've heard him correctly. "Sleep in here? With you?"

He nods emphatically like it's the most obvious solution. Which it is, but still. "I don't even sleep in the same room with my sister. Ever. I like to be alone when I sleep. With shut doors. And dark rooms. And cocoon blankets."

"The tent will be zipped, I can turn off the lantern, and you are free to cocoon. You can even cocoon against me if you'd like."

I toss him a "watch yourself" glare before glancing out of the opened tent towards the remnants of mine and then back to Finley, whose lackadaisical expression *should* concern me because the man is anything but unenthused and uncareful.

"You're not going to take advantage of me, right? Since you wish to date me and marry me and such?" I'm amazed at how I don't actually believe this man in front of me is capable of such things. Finley snorts, then crawls like a predator until he's at my feet, his body rubbing against my calves as he reaches around me and zips the tent. I'm frozen in place as he stands in front of me, my gaze following his smirking face as he rises, his head remaining bent because he's a little too tall for the tent. Which means that I should really angle my face down so that I'm not losing all train of thought into darkened blue eyes and minty breath...

But then he speaks, a twinge of huskiness still present in his voice. "I would never take advantage of you, Leilei. Though I can't deny the fact that you sleeping in this tent with me awakens the urge to..." he swallows, and I mimic the action, afraid of his next words as he grins, "cuddle you."

Despite myself, I laugh, then I slap my hand over my mouth because I didn't mean to laugh. Finley, however, doesn't look to be offended. His grin grows wider as he takes a couple steps backwards from me. "But if you do not want to cuddle, then I will respect your wishes."

"I don't think I would be able to sleep if I were cuddling with you, Finley. Don't take this the wrong way, but touching you is like touching the sun."

"I'm that hot? Way to feed my ego, Leilei."

I glare at him once more. "I said not to take it the wrong way."

He shrugs, wearing a saucy grin. "You calmed down well enough when you were in my arms earlier."

Seems the Prince of Hearts has come out to play. My face heats, my heart reacting to the fresh memories. "I was scared. That's all."

Finley lowers himself to a crisscrossed seated position. "Do you want to tell me about what triggered it?"

"It's," I inhale and release, the heat deepening in my skin, "stupid. Really."

"Stupid or not, you can talk to me." He pats the area beside him. It's then I remember we are still in our gross hiking clothes. Once the storm started, I was too worked up to change, and he was too busy holding me like my life depended on it. My skin starts to crawl at the feeling of grime and sweat and dirt.

"Can we change first? And then I promise to tell you. As long as you promise not to judge me too hard or make fun of me."

He holds out his pinky, and I meet him halfway, wrapping mine with his, laughing.

"Promise," he says. "I'll go to the corner of the tent over there while you change. I also pinky-promise not to look." He releases my pinky and crawls to the corner, covering his eyes and proudly stating, "Ready."

I chuckle and shake my head at his light, childish behavior. It's endearing, really. He says the things and does the things I'd be too afraid to do out of fear of looking ridiculous. And maybe I would look ridiculous if I did, but he surely doesn't.

I dig in my bag until I find the... old sweatpants and holey t-shirt that I brought. Because I was supposed to be in my own tent. Alone.

I don't like people seeing me not put together, but then again, he just held me as I rocked and sobbed over the intense thundering in my brain. He's also seen me wear this back at the house when he picked up Lucy for their first real date. It's just Finley. I'm not trying to impress him. In fact, I am trying to turn him off from me.

Perfect.

With renewed hope that maybe my lack of proper dress will be the nail in the coffin for his feelings, I peel my clothes off, blushing when I'm stripped of my undergarments. I know I wouldn't be able to even attempt to sleep if my thoughts were ruminating on dirty undergarments. I use a wet wipe to brush off the grime, and then I slip into fresh panties and a white sports bra before shrugging on the gray sweatpants and holy white t-shirt. "Ready."

Finley drops his hands and scooches around. He lets out a low whistle as he looks me up and down. "You dress down nicely, Leilei."

"Oh, shut up," I snark, and then quickly begin to apologize for using harsh words.

He stands and takes a few strides towards me. "You do not have to apologize. You had a touch of joking in your voice and I'm aware it was not from malice."

I sigh. "How can you tell those cues so easily?"

"Just the way my brain works. Trust me, it's not all it's cracked up to be. Now, I'm going to change, so you can go sit in the corner like I did or you can watch." He winks, and I sprint to the corner of the tent, mildly stumbling over my backpack. Behind me, he laughs. After a moment, he asks, "Do you want to tell me what happened now?"

I bite my lip as my shoulders droop. At the very least, if he wasn't offended by my clothes, this should be the glaring red light that tells him to stop pursuing me. If this doesn't turn him away, then I really don't know what will.

After a dramatic exhale, I begin. "You already know I'm autistic, Finley. It's not something I necessarily go around thinking about, much less talking about. To me, that term is just a term to describe how I think and process and feel. You know touch obviously gets to me but so do random loud noises. It's more than just getting a scare. It throws my brain into a panic that I can't escape from, and even after the sound disappears in reality, it is still loud and present in my head. Sounding over and over again."

There's rustling somewhere behind me and then the zip of a bag. "How does it make you feel when you encounter the triggering of something?"

"With noises, it makes me want to tune out to everything. It's loud, echoes around in my brain like a ping-pong ball. I can't escape it until I calm down. With touch, it's like my skin crawls. Well, depending on the type. I can't wear certain fabrics, like wool. My brain would explode if I had to experience that scratchy sensation for any length of time. When people touch me, I flinch away because all I can think about is their skin on mine. I'm accustomed to certain people, like my sister, parents, and Hadley. Your touch makes me uncomfortable in the sense that it *doesn't* make me uncomfortable..."

"Why do you think that is?" he prompts.

"I—I don't really know. It doesn't make sense to me. It's almost as if your touch is familiar. Safe. It calms me. Even if the sensation is like touching the sun."

After a beat, he places his hands slowly on my shoulders and begins to rub the knots developed from today's hike. "Is this okay?"

Tension melts away as he hits all the right spots, and I groan. "See. I shouldn't like this. I usually don't. But with you... it feels okay. Hot, but okay."

His hands tighten on my shoulders before he pulls back, clearing his throat. "Are you ready for bed?"

I slowly stand and move around his stiffened frame towards my sleeping bag. His back is still towards me, in his black joggers and black t-shirt, even after I've prepared my sleeping space, three body lengths away from his.

This is it. He's recognized that I'm not good for him.

Why does it feel like my heart is crying?

The silence is unnerving.

I slide into my sleeping bag and stare at the dimly lit red tint of the tent. After a minute, Finley clicks the light off, and then I hear him slipping into his sleeping bag.

"You no longer wish to date me, right?" I finally ask, my brain demanding clarity to the silence.

Finley doesn't answer for a moment, but then he exhales. "I completely want you, Lorelei. That's the problem. I want you more and more with every new thing I discover about you. But I worry you may always try to push me away because of your fears that you are not capable of being loved."

"It's not that I don't feel capable of being loved, Finley." *I think?* "It's more like I fear leaving my safety. And I fear the intense feelings that Lucy always describes and feels. I fear that what I feel for you is only the beginning."

"You—you feel something for me?" His voice is laced with a bit of awe and wonder. "Truly?"

I swallow, wishing for once truth didn't roll off my tongue. "Yes. My heart rate picks up when I'm around you. Your touch brings me comfort. You make me laugh and smile. You're intelligent, kind, and thoughtful. I'm concerned about your dating history, and I am concerned about leaving Juniper Grove and my family and my friends. I'm concerned about moving to a new country. I'm fearful of leading said country. But ultimately, Finley...Yes. I like you. But I don't know if that's enough."

Silence wraps around us for minutes before he whispers on exhale, "That's enough for me. Stretch your hand out towards me, please."

I hesitate for a second but then oblige. I feel around for a moment before my fingers graze his hand. He latches on, holding my fingers because my hand doesn't quite reach his. Then he must move closer because his fingers thread through mine. The darkness surrounds us, and all of my senses are tuned into the way his hand feels in mine: warm, safe, strong.

"I don't understand this attraction and feeling, Finley. It usually takes years for me to open up to people. To be comfortable with them touching me."

He laughs without mirth. "Me either, Leilei. I was instantly drawn to you, and it's only gotten worse. You. Not your sister. Almost as if God has already ordained this."

Fate? Is that what he's speaking of? We were *meant* to be together? "Do you believe in soulmates? To be honest, I never have. I believe love is a choice. You can choose to love anyone, right?"

His thumb rubs circles on the back of my hand. "I agree. Love is a choice. And yes, you can choose to love anyone. But don't you think some people are a little bit easier to love?"

"Yeah, you're right." I smile in the darkness, thinking that if my parents had chosen to love anyone else, the world would have missed out on an epic love story. "I think my parents were ordained by God to be together. I've never seen a love as pure as theirs."

"And what if you could experience that love yourself, Lorelei? What would you do for it?"

His question jolts me. What *would* I do for it? Would I move for it? Would I gain a title for it? Is that sort of happiness attainable for me?

"I guess if I had that sort of love, I'd do just about anything to keep it."

"Me too. And Lorelei, I think we could have that. I'm sorry if it's too forward and not something you wish to entertain right now, but in the name of honesty, I'm falling in love with you."

His hand gives mine a gentle squeeze as his words toss around inside my head. He's falling in love with me. Finley Andersson is falling in love with *me.* Lorelei Raine Spence.

Goodness gracious.

I think I might be falling in like with him. Maybe not love quite yet, but it'd be stupid of me to not admit that I like him. A lot. And what if I can overcome my fears in the span of a couple of months and uproot my life?

Fear trembles in my chest at the thought, and I recognize that it would be no easy feat to erase it that quickly.

But I... *want to?*

Yes. That thought is clear and loud.

I *want* to try.

"Finley, I—"

"You don't have to respond, Lorelei. I don't expect that from you. Take the time you need to process."

"Finley... Yes. I want to try this dating thing. With you. I can't promise that I will be ready to commit to the level you need from me in the matter of a couple of months, but I am willing to try. Is that... okay?"

To my surprise, he laughs. Loud. Though not loud enough to trigger a mental meltdown from me. But still.

"*Prisaa Guud!*" He winds down, a few lingering chuckles escaping. "Thank you. Yes, that's all I can hope and ask for. I have tears in my eyes. Sorry. That probably wasn't manly of me to admit."

I squeeze his hand. "I think that's plenty manly. You'll cry enough for the both of us." I laugh, hoping he catches that I was joking. He does, and he laughs with me. We talk more about the way my brain functions, the way his operates, and then he tells me about his love of antique cars and how he enjoys fixing them up before we quiet down and begin to drift in and out of sleep, his fingers still grasping mine as if it's his lifeline.

Or maybe I'm grasping onto him for dear life.

Lucy's Journal

Saturday, April 3rd * 8:29 p.m. * Seas of sadness wreck me as I lie in bed

My sister is camping with my future king-in-law and they do not have cell service which means I can't text-harass her into all the details. It's driving me mad! And I could really use the distraction because things aren't going to work between me and hot PPO Gabriel. No matter how badly I want it to. He is currently in a plane flying around their camping area because Finley demanded he get to do the hike and camping trip truly alone with Lorelei. The PPOs followed him to the location before jumping in a small plane to periodically check on the crown prince. It was at that moment I realized we wouldn't work. He will have to go back to Korsa, and sure, I could follow, but still. His job would pull him away from me too much, and I know my sensitive soul can't handle that. So here I lie in seas of sadness over yet another failed attempt at love.... To make matters worse, my boss just texted me. He wants me to plan another read-a-thon at the community center. Ugh, he needs to hire a new event coordinator already and quit using me. I'm just supposed *to be the assistant. That's what I was hired for. Granted, I do like encouraging the youth of today to read, and the extra pay is nice. Speaking of, if my sister does move to Korsa, how will I afford this place myself? I really need to sell more books. This $300 a month for my books isn't cutting it. So much to think about, but honestly, I don't want to right now. I just want to throw the towel in on life and say forget it all. Help me out of this, God. Please. I'm slowly losing motivation to keep going.*

Chapter Nineteen

Finley

My eyes blink open to sunlight pouring through the tent, creating a red haze around me. My chest is heavy. In fact, my entire body feels weighed down.

Once my vision fully returns, I realize it's because a human is sprawled on top of me, a nest of red curls covering my face. I spit out a few strands that occupy my mouth before gently combing Lorelei's hair away from my eyes. Biting back a laugh, I bend my neck to look around her head. Her head rests just below my chin, her chest on my stomach, and her legs tangled with mine.

She's literally on top of me.

And how in the world did I sleep through *that* happening?

I lay my head back down and revel in the fact that Lorelei not only said she liked me and is willing to try things with me, but also that somewhere in the middle of the night, she (consciously or subconsciously, I don't know for certain) felt the need to crawl *on top* of me.

The woman who boasted that she sleeps alone. Who doesn't like physical contact with people. Who keeps to herself...

Is. On. Top. Of. Me.

I resist the urge to pump my fists, though I couldn't if I tried from the way she has me pinned down. I know everyone is thinking that this is highly inappropriate and wrong, but I'd like to suggest that their mind is in the gutter because, honestly, this is the most adorable image. Cuter than babies being christened in the palace or, or... puppies.

She feels safe. She feels protected. She feels seen.

By me.

Which is the only reason she'd fall asleep.

On top of me...

I breathe in disbelief, but as I suck in more air, too much flows through the pipes, and a raging cough spews from somewhere deep within my chest.

Lorelei flails and scrambles to her feet, her hands pressing into my chest as she uses me as push-off. She trips on my feet as she goes to move away, and as she falls down, I'm too immobilized to catch her.

But have no fear...

She tumbles down and down, right back into her starting position on top of me.

I grunt in pain as her head slams into my chin, her body sinking into mine as I lay on the hard ground of the tent. A Korsan curse slips through my lips.

"Are you okay, Lorelei?" I wrap my arms around her to move her off me, gently placing her to my side as I shove down the muscle pain and the possibility of an entirely bruised body. I sit on my knees and examine her, her messy hair covering her face and her shirt riding up enough so that the pale skin of her stomach shows through.

She has freckles on her stomach.

How blasted adorable.

Boisterous laughter rips my attention from that sliver of skin, and Lorelei is starfished out on the ground, heaving and coughing with laughter.

"I can't believe that just happened," she exclaims, dragging her hands to cover her face. She mumbles through her laughter about Lucy getting story fuel from this scenario. "So embarrassing."

Giving her one last look over to make sure she's okay, I allow myself to laugh at the situation, too. And once I start, I can't stop. The joy is immense. I mimic her pose and starfish out on the ground, my hand finding hers like it's my lighthouse on the ocean. We laugh and laugh until we're facing each other, clutching our stomachs, with tears streaming down our face.

Her hazel eyes are bright, her cheeks pink, as I trail a finger down the side of her face and catch a tear. "Good morning, bae," I finally manage to say as my laughter dies down.

She sucks in a breath and whispers, "Good morning. Did you know that saying good morning is a wish that one's day would actually be a positive and eventful one? It's not simply a nicety."

I grin. "Then I wish you the best of mornings. I hope your morning is positively the best one you ever experience, despite how we awoke."

"I think because of how we awoke, this will be the best morning I've experienced." She beams before schooling her expression.

"Even better than Christmas morning?"

"Hm..." She lifts a finger to her chin. "Yes. I think so. I've never laughed so hard. Oh!" She sits up on her knees, suddenly alert and inquisitive. "Are you okay? I must have hurt you."

I rise to my knees and shake my head. "I'm perfectly okay. Waking up with you sprawled on top of me was... something."

She tilts her head. "Something in a good way or bad way? Sorry, I can't tell."

"Don't be sorry." I take her hands in mine. "Something in the best way. Waking up to your hair in my mouth and suffocating me is the absolute highlight of my existence. And I mean that with zero sarcasm. You can suffocate me every morning."

She rolls her eyes. And after taking a deep breath, she gently pulls her hands away from me and combs her fingers through her hair before taking the black ponytail holder on her wrist and whipping the frizzy mess into a bun on top of her head. "We should get ready to head back. The trail will be more difficult due to the storm last night."

"We'll make it to the end. Together."

She smiles softly, a certain calmness to her being that wasn't present yesterday. "Hopefully so."

"Lorelei, I have to ask. Did you truly mean what you said last night? That you are going to try with me? We won't get back to Juniper Grove and you'll disappear?" This moment feels too much like a fever dream; my overthinking brain is a smidge worried.

She stands and holds out her hand to me. I take it as she hoists me. The petite woman is stronger than she looks. "I meant it. I don't make decisions lightly and unless I'm positive. I also don't say things I don't mean."

"I'm learning to trust that. So many women have led me on in the past, so please forgive my hesitancy."

"Why don't you tell me more about your fears as we pack up? You learned about mine last night, and I would like to know yours. I'm going to change real quick." She motions for me to turn around, so I do.

"I've dated a lot, as you already know. I've always been a hopeless romantic, like your sister. I didn't want to get married just to get married or to unite countries or for simple convenience. I wanted to marry for love, and the only way to find that love was to search for it. It was easy for me to get dates. I am a prince, after all. But I quickly learned many women will use a person for their own gain."

Her bag zipper sounds in the background. "I'm listening," she says, prompting me on. I stare out of the side of the tent, able to see shadows from the sun reflecting off the red fabric.

"Mamma has been pressuring me to marry Her Royal Highness Princess Karin of Vespen, a neighboring and friendly country of ours. She believes Karin is perfect for me and that a union between us would be beneficial to both countries. I, however, do not think Karin is good for me. She's conceited, materialistic, and demanding. She suffocates me when I'm home or visiting Vespen for state affairs. I don't love her and I wouldn't choose to love her."

Silence ensues for a moment. "I'm done," Lorelei says, and I turn around. She wears a new pair of black leggings, an olive green athletic shirt, and white ankle socks that will be brown by the end of this hike. She maneuvers to my corner and sits, motioning me to go ahead and change. "Do you think your mother will accept a commoner?"

Like me hangs between us.

"She will," I reassure her as I grab my bag. "Mamma loves me dearly. She loves me so much that she wants to control my happiness to make sure I am happy, but I've learned how to stand up for myself and say no where I need to. She respects my decisions even if it takes her a while to come around."

I strip my clothes and slip into new black joggers and a heather gray t-shirt with our family crest on it. I continue, "Father is already overjoyed that I've found you. And yes, I've talked to them about you. As Lucy and Lorelei. They know about the switch. I don't really keep secrets from my family."

"I like that about you," Lorelei says. "It killed me pretending to be Lucy and hiding that fact from everyone. Including you."

"I understand why you did it. It wasn't your secret, but your sister's. You love her deeply and wanted to protect her."

Lorelei sighs. "Yes."

"I'm ready," I say, shoving my folded night clothes into my backpack. She stands and examines the tent, then sets to rolling up the sleeping bags. Both of ours. Like we are truly a couple.

Which I guess we are now. The thought warms my soul, and inexplicable joy encompasses me.

"Lorelei," I say her name in a whispered breath, take two long strides, spin her around, and wrap her in my arms, holding her tightly against me. After a moment, her hands come to rest on my hips, then she slides them around and up my back until she's squeezing me in a sturdy embrace. I'm already so in love with her, and I don't know what to do with myself.

She breaks free and pulls back, so I let her, my hands moving to grasp her forearms as she does the same. She's smiling wide with a sparkle in her hazel eyes. "We should get going, Finley."

"Right. I just can't seem to let you go. Physical touch is my love language, just so you are aware."

"Of course the man I end up with enjoys physical touch." She laughs, dropping her hands. Then she twists her lips. "I don't know what my love language is..."

"We can try to figure it out on the way back."

"Agreed," she says with a firm nod of her head. "But first. Food."

"I'm so sorry, Lorelei. I don't know how this happened."

A helicopter hovers above us, trying to get as low as possible without hitting the trees. I know it's Gabriel and Anders, but I don't know why they are here as we have zero phone service out here. I trust them, though, so as they toss a long rope ladder down, I begin to mentally prepare to climb it.

"Finley, I don't think I can do this." The quiver in Lorelei's voice tightens my chest. I wish I could snap my fingers and get us up this rope, but it's not going to be that easy. She has her belongings at her feet and is pressing her hands against her ears as if she's attempting to pop her head open with pressure.

I toss onto my back the backpack that has my tent rolled up and clipped to it. Then, I grab Lorelei's from her, which has a cooking pot attached to it, and slip my arms through it so that it's on my chest. I finagle the bags around and lean in as close as I can to her and say, "I'm going to climb up with our stuff, and then I will come back down for you. We've got this. Everything will be okay. If Gabriel and Anders are doing this, it's for a reason. I trust them."

She begins to say something else, but I need to be quick, so I reach for the rope, the end of it dangling right at my kneecaps. I climb, my stomach dipping at the swaying motion. The closer I get to the helicopter, the harder it is to climb. The rope sways even more as I push through the force of the wind the blades are creating. I reach the top, and Gabriel and Anders help hoist me onto the helicopter. It's impossible to talk without a headset, so Anders holds up his phone, and I scroll through articles stating that I was out here hiking and camping that leaked this morning. Then, Anders types that people are hiking out here to meet me and that others are gathered around my car in the lot at the head of the trail.

Curses rip through my head as I chunk the bags off me. How did this happen? Only a handful of people knew we were coming here. I've gone a few months without being noticed here in Mississippi. Why now? What changed? Karin? Is this her doing somehow?

Breathe, Finley. Let's get out of here first.

I take Anders' phone from him and type that I need to go back for Lorelei and I need a headset for her. He hands one over to me, and as I go to step down the ladder, I notice Lorelei is mid-way hanging on for dear life, a look of unadulterated terror covering her face. Cursing once more, I quickly climb down, moving around to the opposite side of the rope ladder. Once I reach her, our faces across from each other through one of the rung spaces, I loop one arm through the ladder and take the headset off, using one hand to place it over her ears. Which is as difficult as you can imagine it would be. Her hair is a disaster once I finally get both earpieces on her.

Her knuckles are white against the rope. I motion upward, telling her she has to climb. She shakes her head with enough force to swing the rope. Her eyes bulge with fear. I mouth, "It's okay. I've got you."

She tilts her head in confusion, but I look up where Anders and Gabriel are poking their heads out the door. I signal for them to pull the rope, and they give me the okay sign.

Making sure my feet and hands are secure, I move around the ladder so that I'm pressing against Lorelei's back, forming a cage around her. I place my hands over hers and tuck my knees into the dip of her legs, creating a seat of sorts for her. At that moment, the rope is jerked. Lorelei goes still underneath me, and I wish I could whisper in her ear that I have her. I hope she feels every ounce of me pressed against her right now. She's safe. Even if she let go, she'd fall against me.

The rope jerks again and again as we are hauled up. Once we reach the top, I force Lorelei's fingers to free the rope as my PPOs reach for her. She takes their hands and they lift her onto the helicopter before they grab me.

Once we are both on safely, I face Lorelei, whose face is abnormally pale, tears springing in her eyes as she breathes erratically. I open my arms for her, and she topples onto me, her arms wrapping around my waist and squeezing as if she's still on the rope and may fall. She sobs into my chest, and I press one hand into her mid back while the other tangles into her hair. We stand there for a moment before Gabriel gently places a hand on my shoulder, indicating that we should get going.

Desperate to know the answer, I pull out my phone and type out the words: Why did you climb?

She looks at me through watering, hazel eyes as she takes my phone and types underneath my question: I couldn't stand the thought of not pulling my weight to help out your heavy load.

My heart simultaneously leaps and sinks. She was thinking of me. Thinking of helping me. Even though the sound was deafening, she braved it. She took a step. She started the climb for me.

Little does she know that I would haul her anywhere, though. That I would climb a million rope ladders to keep her safe and at peace.

I love her, and by her actions today, I think—

I think she might love me, too, even if she can't admit it yet.

She climbed the ladder...

Finding too much meaning within the clouds, I strap Lorelei into a seat, then I sit next to her and hold her hand the entire time on the ride back to Juniper Grove.

Lorelei opts to have her communication capabilities silenced in her headset, so I communicate with Gabriel and Anders through our headsets as they fill me in on the totality of the situation.

Someone leaked that I was here, they haven't found the source yet, we will come back for my car the moment everyone clears, Lorelei's face is in the tabloids as the woman I am dating, Mamma is livid, Karin has nothing to do with this one, and Father is wanting me to come back home until things blow over.

And he wants me to bring Lorelei.

CHAPTER TWENTY

FINLEY

I grit my teeth as I read Lucy's text.

> Reporters are outside the apartment again. I'm going out as Lorelei with Karoline by my side while Hadley escorts my sister to work. She is refusing to stay home again.

This is all my fault.

Though, I technically know it isn't. It's been three days, and we still haven't figured out who leaked the information. After questioning our friends, which we didn't suspect at all but still needed to be sure, we turned it over to my capable PPOs to do the digging. At this point, I think I need to ask the local police to step in to keep reporters off Lorelei and Lucy's doorstep.

Meanwhile, I'm now tucked away in Mason's vacation home. I asked the twins if they'd like to move in here for a little while, but Lorelei said no, even at Lucy's nudging. It would be too much of a routine change for her right now when she needs her routines the most. Karoline and Hadley have been on rotation making sure the girls are safe; Braxton, Mason and I are stepping in when needed. Well, I'm stepping in because Lorelei is my girlfriend, and I dare anyone to try and attack her or get pictures of her without her permission.

Watch out, world. Angry Prince of Hearts is coming out to play.

I'm so grateful for Lucy. She's been generous with her time and energy, pretending to be her sister to distract reporters. I'll definitely have to do something to help her with her writing career after this.

My phone buzzes; Father is calling.

"Hello," I answer. "Any news?"

He sighs. "No, not yet. When are you coming home, Finley? I get worried with you across the ocean and only two PPOs to protect you. I can send more—"

"No, I'm fine," I interrupt. "I'll come as soon as I know Lorelei is safe and/or decides to come with me. So far it's been a moot point. She's already frazzled and doesn't want to be flown across the world to an unfamiliar place."

Father is quiet on the other end of the line. "Do you think, when the time comes for you to move back to Korsa permanently, that she will come with you?"

He asks the question I've avoided thinking about for a while. The truth is: I don't know. I honestly have no idea if Lorelei will be ready to come back with me by the end of June. Yes, she has agreed to date me, but even then, she made it perfectly clear that she doesn't know if she will be ready. Lorelei is not one to lie. She means it. She doesn't know, and neither do I.

"I'm praying for it, Father. It's in God's hands alone. I won't force her, but I'm doing absolutely everything I can to put her at ease, though this leak of my location and our date isn't helping matters."

"I'm sorry, son. I hate you're going through this, but think of it as a lesson and an opportunity for growth." My father, ever the wise, loving man. How does he remain calm? I'm ready to tear my shirt and crawl on all fours to rip the head off of whoever did this. I want to beat my chest and howl and seek animalist revenge.

"How are you not as angry as me?" I ask, defeated.

"Years of practice controlling my emotions. Being a king is not for the faint of heart, but I know you are up to the task. You will make mistakes, you will act on your emotions at times, but at the end of the day, apologize where you need to, stand strong in your decisions, and forgive readily. Allow God to continuously lead you down the path He has set forth and called you to. That will make you a grand leader."

Tears form in my eyes at his advice. His soft-spoken, gravelly words are sanding off the rough edges of my mood. *Thank you for a father like him, God. For a good leader and example to follow.*

I wipe my eyes with the backside of my hand before telling him I would be home soon and hanging up. I need to talk to Lorelei about everything. She has only texted me a handful of times since we made it back Sunday afternoon, and I've only seen her on Monday when she stayed home from work. That's when I asked her about flying to Korsa with me, and the visible panic in her features gave me the answer.

But maybe she's had time to sit with the idea now?

Either way, I've got to try one more time.

Plus, I miss her.

I send her a quick text stating that I am preparing dinner for us tonight at her place and that it will be ready when she gets home this evening.

As I begin to get ready to leave, she texts back a simple, "Okay."

My head spins, wondering if it's simply "Okay, sounds good" or "Okay, but I'm upset with you" or "Okay. This will be the last dinner we share." I shake the thoughts away, toss on an awful black wig, use a brow pencil to color my own eyebrows black, and pop in dark brown colored contacts. Once I effectively look like I've stepped out of the Addams family, I hop in the black, lifted Tundra that looks a lot like Mason's (he was the one to suggest this as my new vehicle for the time being) and head to my first destination of the day: the Juniper Grove Police Station.

At the very least, I'm getting those flies away from Lorelei's doorstep.

"Oh, they were mad, Lorelei." I drag out the word *mad* for emphasis as I fill her in on the biggest flytrap of this century. "The Mississippi branch of the FBI and police and Anders and Gabriel, on behalf of Korsa, of course, were a force to be reckoned with. The reporters flew out of the area."

She shoves a bite of chicken marsala into her mouth, an amused expression twinkling in her eyes. The fact that she could come home from work and not have to go roundabout ways to get into her apartment made her the happiest I've seen her since the morning she woke up sprawled on top of me.

I take a bite of garlic bread, relishing in the joy of this moment. Turns out "Okay" meant exactly what the word is supposed to mean. She was perfectly content with me coming over and cooking dinner for her.

"Thank you for going through the trouble, Finley. I feel a little more at ease now."

I swallow my bread then take a sip of lemon water. "At ease enough to possibly fly to Korsa with me this weekend?"

"I don't think so. My life just started getting back to normal tonight."

"Look at how well you've managed and handled everything, Lorelei. I am proud of you. Thank you for sticking by my side and not abandoning me through this. I know it's been difficult for you. Probably more difficult than you've let on."

Her eyebrows knit together as she tilts her head. "Why would I abandon you? I told you Saturday night that I wanted to give this a chance. I knew that came with the possibility of the spotlight, though admittedly, I wasn't expecting it this soon."

"I'm sorry it was this soon and that I hadn't properly prepared you for it."

"All is forgiven. This chicken marsala is delicious." She grins.

I fiddle with the collar of my white short-sleeved polo. "Is breaking your routine and rhythm of life the only thing keeping you from traveling to Korsa with me this weekend?"

"I think so. It's scary to think about going somewhere new with someone of your capacity. Won't the spotlight be even brighter there?"

Her hazel eyes, which air on the side of brown tonight, perfectly suiting her mocha blouse, ask a thousand more questions that even she seems to be unaware of. *What if I'm not accepted? What if I don't like it there? What if I'm too socially awkward to rule a country? What if...*

I open out my hand to her across the wooden table as one of her cats meows from the corner of the room. She places her hand in mine without hesitation as a warmness fills my soul. "You are an amazing woman. And so strong. Capable. I know the thought of moving to a new country and becoming a queen is scary, but you are trying. I appreciate your effort. And for the record, I think you will be a brilliant queen and will adjust well to Korsa. Yes, there will be a spotlight on us, but I can get us from the airport to Stjarna Palace in secret. I can move us around that entire country in secret. No one even has to know you are there this weekend. That's why I'd like for you to visit with me, even if it's just for a few days. I would like to show you around. That way you can make a well-informed decision." I don't say that I desperately need her to stay with me, but man, I truly do.

She squeezes my hand before pulling away; a dazzling, toothy smile illuminating her expression despite the fact that she has dark spots under her eyes. "Do you really believe that about me, Finley?"

"Of course I do. Will you please come to Korsa with me?"

Her cat meows again, and Lorelei turns her attention to it. "What do you think, Frizzle? Do I take the prince up on his offer to whisk me away to another country?" The cat meows.

"See, even Frizzle agrees you should go."

Lorelei narrows her eyes. "How do you know that was her yes?"

At that moment, Frizzle jumps into my lap and starts licking my chin with a sandpaper tongue. I gesture to the cat as Lorelei laughs and feigns a betrayed expression.

"Okay, okay. You've made your point. As long as we stay in secret outside your family, I will go with you. Oh, and one more condition."

I arch an eyebrow, which is now back to its original golden blond color.

"Lucy comes with us. I need her. She has to be my constant in the midst of change."

Biting my tongue to stop myself from saying, "But I can be your constant," I nod. Then I actually say, "That can be arranged without issue. Plus, you know she'd love it."

"Exactly," Lorelei says before scooping another piece of chicken into her mouth. One day Lorelei will consider me her constant. I can tell I'm a safe place for her now, but I understand Lucy is her constant, her bridge back to home.

I spend the rest of the evening answering every question she has about the country, royal etiquette, and security protocols. We laugh, lightly touch, do the dishes together, use a laser to play with the cats, and at the end of the night when I leave, she lingers in a hug, her gaze falling to my lips more than once. I lean in, but she stops me with a hand on my chest. At my obvious disappointment, she says, "I promise we will try soon. Just give me a little more time. I want it, I truly do."

The fire blazing in her eyes verifies her words, and I take it as a win that she embraced me for a solid two minutes without pulling away once.

On the way home, I call my father to let him know that I'm getting on a plane Friday night with Lorelei and Lucy. And he informs me that he found out it was the original stalker who leaked the news that I would be hiking.

A stalker that finally came out in the open.

Who secured a job to spy at a place I frequented.

A woman who went by the name Selene.

And who, once caught, verified that she was not hired by Karin as we thought.

But by my own mother.

CHAPTER TWENTY-ONE

LORELEI

"This is the only way I will fly from now on." Lucy says after she picks her jaw off the ground. Or, more accurately, off the floor of our private jet.

No, not our.

Finley's.

It's not mine.

Yet.

Oh, hush up, brain.

The man has me wrapped around his finger. From his heroic rescue with the helicopters, to giving me space, then cooking me dinner and reassuring me verbally and with his presence that everything will be okay.

I've got a big, Lucy-style crush on Finley Andersson, and that's why I'm on his private jet, strapped into a very comfortable gray leather seat with a plate of strawberries, bananas, oranges, and grapes in front of me on a sturdy metal tray. A giggle escapes my lips as I stab a grape with a fork, lifting the plump, purple deliciousness to my lips.

My heart feels the lightest it has in days, all because a man said some nice words to me. I sneak a glance at Lucy who is sipping a glass of champagne in the seat adjacent to me. I think she's rubbed off on me some over the past week. She has been a saint—constantly remaining by my side, taking off her own work to sit in the office with me when I needed her, and pretending to be me when we had to distract reporters.

And through it all, she's gushed over my relationship like it has become the sole focus of her own life. She has sung his praises, has helped me work through these new, confusing emotions, and has spelled it out for me: I am falling for this man.

Falling some kind of hard.

Knowing it and accepting it are two different things though. I believe I'm on my way to accepting my feelings, but I'm not quite there yet. Maybe this trip to Korsa will help. Which is another reason I agreed. Dating Finley means there is a possibility of marrying Finley. Marrying Finley means moving to another country and running said country alongside him.

My sister has told me over and over that I am built for such a job because of my patience and intelligence and logical brain.

But I'm not so sure.

An autistic queen?

Does Korsa really want that?

"*Mysaa*, is your head crowded?" Finley asks, taking a seat next to me and popping a strawberry into his mouth. "Unload on me, please."

I stab another grape and chew while I contemplate telling him what's on my mind. He doesn't rush me to speak; in fact, he continues to eat fruit alongside me, giving me the space to think. Another wonderful quality that I admire about this man. So many people in my life have gotten offended or frustrated with me when I have responded or answered in a manner they deemed untimely.

"I'm worried that Korsa would reject me as a queen because I am autistic."

Finley doesn't skip a beat in his response. "Who says neurodivergent people can't make great rulers? It doesn't have to define you, and from what I've seen, you make it a priority in your life not to let it define you. You simply are who you are. I adore that about you. And I believe the very things you don't like about yourself are the qualities that will make an excellent head of state."

I stare at him, a strawberry pressed to my lips, mouth agape. "Really?" *Brilliant response, Lorelei. See. You're not as clever as he believes.*

"Really, really." He meets my gaze, his lips ticking up in a smile. Slowly, allowing me plenty of time to stop him if I wanted, he reaches for the strawberry pinched between my fingers. He takes it from me, then holds the plump, red berry in front of my mouth. "Open up," he commands. He slips the strawberry through my lips, and I bite down. His eyes never leave mine.

"Good girl," he whispers, and two things happen simultaneously: Lucy begins to choke while my toes begin to tingle. The feeling travels up my legs and spine, into my arms, and finally spreads throughout my face, causing my nose to scrunch. There's also something unsettling about the words that I can't pinpoint.

"Man's got game," Lucy blurts. I snap my attention to her as Finley sighs, sitting back in his seat. "Oops." She covers her mouth, giggling, turning back around in her seat.

"What's she talking about?" I ask Finley. Judging by his irritated glare in my sister's direction, she has greatly offended him with that statement.

He shakes his head, bright blond hair swishing around with the motion. "When someone says that they have 'game,' they are typically stating that they know how to win another person over romantically."

Huh. "Is romance supposed to be a game?" I don't know if I like that train of thought.

"No." Finley laughs through a grimace. "Romance is not a game. And furthermore, I don't believe you can necessarily 'win' somebody. People are gifts in our lives, not something to be owned. Hear that, Lucy?" he asks in a louder voice.

"Roger that." Her hand flicks from the edge of her forehead like a salute even though she's not facing us.

I smile, loving where this man's heart is with every passing second. "I would agree with that." I reach for his hand, and he easily slips his long fingers through mine. He looks down at me wearing a proud smile. I continue my line of questioning, "But why did she say that in response to you telling me 'good girl?'" *And why did I tingle so much?*

His smile turns saucy. "How did you *feel* when I said that?"

My cheeks heat, and I avert my eyes. I find myself not wanting to tell him, but if I'm ever going to figure out how to be romantic and such, I need to be open and honest. I have to *learn.* And learning is nothing to be ashamed of. "I felt tingly. It started in my toes and traveled up my body."

"Then it had the effect I wished it would." He winks. "I'm thrilled to know it's something you like."

Do I like it? That feeling?

"Say it again."

His eyes widen before they hood over. Finley leans down as I stare straight ahead, preparing myself for the feeling again. His breath tickles the hairs on the back of my neck before he whispers in a raspy voice, "Good girl, Leilei."

I tingle once more, but I'm cautious now. As much as I do like this feeling, I pinpoint the reason the words unsettled me. The words feel a bit demeaning, like when doctors spoke to me like I was a little girl when I was eighteen years old simply because they saw the word "autistic" on my medical reports.

I shake my head, also trying to calm down the blush coating my cheeks. "No. I don't like those words, but I like the feeling associated with them. Are there other words that could create the same feeling?"

Finley strokes the back of my hand with his thumb, and I realized I've been holding his hand for longer than normal.

So much so that I forgot I was holding it.

And now that I remember, my hand is set aflame, and I remove it from his.

His smile doesn't falter. "Oh, there are so many words I can use to recreate that tingly feeling for you. We will experiment as we go."

My heart warms. "Thank you. I'm sorry I don't know what I like when it comes to romance."

"Don't apologize, pretty woman," he says, a gleam in his eyes. "I vow to help you explore all the romantic things. In fact, I'm going to have a lot of fun doing it."

"Pretty woman. I like those words."

"Noted." He laughs, but then it dies out as he folds his hands together in his lap.

Noticing the shift in his mood, I ask, "What's wrong?"

"I'm going to be face to face with my mother soon."

I sit quietly, waiting for him to elaborate, but he doesn't. "Have you spoken with her since you found out she hired Selene?"

He shakes his head, a contemplative expression on his face. "I don't—" He pauses, sighs, and closes his eyes. "I don't know how to approach this. She's my mother, Lorelei. Karin was easy to approach. But this... I can't believe she has taken this action against us. Against me."

His words sting. I can't imagine how I would feel if I found out my mom had betrayed me in such a way. In fact, I probably wouldn't be able to feel at all—I'd shut down until the situation no longer bothered my brain. But knowing Finley, he is going to continue to feel this betrayal. Down to his bones. Deeply and painfully.

"I'm here for you." I place my hand on his bouncing leg, which instantly settles him. "I'm sorry I can't enter into your feelings with you, but I can be of assistance in the advice department. I can listen and help you formulate how to approach her when you're ready."

He smiles sadly at me, tears in his eyes. "You truly don't understand how much of a blessing you are to me, Lorelei Raine. I love you."

Love.

He's told me before that he was falling in love with me, but this is the first time he's said those three words so plainly.

And I—

No.

I can't love him just yet.

But as I look at his vulnerable, despondent frame, my heart sings a different tune. He's been more than I could ever hope for in a man. He understands me, has stuck around and continues to pursue me even when I'm not the easiest to deal with, and has trusted me with his heart.

Is this love? Is this feeling of immense gratitude and hope and some unknown stirring deep in my gut actually love?

Love is a choice, right?

So I can't love him until I make the choice to stay by his side and become his queen. I can't love him if the thought of still walking away from him is prevalent.

We spend the rest of the flight talking about the best way to approach his mother, whom I desperately do not like at this point, which is unfortunate because when I don't like a person, I have a difficult time not letting them know.

The plane lands, we awaken Lucy who passed out after a glass of champagne and indulgence of fruits, and Gabriel and Anders prepare to escort us through the backside of the palace for good measure. We all agreed it was best to keep my presence here hidden until I've had a chance to meet the family.

I need to make a good impression for Finley's sake, even if I don't end up by his side. I don't want his family thinking he went off his rocker in choosing a woman like me. But everything his mother has said and done to him is souring my view of her. "Finley," I grab his arm before we step off the private jet. "I'm sorry if I'm rude to your mother. I am going to try my best, but she hurt you, and I feel righteous revenge bubbling at the surface."

To my surprise, he laughs. "Righteous revenge? Maybe I should send you in to chat with her."

"Finley, it's not funny. I have a hard time controlling my tongue when someone I love has been hurt."

Love.

The word slipped out.

Because, dang it, I *do* love Finley Andersson. It's time to stop trying to make it black and white.

It's more than a choice. It is a feeling. A deep, unwavering feeling to protect, encourage, and stand by his side. For the rest of my life.

"You love me?" he asks, his eyes wide, hopeful, and full of awe. He covers my hand still grasping at the soft, navy blue fabric coating his arm.

"I—I," I swallow the stutter. "Can we talk about this later?"

He grins brilliantly. "Oh, we will, pretty woman."

A shudder runs down my spine. Now is not the time for those feelings. I have something to take care of first. "But first, let's handle your meddling mother."

Chapter Twenty-Two

Finley

Mother sits across from Lorelei and me at the long, rectangular table where we typically host state dinners. Father is beside Mother, looking every bit as tired and conflicted as I feel. I tried to deter the woman, who is dressed in a navy gown lined with gold swirling designs with gray hair adorning the top of her head under her golden crown, to allow us to speak in a more private, comfortable, low-key location, but she wouldn't have it. A boiled turkey sits at the center of our small gathering of four with endless side dishes that could feed a small village.

Excessive.

But that's Mother when she's attempting to stand out. Which is also why I asked Gabriel and Anders to keep Lucy company. She doesn't need to experience this side of my family. If I could shield Lorelei from it, I would, but she needs to get accustomed. They will hopefully become her family, too.

"Why did you go through all of this?" I finally ask, breaking the uncomfortable silence. I squeeze Lorelei's hand, and she squeezes back. I've already whispered apologies to her countless times as the food was being whisked in and Mother threw sharp glances her way.

"You brought your girl home finally. I wanted to make a good impression." Her voice is high-pitched with undertones of "how dare you question my intentions."

"We both know you wanted to undermine Lorelei by showing off your wealth and status. Don't lie, Mother."

She doesn't even flinch. "Believe what you will, son. But I simply wanted to impress the woman you have deemed worthy of becoming the next queen of Korsa."

My hand tightens around Lorelei's, and she winces. "Sorry," I mumble in her ear then release her hand. I know I'll be making fists again in no time.

"Thank you for going through the trouble for me, Your Highness," Lorelei says with a slight bow of her head. Her voice is steady and sure, and the only thing impressing me in this room is her. "I'm in awe of your lovely dining area."

Was that... sarcasm? I shift my eyes to Lorelei, who shows no sign of misgivings or intentional pushback.

Mother, however, must have interpreted what she said as I did because her overly pink lips turn down slightly. She clears her throat, switching to Korsan even though I asked her to please speak English in front of Lorelei. "*Taak.*"

"*Vaarsaagood,*" Lorelei replies with the slight dip of her chin. I grin, loving the way Korsan sounds in her voice. She hasn't learned a lot, but she's mastered pleasantries. In fact, she's gifted in the sense she can pick up languages easily. She'll have Korsan down in no time at all.

"You speak Korsan?" Father asks. "Finley has not informed me of that."

Lorelei's firm but welcoming expression never changes. "Not yet. I intend to speak fluently, however."

"Wonderful," Father says through a warm smile. My heart is thankful for a moment before Mother captures my attention again.

"Of course the queen of a country should be able to fluently speak its language," she dismisses Lorelei's efforts as if they aren't enough. But that's the thing with Mother... Nothing is enough unless we do exactly what she wants of us. What she insists is fit for us.

"Enough," I state, my voice firm but respectful. "Mother, we need to address why you hired a woman named Selene to stalk our dates, why you decided to place the blame on Karin, and why you had Selene disclose our location to the press."

The mood in the room instantly shifts, and I wonder briefly if Lorelei can feel it. I look her over once. She's stern, sitting up rod-straight, her hands folded on top of her navy pencil skirt. I bought her this outfit (with Lucy's help) before we left for Korsa. It's the correct color of navy that matches our family crest. She has a white button down tucked into the skirt, and a matching navy blazer with gold buttons tops off the outfit. And because she is Lorelei, she wears her white sneakers and her hair in a ponytail.

She's every ounce the queen that Korsa needs.

"Finley, I did not ask nor demand Selene to disclose your location. She did that of her own accord."

Despite myself, I scoff. "Am I supposed to believe that after you made Karin take the fall for you?"

Mother sighs, and Father places a hand on her back as she hunches over in a show of defeat. "You're right. I do not have ground to stand on because of my previous deception, but I am being honest. That was all her, and she is now in custody with our court."

"Why put her in court when you are the one responsible for hiring her in the first place? Will you own up to your actions in front of the court?" The sharpness in my voice could carve the turkey in the center of the table, but I will no longer allow Mother to believe she has a right to control my life in this manner. I've skirted around her wishes long enough. It's time to put an end to it.

"We will handle it, Finley," Father replies in her stead. My eyes don't move from Mother, whose gaze is fixated on the empty porcelain plate in front of her.

"I want to hear it from her, Father."

"I understand, but your Mother is under great pressure right now, and—"

"Is she?" I bite. A laugh of disbelief bubbles out of me. I realize I'm crossing a line, allowing my indignation to speak on my behalf, but I simply don't care right now. "Is *she* the one becoming King of Korsa in less than a year? Is *she* the one being forced to marry because an outdated piece of paper commands it? Has *she* dealt with her dates being stalked? Experienced the fear that the person *she* loves may be in danger? Had to be lifted out of a campsite via helicopter?" My breaths come heavy, and then I feel Lorelei's hand rest on my thigh. All the anger, frustration, and hurt dial down by ten notches at the warmth radiating underneath her palm. My next words are a plea for Mother to see me. "You both gave me permission to pursue the qualifications of kingship on my own terms for three months. You both stated I could have this time. We all agreed. We agreed if it didn't work out that I would marry Karin. And then... Then you, Mother, tried to once again take my choice away. You didn't trust me or have an ounce of faith in me. And that is what hurts me the most."

I hang my head, closing my eyes and attempting to push back the tears threatening to fall. Placing my hand over Lorelei's brings another wave of reprieve from the heavy cloud of painful emotion smothering me. The room has fallen silent, not even the sound of movement typically present outside the tall, double doors can be heard. Slowly, I raise my head and open my eyes. Mother is staring at me with water prickling at the edges of her blue eyes. Father is watching Mother.

I glance at Lorelei, who is watching me.

The scrape of a chair jolts my attention. Mother raises from her seat, Father following suit. Lorelei and I jump to our feet out of respect, but without another look in my direction, she walks away, the heavy click of heels on the granite floors bouncing off the four cream walls of the large hosting room.

Father hurriedly apologizes to Lorelei and me before giving me one last look of desperation and scurrying off after my mother. We sit down in silence after the doors click shut.

And then I lose every ounce of restraint, plunging my elbows onto the thick, wooden table and covering my water-filled eyes with my hands. I choke on the sobs as they overtake my body—the pain caused by my own mother has become too unbearable to shove down.

Lorelei places her hand on my back at some point; I'm vaguely aware of the way she rubs circles while patting my thigh with her other hand. She doesn't speak but lets me get it all out, her touch alone keeping me from collapsing to my knees. Once I can no longer force a teardrop from my eyes, I wipe my face with the cloth napkin beside me and face Lorelei, whose expression is one of sorrow and understanding. Not an ounce of accusation or disgust at a grown, sobbing man to be found.

In fact, when I give her the smallest of smiles, she tilts her head and asks, "Feel better now?"

A genuine laugh escapes me as I admire this lovely woman the Lord has gifted me with. "A little more weightless, but this isn't over yet."

"You're right." She furrows her eyebrows and purses her lips in thought. "It wasn't cool how she walked away without saying anything, but I guess people process differently."

"That's my mother for you. If she isn't in the right or given what she desires, she will make sure no one else is happy. I don't know if I've ever truly heard the words 'I'm sorry' from her."

Lorelei removes her hands from me, but she continues to angle herself towards me, her knees inches from my legs. "I wonder what made her that way. Everyone has a story."

That phrase jolts me. What is my mother's story? My entire life, she's been the controlling, demanding Queen of Korsa whom I knew loved me though she never showed her love for me in the ways I receive it best. She hardly ever hugged me, told me she loved me, or praised me. But I knew she did because I learned to see how she loved—action and service to others. She took care of me, stood up for me, and made sure my every need and most desires were met. Because I knew she loved me, I often gave in to her wishes and appeased her demands.

But somewhere underneath all the knowledge I have of her love is a little boy who only craved the warmth of his mother's arms. A teen who desired to be praised for his good actions, grades, and talents. A young man who wants to hear the words 'I love you' from his mother's lips.

And maybe I haven't stopped to think about what made her this way. *Who* made her this way? I've been blinded by my own hurts to ask her about hers.

"Finley?"

"Hm?" I answer automatically to the sound of Lorelei saying my name. My thoughts drift away as I lose myself in the freckles of skin and the sparkle of her hazel eyes.

"You're okay," she whispers, taking my hands between hers. "We will walk through this. Together. I'm going to stand by you. My space is always a space for your tears and your pain and your insecurities. If you can somehow manage my sensory overload breakdowns, then I can manage your tears."

My heart explodes with immense love for the woman beside me. Before I can stop myself, I whisper, "You're beautiful, Lorelei. Your body, your brain, your heart, and your soul."

A faint blush coats her cheeks and nose, but she doesn't look away. My lips ache to kiss the pinkened skin, every freckle, and her parted lips.

I clear my throat. "Does this mean you are saying yes to me? Yes to everything it means to be by my side? Yes to dating me with intentions of marrying me?" Hope swells in my chest, and I dare to believe a woman like her will marry me.

"Yes, Finley." A confident, broad smile takes over her features. But then she tilts her head, her ponytail falling to the side. "But this doesn't mean we are engaged, right? I need more time than that, please. I'm still trying to figure out this dating thing."

"Oh, Leilei. You'll know when I propose to you." I laugh freely, the pain from earlier a wisp of a bad dream. I know I'll have to come back to it, but right now, in this moment, I will live for the bliss of it all. I stand, tugging her up with me. I wrap my arms around my person, determined to never let her go. The tea tree scent of her hair fills my senses, and I can't wait to smell that as I fall asleep for the rest of my life. The physical ache in my bones reminds me of one important detail that I need clarity on when it comes to a married life with her. "Bae?"

She rolls her eyes at the term of endearment but gives me her attention. Her face is so close to mine; a few inches would connect our lips. My nose would fit perfectly against hers. My hands slide to cup her face, her skin soft beneath my touch. The ache for her streams throughout my nervous system.

"As you know, I need physical touch. And as I know, you are quite adverse to it. So I have to ask, if we married, will we be able to... you know? Make love?"

Her eyes grow wide while the remnant of the last blush deepens. "I, um, well..." she stutters. I give her the time to process and formulate, and she finally says, "I believe so. But it might take some easing into."

My cheeks hurt from smiling so big. "Practice makes perfect, sweetheart." I wink, and she shoves away from me with a laugh of disbelief.

"Finley Folke Andersson, you will be the death of me."

I pull her close again, engaging her in my arms and discreetly sniffing her hair. "I pray to be the life of you."

She chuckles. "Sorry. God is the life of me. But you can come second."

"That is the only spot I'd aim to be in," I affirm, sending a prayerful thank you to Him for this blessing in my arms.

We stand in silence for a moment before Lorelei pulls back from the embrace. A panic runs through me as our eyes meet. She looks worried and hesitant. "What's going through your mind?" I ask.

She swallows, her eyes shifting away from me for a millisecond before snapping back. "I think I'm ready to try."

"Try what?"

"Kissing you."

Chapter Twenty-Three

Lorelei

My boyfriend looks shell-shocked.

Boyfriend.

Huh.

Weird how that little word no longer makes my brain squirm. In fact, I quite enjoy it.

But Finley Andersson is so much more to me than a mere boyfriend.

Something snapped in my weirdly wired brain today when I sat at a table of admittedly delicious-smelling food and watched him interact with his mother and father, saw Korsa with my own eyes, and noticed that this manly, strong, capable prince is stepping up to the throne to protect his siblings all the while fulfilling a duty assigned to him at birth.

When he told his mother all he wanted from her was her trust and faith, my heart shattered into pieces. I saw Finley. For the first time, I saw a part of him that I'm certain no one else has seen. He was vulnerable. Hurt. Insecure. And in need of love.

We will give him all the love, my brain shouted. And I knew. It's as if God allowed the walls to fall. Being with Finley makes sense. He makes sense. He loves me for me. He believes in me.

And he needs someone to believe in him. I do. I believe he means it when he tells me that I would be a great queen. He isn't new to this royal life. He knows what it takes. And if he says I have it, then I have to believe him. He needs me in his corner the same way he has been in my corner. Heck, the man wanted me before he knew I was actually me. I see it all now. Very clearly.

But I think I broke him...

"Finley? If you're not ready, then okay. That's fine. I just thought—"

"I'm ready!" he interrupts in a high-pitched voice, then he coughs a few times. His next words come out in his normal, deeper voice. "Sorry, I mean, yes. I am ready to try if you are absolutely sure."

My lips twitch, amusement washing over me. "But first, let's eat this lovely food your mother has prepared for us. I would like to be in my room when we try. Just in case it doesn't go... well."

Finley swallows and nods a little too eagerly. I settle into my cushioned seat and call Lucy to come down. Minutes later, she arrives with Gabriel and Anders flanking her sides, a look of whimsical awe in her every movement. She wears a navy dress with a hemline that rests above her knees, her feet donned with matching shoes. Golden buttons run from the top to the bottom of her fitted dress. Her strawberry blonde hair is curled in big waves that cascade down her shoulders, her bangs swooped to the side.□

My twin is immaculate.

Gabriel's constant gaze on her says that he thinks the same thing.

Part of me secretly wishes the two of them would have continued on and Lucy could move here with me, but she was adamant that Gabriel's career was too high-risk for her sanity.

"Ugh, Lorelei. I hate you. You will eat like this every single day."

I laugh, then I whisper, "You could, too. Date Gabriel and move here. Room next to me. Never leave my side." I'm joking with her, but only partly. My heart aches at the thought of not being next to my sister every single day. We've only ever spent a few days apart at most. We roomed together in college. She is my person.

She brushes me off. "I've already explained that one. So," she leans in to me, "did you decide you will stay?"

I grin, recounting the events that recently unfolded to secure in my head that I do in fact belong here. If Finley thinks I do, then I believe him.

"Wow, so are you two going to make nice with the queen?" Lucy asks.

Finley nudges into our conversation. "My mother will come around. She may have engaged in unfavorable actions, but I know she's only trying to do what she perceives is best. I'll hold my ground, and she will learn to accept reality."

We spend the rest of the meal talking, laughing, and making this place feel like I can actually make it a home. At the very least, this room. Lucy says we will walk every hall of this palace, which is soaked in history by the way, until I feel at home.

Finley meets Lucy and me at the opening of the Royal Garden around dusk. I'm tired from the time change, stupidly delirious from consuming so much history as I walked the halls of Stjarna Palace, and my brain aches from trying to understand Finley's explanation of his antique car collection. Regardless, I'm feeling freer than I ever have in my entire existence. The fears I had surrounding coming here have vanished. Everyone except the queen has made me feel completely at ease. Furthermore, physical touch doesn't seem to be a big thing here like it is in the South. Personal spaces are respected amongst everyone, and that is something I can totally get used to.

"Look!" Lucy squeals, pointing in front of us at an archway, white with ivy winding up the sides, chrysanthemums poking through the green. A memory flashes across my vision as I catch sight of Finley standing underneath it wearing a white three-buttoned dress shirt and navy dress pants. His hair is in its typical disheveled form, and he looks every inch the Prince of Hearts with his roguish smile and heated eyes directed at me.

My dream.

Not quite the same, but mighty close...

The haze around the forgotten dream lifts, and I vividly remember kissing the prince. My face heats, but Lucy nudges me, breaking the hold the image has on me.

"Your favorite flower." She waggles her eyebrows. "With your favorite man underneath them."

The blush deepens as we approach Finley. Gabriel stands behind him as Anders was the one to escort us to the gardens. Once I'm directly in front of the grinning, happy man, I walk right into his outstretched arms for a life-giving hug. With every moment of contact between us, and everytime I choose to linger instead of pull away, I'm growing more comfortable and accustomed to his fiery touch.

"Are you ready to meet two of your biggest fans?" he whispers in my ear before breaking our hug.

"Huh?" I cock my head to the side and look past him. The plants catch my attention first. There. Are. So. Many. This is *heaven.* Shrubs are shaped to resemble different animals and objects, and the fountain at the center of the garden is spewing like a geyser around a statue of a mermaid and merman, strong and unwavering. Absolutely beautiful. The aroma of fresh, misty water mixed with florals is intoxicating—natural, sweet, and earthy.

I tap Finley's shoulder then point to the fountain. "Have you heard of the myths surrounding the Nephilim mentioned in Genesis six?"

He nods, following my gaze to the intertwined merpeople. "Are you about to tell me about how the merpeople are by-products of the supposedly fallen angels that mingled with humans?"

I tuck a strand of flyaway hair that's invaded my vision before smiling at Finley. The man just gets me sometimes. "Yes. But it seems you are aware. What are your thoughts on that subject? Do you think that the origin of fae creatures stems from Nephilim?"

"Something to consider. Legend has it that the fae are guardians of this world for God. The merpeople guardians of the waters, perhaps," he states, placing his hands on my hips and turning me towards the swings off to the side of the fountain. "But we won't know on this side of heaven. You can, however, get to know my siblings."

Peeling my eyes away from the colorful beauty of this place, I spot two people, a man and a woman, who both resemble Finley. Instantly, I catalog them as Johan and Astrid, his older brother and younger sister. The young woman waves with both hands, an excited smile across her perfect, sharp face. The thought crosses my mind that if Finley was a woman, he would look like his sister. Next to her, sitting down on a rather big swing, is Johan.

I wave timidly and pray she doesn't want to hug me, but the way she's bounding up to my side diminishes my hope.

Finley sticks his hand out in front of me right as Astrid goes in for a hug. "Remember what I told you? Ask permission before you embrace her."

My soul melts.

"Right," Astrid says. Her accent is thick, but I can still make out her quick words. "May I hug you quickly, Lorelei? I've been dying to meet you! I thought I'd have to come down to Mississippi to persuade you to date my big brother. He's a tool sometimes, but I promise you won't find a better man." Astrid's rambling and buoyant personality reminds me so much of Lucy, and that thought alone brings a wave of comfort and ease to my nerves.

But not enough for physical contact.

"Thank you for asking, Astrid, but I don't think I am prepared for that at the moment."

Her face falls only a fraction, but she rebounds quickly. "No problem! I plan to win you over quickly." She laughs, and I join. She truly radiates light—I glance at Finley, who is smiling at his sister—just as Finley does. Then she glances behind to my sister. "And you must be the twin Finley was supposed to date."

"That's me," she says through a laugh. "And I am a hugger." Lucy steps around me and embraces Astrid. Astrid immediately begins to compliment Lucy's fashion while Finley whisks me away to where his brother sits on a huge white swing with a bed of ivy and wildflowers covering the top of it.

Johan stands, slightly shorter than Finley is, and introduces himself, his hand outstretched.

That I can do. I shake his hand briefly and introduce myself, noting how different Johan looks from Finley. Where Finley and Astrid resemble their father, Johan looks a male version of his mother. But his warm smile and welcoming tone is lightyears away from what I experienced with the queen at lunch time.

"You have no idea how prayed for you are, Lorelei," Johan says in accented English. I shift my eyes to Finley, who has gone a little pink in the cheeks. It's a cute look on him. "We thought this man here would never settle down. Scared the daylights out of me when I was diagnosed with Parkinson's and learned I'd need to pass the crown prince title to him."

"Not cool, *broor.*" Finley playfully shoves him.

"Not because you aren't capable." Johan laughs, his eyes lighting up the same way Finley's does when he's amused. "But because I didn't think you'd find someone who would want to marry you in time to ascend the throne. You're a picky man."

I raise an eyebrow in agreement. "He's dated half the world."

Johan laughs while Finley looks upon me with disbelief. Finley retorts, "I dated often because I am picky. You are the only woman I've asked to date me with intentions of marriage. You are the only woman I've presented a handmade gift to as per Korsan tradition to make intentions known."

"That's what I was saying. I was agreeing that you are picky," I state, perplexed by his explanative response. "What did my tone sound like?"

Now Finley laughs. "Ah, that makes sense. I thought you were being sarcastic stating that I wasn't picky because I have dated so much."

I shrug. "Nope. But thanks for the clarification."

"Always, Leilei. We will continue to get to know each other until I can read your speech patterns the way you read *Common Sense.*"

"Too cute," Johan coos. At that moment, Lucy and Astrid join us. We all stroll through the gardens, laughing and getting to know each other. I thoroughly enjoy Johan's calm steadiness and Astrid's bubbliness. I think... I think I will fit in just fine here.

After about forty-five minutes, we part ways as the sun fully sets. Finley navigates us through the palace. Instead of Lucy coming into our room with me, however, she detours and goes to visit the pool hall with Anders and Gabriel. I think Astrid planned to meet her down there, too.

But I am perfectly okay with that because as Finley and I stand in front of the wooden door with stars carved into it, my nerves begin to buzz with excitement. We haven't said much to each other as we've walked through the halls hand in hand, the tension between us thick and heavy. And now it's time to break it.

I clear my throat. "Will you come in with me for a little while?"

Flames flicker across his eyes, and I fear briefly that this kiss will burn me alive. "Yes," he responds in a voice that's rough as sandpaper.

I push open the door, and he quickly takes the weight of it by placing his hand on the smooth, stain-coated wood. I walk into the room I barely got to know earlier today as I've been whisked around the palace. The walls are a shimmering light gold with white trims, a massive bed with navy sheets and a white quilt rests against a wall, middle aligned.

A white loveseat is against one wall while a desk area opposes it. I don't know if I want to stand or sit, so I opt for standing. I had slipped my shoes off before stepping into the room, but I go ahead and take my socks off and allow my feet to press against the cool hardwood floor. I pay attention to the smooth ceiling, the feeling of Finley's hand resting on my hip, and the large window in front of us. Grounding myself before the sensory experience that is about to happen.

Despite my best efforts, my nerves are shot and my body buzzes with anticipation. I say a silent prayer that I can handle this and that everything will be okay. But there's ultimately only one way to find out...

I turn to face Finley, who is looking at me with the most tender expression. The corners of his lips tug into a light smile and his eyes glisten with wonder. Instantly I'm at ease, that is until his other hand comes to a rest on my other hip and he tugs me close to him. My tilted chin is inches away from his downward gaze. He doesn't speak, but his eyes are seemingly asking permission to move closer. I swallow my fear and nod ever so slightly. One hand slides up my arm until he cups my face, the other hand splaying across the small of my back and he brings me closer. I press my hands against his chest, not to stop him, but to stabilize myself. He hesitates at my movement, so I whisper, "Kiss me."

Then I close my eyes and give myself over to the heat radiating off his skin and the smell of mint on his breath. His lips press against mine as if they were a feather brushing the tip of a blade of grass. I'm frozen as he lingers, my brain short circuiting on what to do next, so I stand there, committing the feel of his lips on mine to memory.

A moment later, he pulls away, resting his forehead against mine. He isn't smiling; in fact, he swipes his tongue across his bottom lip, an obvious hunger for more raging within him.

I handle the texture of his lips just fine.

Maybe I can try more?

I *want* to try more.

I wrap his shirt in my fist and drag him down to my lips again, as if it's an action I've done a million times in my life. When his lips crash against mine, he groans, forcing my lips apart as the tender kiss from before disappears into a deep, longing slow show of passion and desire. I move naturally against him, as if my lips were made for him, but then a feeling of a thousand needles pricking my skin overtakes the pleasure of his kiss. I shove him away, my breaths labored and heavy as I fight to maintain mental clarity and focus.

Finley reaches for me, but I hold out a hand to stop him.

"Lorelei?" He questions in a broken, breathless plea. *Are you okay? Did I hurt you? What can I do?* I can hear all those questions racing through his brain.

"Give me a moment," I manage to say. I evaluate my surroundings again. My feet are cool against hardwood. There are white and navy thick curtains lining the large window. A painting from Swedish painter Carl Frederik Hill called *Apple Tree in Blossom* is prominently displayed above the king-size bed. "Did you know that the artist who painted the landscape oil painting above the bed was rejected so much that he became severely depressed and was eventually put into an asylum for schizophrenia and constant hallucination? It's a shame, really, how the world appreciates art after the artist has passed and gone. What an insufferable life."

Spewing the random fact helped to calm my nerves, and the sharp, prickling feeling has dulled to a phantom pinch. I finally snap my gaze to Finley, who is looking at me with love, understanding, and patience.

"Humanity doesn't appreciate the dark parts of life until they can no longer be impacted by them. When the dark parts are alive and well, it's frightening to others who wish not to experience the emotion associated with voids." Finley moves to stand closer to me, but he doesn't touch me. "I appreciate your dark parts, Lorelei. Thank you for gifting me and trusting me with your first kiss." He smiles wickedly. "It was mind-blowing while it lasted, and I can't wait to help ease you into longer, deeper, desperate passionate kisses. I am up to assist you whenever you call, my Leilei."

"I—I love you," I blurt. Finley opens his arms, and I'm at ease enough to slip into them, my hands grasping at his back as I pull him flush against me. I bury my head in his chest, breathing in his scent that smells like rain on the horizon.

"You are my life now, pretty woman."

And dang it.

I believe this man.

I am his.

He is mine.

Forever.

I take a deep breath, then I knock on the door Astrid led me to—the Queen's sitting room. The moment I knew I wanted Finley forever, I was burdened to come speak to his mother. Seeing that hurt etched all over his face, tainting our day no matter how hard he tried to hide it, nearly killed me. I may be overstepping a boundary, but honestly, I want justice for the person I love. The man I love.

And ultimately, even if it was Lucy who actually encountered the stalker, this has to do with me.

"Lorelei," the queen acknowledges with a slight dip of her head and a plastic smile. "Astrid mentioned you would be stopping by tonight. How can I be of assistance?"

"May I come in and speak with you regarding Finley?"

"Whatever for? Has he done something wrong?" Her Korsan-accented tone is considerate but something in her glinting eyes challenges me to misstep.

I square my shoulders. "No, Your Highness. But you have."

Her silver brows hardly lift. Her thin smile never fades away. "Come in, Lorelei. It seems we have much to discuss."

I gulp as I cross over the threshold. No matter the bravado I'm summoning into existence right now, this woman is still the queen of a whole entire country. And she still reminds me of an ice queen.

The room is full of books. That's the first thing I notice. It's no library, but it must be her personal collection. An entire wall is dedicated to red oak wooden shelves. She has two golden-tufted chairs that sit on either side of a matching couch in the center of the room. A large window with a lovely nighttime view of the garden is on the backside of the room, and finally, on the wall opposite of the bookshelf, is a portrait of the entire family, including what I assume to be grandparents. The ceiling is high, the corners of the walls an intricate knotted wood design.

"Take a seat." The queen instructs, gesturing to the couch. I obey. "Racinda, please bring tea."

A woman I hadn't noticed standing behind me scurries off.

The quiet is so loud, echoing as if I was in an empty ballroom, and I resist the urge to cover my ears with my palms to comfort myself.

"What kind of mother would sic a stalker on her son?" I blurt the question just to clear the obnoxiously beating silence.

The queen doesn't even budge, but I do notice her shoulders tense. She looks away from me as she says, "The kind who is looking out for his well-being. You don't know Finley like I do. The responsibility he is having to take on."

"With all due respect, I do. I know Finley is warm-hearted and kind. I know he looks out for the people he cares about. I know he makes people smile wherever he goes. He's easygoing and loves to laugh." I pause for a moment, thinking about the man I've fallen for. The queen turns her gaze back to me. I clear my throat and continue. "But underneath all that, he's anxious. He's insecure in areas of his life, and he needs constant reassurance and affection. He understands the role he is acquiring, and he wants to be the best possible king he can be. He wants to follow in his father's footsteps."

The silence returns with a screaming vengeance, and I pray that the Lord will make this queen open her mouth to talk.

Or command a banshee to screech.

Something.

The door swings open, and the woman who left earlier is back with a tray of tea. The clanking of the white glass cups against the shiny golden tray brings a welcome reprieve.

"Thank you," I say to the older woman as she hands me a cup of steaming tea. It smells like chamomile, and I silently commend the woman on her taste.

After she leaves, the queen sighs, taking a sip of her own tea. "It seems you know my son. Better than I thought you did. And the simple fact that you dared to approach me in this manner says a lot about your character, Lorelei."

"I'm sorry if I've come off as blunt or rude. That was not my intention. But I did feel the need to defend the man I love and care deeply about. Finley is important to me, Your Highness."

"Love? You—you love him?" she stutters over her words, her icy gray eyes rounded and jaw slightly left hanging open.

I nod affirmatively. "Yes. I love him. And I choose to stand by his side as he chooses me."

And to my utter shock, the queen smiles a genuine, dethawing, toothy grin. "I'm so pleased to hear that, Lorelei." She sets her tea down and claps her hands together. "Please allow me to explain my actions. So many women in the past have tried to use Finley. They wanted his money or his title. He was too much of a gentleman with a heart of gold to see the blackened souls of those who attempted to have him. The princess of our neighboring country, Karin, is as sweet a soul as Finley is, if not a little more abrupt in nature. She agreed to take the fall if my plan went south, which it obviously did, and I plan to make everything right with her.

"But I digress. I wanted to make sure Finley found a woman who could be his counterpart. You see, my husband is the older version of his son. We are opposites in many ways, but that helps us. Whereas he is spontaneous and full of laughter, I am structured and serious. Where he is anxious and questions his decisions, I stick to decisions once I arrive at them. There are many other things I could say, but I see that you and Finley will interact in very similar ways to me and my husband. You will be good for him, Lorelei. I can tell from what his siblings and father have told me and from what little I've seen in you myself."

I feel like I should want to cry, but I don't. Instead, I'm just purely thankful. I'm thankful she is accepting me, is doing me the honor of explaining herself, and is welcoming me into her life.

"Thank you for sharing that with me," I say to the queen. I don't offer more because I'm unsure of what to say. So, I end with, "Please explain everything to Finley. He is very hurt by your actions and just wants you to trust and believe in him."

The queen's smile softens as she tilts her head. The simplistic nighttime gown she wears is navy, contrasting against her pale skin and silvery hair nicely.

"I will, Lorelei. I haven't done a great job in the past of trusting and believing in him, but it wasn't because of him. It was because of my own controlling nature. I want what's best for my son. And that does appear to be you. I know he wouldn't settle for just anyone."

"He wouldn't," I agree. "Nor would I."

She smiles again then rises. I stand with her. Then, she opens her arms.

Despite not wanting to hug, I embrace the queen. I feel like she needs this hug more than I do judging by the water pooling in her eyes. Thankfully, she breaks the contact after five seconds.

"Thank you, Lorelei," she says in Korsan.

I respond in Korsan, bowing my respects to the Queen.

As I turn to leave the room, she speaks up in a voice that has warmed like a kindling fire since I first walked into this room, "Please, call me Sylvia."

Lucy's Journal

Saturday, April 11th * 11:09 pm CET * underneath the silkiest sheets I've ever experienced

I'm in KORSA. In a PALACE. Where my SISTER will become QUEEN in less than a year. We are only here for a few days, but this will become her life soon. Wow. That is something, I tell you. How quickly life can change...

Astrid is really cool. She's already given me her personal number, so I'm excited to keep in touch after I leave. I fear Lorelei might not want to come home at this rate. She's completely enamored with this place and its rich history, not to mention her prince. I'm kind of reconsidering Gabriel, but honestly, I know myself. I wouldn't be able to handle it when he's gone. I need a man who can come home to me every single night, and with his career, he wouldn't be able to. But honestly, being here has been such an experience. And I still have two more days to go until I fly back to reality and my stupid career and my frustrating boss. Maybe I can use all the fodder I'm gaining on this trip to write a bestseller. Then I quit Stone Harper for good. Speak of the devil... looks like I got a text from him. Ugh.

He asked me to organize an event for the community baseball team. Which is now my actual job since he combined event coordinator duties with assistant duties into a decently-paid role, but still. I'm on vacay. Can't it wait? I better get to it so he doesn't keep pestering me. I swear this is simply an attempt to keep him on my mind while I'm away. He did tell me not to go fall for a prince or duke or other rich, titled fellow. UGH. Why does he even care?

CHAPTER TWENTY-FOUR

FINLEY

"Finley, breathe," Lorelei instructs, gently squeezing my hand. "Everything will be okay. I may have spoken with your mother last night when I slipped away from dinner."

An error message flashes across my vision. "You... what?"

She smiles sheepishly. "I should have told you last night when you stopped by to tell me goodnight, but I was still processing. We had a good conversation. I wanted to tell her that I'm staying by your side no matter what. She apologized to me, Finley, and I'm certain she is ready to do the same for you."

We stand outside Father's office. Beyond that door is a king trying to manage the land while his wife tries to manage her son. And today we have to get to the bottom of everything because Lorelei will remain by my side no matter what Mother wishes. But apparently Lorelei has already embarked on that mission. I stare at the woman I will call my wife in less than a year. She is brilliant, lovely, and confident. She utterly amazes me with every day that passes.

Mother has to be impressed with Lorelei if my woman waltzed into my mother's space and spoke clearly with her. From the outset, I believed Mother would like Lorelei if given the chance to know her like I do; I think her dilemma was not having control over my life like she was used to doing. The lack of control made her do something irrational. That's what I'm choosing to believe.

"I trust you, bae," I say to lighten the mood. "Let's get this over with." I squeeze Lorelei's hand back. I look at my girlfriend who is dressed in a black pantsuit that fits her curves in all the right places. Her hair is tied back in a ponytail, and of course, she is wearing her white sneakers. My woman means business today, and I'm a little afraid of what she might do to my mother if Mother doesn't do whatever it is she led Lorelei to believe she would.

I never once feared Lorelei would be worrying about how to impress the queen. My Leilei is who she is. She only feared that who she is wouldn't be enough, but she never set out to change that. Something has shifted though, and it's as if Lorelei finally believes that she is absolutely enough for me and is fit for the role that is demanded of her if she marries me.

Correction.

When she marries me.

A spark of thankfulness jolts my heart, and I bend to plant a light kiss on her lips before knocking on Father's door. I've been kissing her lightly every chance I get since our first one two days ago, trying to help make her more comfortable. So far, she hasn't pushed me away. In fact, earlier this morning, she pulled me back for a longer, lingering kiss. It was closed-lipped, but it's still a win.

The door swings open, and Henrick, Father's regent, ushers us into the small, cluttered room. I sit down on one of the golden velvet chairs in the corner of his office, and Lorelei sits on the one located on the other side of the side table between us. Mother stands beside Father's large desk while Father sits in his rolling chair with his fingers templed under his chin. The air is thick with apprehension; it could strangle a person.

"Son, I—" Mother says at the same time I attempted to address her first. I motion for her to continue. "I am sorry." She drops her head and folds her hands in front of her. The silence in the room is deafening. I was prepared for a long, drawn out argument... Not this.

"I'm sorry for not honoring the decision we made as a family to allow you time to find a love match. I am sorry that I spied on you and attempted to ruin your dates in order to get you to come back home and marry the woman of my choice. I am sorry that the person I hired went too far and disclosed your whereabouts to the media. Finley," she chokes on a sob before finally meeting my eyes, "I'm sorry for not believing that you were capable and trusting you with the responsibility of your own life."

Father stands and hugs her while my mind spins like a hamster on a wheel. This is the last thing I expected to happen, but I couldn't be more thankful. I glance at Lorelei who smiles broadly at me with a shrug of her shoulders. This is because of my amazing, capable woman. She leans and whispers, "Go hug your mom."

I do as she says, and when my arms close around her, she crumbles in my arms, apologizing over and over. Tears spring in my own eyes as I hold the small but fierce woman tight. "I forgive you,

Mamma," I whisper, using the term I've called her my entire life up until she cut me deeply, squeezing her one last time before letting her go. As we break apart, she clutches on Father's arm as he smiles lovingly and warmly upon her.

Lorelei moves to my side and places her hand gently on my back. She's been so good at little touches that offer reassurance. *God, I'm so thankful for her.*

"I do wish to talk more about why you felt the need to do what you did if you are willing to," I mention. Mamma nods as I add, "But we can do that later. I believe we should all start over with Lorelei." I throw an arm around Lorelei's shoulders. "Mamma, Father, my king and queen, I wish for you to meet Lorelei Raine Spence. She is the love of my life, the most intelligent and beautiful woman I've ever met, and she will become my wife and the next queen of Korsa."

Lorelei trembles at my side, but she pushes through and bows to my parents before reaching out her hand to shake each of their hands. "It's a pleasure to meet you both," she says with full confidence. "I love your son, and you have raised an outstanding human being."

Father and Mamma glance at each other, exchanging a look of "huh?" as Lorelei would say when something perplexes her. I laugh and my parents smile. Father shakes his head and rubs his white beard. "I believe there is only one thing left to do at this point, then, if you are certain, Son."

I nod with assurance. I didn't tell Lorelei this would happen, though mainly because I didn't expect that it would happen today.

Eventually, yes. But I'm still reeling over the fact that Mamma was genuine and open in her apology to me.

My parents dip into a low bow, speaking in Korsan in unison, "We acknowledge you, Lorelei Raine Spence, as the future wife of His Royal Highness Finley Folke Andersson. May you rule side by side in integrity, faith, and humility."

"What's happening?" Lorelei asks, looking up at me with confusion.

"They are acknowledging you as my future wife and the queen of Korsa." I instruct her on what to do, bowing and reciting the ancient oath of Korsa. She speaks the Korsan words with confidence and ease. The woman's brain is truly a wonder. Her ability to catch on to a new language is fascinating.

"Welcome to the family, Lorelei," my father says.

"It is your last day here. Shall we get to know each other better over tea?" Mamma asks.

I sneak a glance at Lorelei who lights up. "Yes, please!" she says.

I chuckle at her cuteness and then mouth a "thank you" to my parents as we all exit the office. We make our way down through the halls, and as we pass portraits and statues, memories surface of running around this place playing hide and seek with my siblings. There are literally a million places one can hide in this drafty, old palace. Lorelei and I, hand in hand, follow my parents to the library. I watch her reaction as we step through the doors and into the room stacked full of dusty tomes, lifetimes of history, and that curious old book smell that doesn't quite smell like anything else.

Lorelei's eyes bulge out of her head, and she releases my hand, darting to the first wall of shelved books. Her hand caresses the eye-level books in the Korsan history section just as Lucy and Astrid appear beside me.

"Can I—can I have my *Beauty and the Beast* moment?" Lucy asks, awestruck at the rolling ladder next to Lorelei.

Astrid says, "Oh, I want to record you!"

The two women race towards the ladder while Lorelei disappears down another aisle of books.

"Those two are very identical in their looks," my father says.

"But their personalities are extremely different," I comment. Astrid whips out her cell phone as Lucy practices the hop onto the ladder while pushing off. She had to take off her heels, but I can't help but feel a sense of joy at the sight of her having fun and letting loose like this. In fact, I'm surprised Lucy didn't acknowledge Mamma and Father in the room. She had a zillion questions on the plane about how to act in front of them, then when she finally meets them, she zooms right past them for a rolling ladder.

Maybe Lorelei and Lucy both share a sense of hyper-focus on things they love.

The tea arrives while the ladies are exploring the library, so Father, Mother, and Johan, who just arrived, sit down on couches and chairs in a reading section of the library.

"You are smitten with her," Johan says, sipping Earl Gray.

"Just like you were with me," Maria, his wife, says as she sits next to him and is given a cup of tea by Hannah, an older lady who has served our family for years.

"*Haalaa,* Maria," I greet the brunette woman with kind eyes and a red-lipped smile. "Long time no see."

"Tell me about this woman of yours. It's the first time we are getting to meet a lady you're interested in. You know how Johan is. He's only told me that you're going to marry her."

"Shouldn't that say enough?" I tease, and she rolls her eyes with a playful smile.

"But I am a woman. I want to hear all the details. I know you like spilling details."

I shrug, laughing. "You're not wrong. It started when she went on a date with me that was meant for her twin..."

By the end of the night, Lorelei has charmed my entire family by being herself just as I knew she would. We took frequent breaks so that she could decompress from the interactions, touring the gardens not once but twice today. Safe to say it's her favorite place.

The library comes in second place. We spent almost half the day there, even after my parents had to leave to attend to business.

Lucy's favorite place coincides with Astrid's—the Royal Treasury, where we keep all of the family jewels, crowns of previous monarchs, and priceless heirlooms.

Beside me on the loveseat in her room, Lorelei sits looking like a queen in her baggy sweatpants and holey t-shirt, her hair in its classical low ponytail. She types away on some cases she had started at work while I look through different documents on their way to the governing body, *Riiksaag*. I definitely could get used to a routine like this, but I wonder what Lorelei is going to do about her job. Has she thought about it? Of course she has, she's Lorelei Spence...

"What are your plans for your career since you have decided to stay by my side?" I can't quit saying that phrase. It brings great joy to my heart.

She speaks as she continues to type away at something on her laptop. "I'm going to talk to Mr. Austen when we arrive back in Juniper Grove tomorrow. I want to wrap up the cases I'm currently working on, but I will not take on anymore. I have until June, right?"

"That's the plan," I state. "But honestly, we don't need to wait until June. That was my deadline. We can come back soon—"

"No," she interrupts, frenzied eyes boring into mine. "I need until June. I need time to make sure I have everything together, all my ducks in a row so to speak. Plus, I'm a bridesmaid in Karoline's wedding. Speaking of, aren't you a groomsman?"

"Mason hasn't said anything..."

She covers her mouth with her hand. "Oops. I guess he hasn't asked yet."

I can't fight back the smile at the thought Mason will ask me to be an integral part of his wedding after knowing him for only a short while. I guess it's true that living with someone draws souls close together. He's definitely become one of my best friends. I love that redneck man. "I guess we are staying in Juniper Grove for another month and half, then. I will need to slip out to get pictures of myself here in Korsa. That way people will think I've returned home for the meantime and won't flock around us in Juniper Grove. We will have to stay on the down low."

"Thanks, Finley," she says, reaching out to pat my thigh. I grab her hand, our eyes lock on to each other, and I tug her arm, causing her to fall on top of me, her laptop and mine sliding to the floor.

"What the—" she says, shock written across her face, so close to my own. I want to kiss it off.

I waggle my brows. "Let's practice some more, love."

She laughs breathlessly, but then she places her thin hands on either side of my face, her elbows resting on my shoulders—but I won't complain of the dull ache it's causing. Lorelei closes her eyes and leans in, her lips causing a sweet, delicious fire in my veins when they meet mine. She lingers for nine seconds (yes, I'm counting) before pulling away.

"Are you well?" I ask, as I have after every "practice" I've initiated.

She grins, her freckles shining through her flushed skin. "Very well, actually." And then she surprises me by pressing her lips to mine again, forcing mine slightly apart. I gasp against her mouth and melt into her kiss, my hands roaming up her back, one tangling in her ponytail while the other grips her hip. My head is swimming, all thoughts of counting forgotten. I take control of the kiss and whisper her name. She sighs, her body sinking into mine, her fingers gripping my hair. My world is spinning as I feel the love radiating from this beautiful woman. I can't believe she's mine. All mine. I love her so much, and *God, I am so grateful to know her.*

We continue to kiss and explore for what seems like mere minutes but also hours upon hours. When she finally pushes off my heaving chest, I'm left as a thoughtless ball of mush, unable to say anything other than, "Wow."

"I want more," she whimpers. "Will I be able to handle more?" It's as if she's speaking her thoughts aloud, not necessarily fishing for an answer from me. I let her continue to catch her breath outside of my touch, though I crave to have her hands in mine or to hold her in my arms.

"Finley, I lasted," she says through a beaming smile. "I kissed you. Really kissed you. And I didn't feel icky!"

I snort, but laugh. "I'm proud of you, Leilei. And that was the best kiss of my existence. You should know that. Kissing is worthless if it isn't with someone you truly love."

"If what we just did is representative of that belief, then I would have to agree." She laughs, a cute, breathy sound. "Thank you for being patient with me. Please continue to do so. I never know if I will get stimulated or not, so it will always be a gamble when we kiss."

"Always, Lorelei. I will protect you. And when I fail to, I pray you will be forgiving and patient with me."

"Always, Finley," she reiterates my sentiments. "And please know I will protect you as well."

"You went toe-to-toe with my mother behind my back. I fully believe you will protect me." I scooch closer to her and fiddle with the hair that's fallen from its black constraint band. "Thank you for that, by the way. I don't know if I've properly said those words to you. It's been such a whirlwind having you here in my world. Not to mention this world is one I've avoided for a long time."

She rests her head on my shoulder, and I move my hand to clutch hers. She sighs. "I protect and defend those I love. And I just so happen to love you very much. I'm still unsure of how it happened. Was it slow? Quick? Did we float? Crash? The truth seems to lie somewhere in between. Either way, Lucy was right. Love comes for you. And then it's up to you to choose it. Thanks for choosing a girl like me, Finley."

I couldn't wipe the stupid grin off my face if I tried. Everything about this moment feels so right. Like she's my missing puzzle piece. Life just makes sense with her. "There's only one of you, Leilei. You are not a girl *like* you. You *are* you. The only one of you. Perfect. Lovely. Brilliant. *Weird.*" I nudge her and she laughs. "But your weirdness is everything I've prayed for, so thanks for staying true to who you are and not trying to diminish or change yourself. I love you." I kiss her temple. "I can't say that enough. I love you so much, Lorelei Raine."

"Too much emotion," she hums. "My brain is struggling to keep up. It wants to float into Happy Land and relive our kiss over and over."

"I can give your brain more fodder if you wish." I kiss her temple again, running my fingers up her arm.

"I think I'd die," she says, not a trace of a joke. "It's time for space, Lover Boy."

I stiffen. "Did you just call me Lover Boy?"

She turns to look at me, humor and amusement dancing in her hazel eyes. "You call me by that ridiculous 'bae' name. I've never been one for nicknames, but I decided you needed one. Lover Boy suits you. You are very much the embodiment of the term. Go grab a dictionary. Your face will be next to the entry."

I laugh, soaking in this side of Lorelei. I stand and grab my laptop from the floor, prepared to allow her the time she needs to process everything that's happened emotionally between us tonight, but before I leave, I tell her, "You can call me whatever you want as long as you never let me go."

Chapter Twenty-Five

Lorelei

"You are stupidly in love," Lucy pokes me in the arm as we lay in bed, deadened bodies with overactive minds. We got home earlier this morning, and we are both exhausted from traveling. Our bodies don't know if we should be in Central Time or Central European Time. We are caught somewhere in between right now.

"I'm stupidly tired," I retort. "So get out of my bed so I can sleep."

She clicks her tongue, rolling over on her side to look at me, propping her head in her hand. "I'm happy for you, Lor. Jealous, yes. But very happy. Plus I have a lot of story inspiration from our trip to Korsa. Did you see the massive mermaid fountain in the gardens? I can use that somehow in my merman and female pirate story. Maybe the merfolk are connected to Korsa somehow..." she teeters off, deep in thought. "Oh! I've got it. I need to go write it down."

"Yes, yes! Go write down your epic tale, Lucy May." I shove her, and she rolls her eyes but scrambles off my bed and through the door. To my dismay, Frizzle takes her place.

I groan. "What does a girl have to do to get some peace and quiet around here, huh, Frizzle?" She answers with a rumbly purr before settling in next to me. "You're coming to Korsa with me, right? I forgot to ask if pets were allowed in the palace."

I grab my phone from the stand and open Finley's text thread. We don't text often, as we are typically both busy with work when apart, but the thread is still pretty lengthy.

Can Frizzle move to Korsa with me?

He doesn't respond immediately, so I set my phone down and allow my brain space to spiral. I'm moving in a little over a month. A week after we travel to Dallas for Mason and Karoline's wedding. That's a lot of travel crunched closely together. Will I be okay? My routines are going to shift so much. I lost it last night while in Korsa when I woke up to take a few steps around my bed to go to the bathroom, but the bathroom wasn't there. I ran into a wardrobe instead. I freaked out, ran in my night clothes to the room next door because through the fog I remembered that's where my sister was, and cried uncontrollably for at least an hour, probably longer, before I settled down and slept with her the rest of the night. She told me a story to calm me down, one about a brave woman who stepped outside of her comfort zone to create a new and better comfort zone.

Yes, she was definitely speaking of me, but as I listened, I realized she was right. I've been stuck my entire life. Chained to my routines. They are good, and I do absolutely need them to stay sane, but I can deviate sometimes. I can allow myself to change. I can take on big tasks. I don't have to allow my weirdly wired brain to hold me back from something I love.

Someone I love.

I check my phone.

> Yes. Will Frannie be joining our happy little relocation?

I chuckle before quickly typing back that I have to leave her with Lucy. Finley has started using that term, *relocation*, since this morning when I told him of my meltdown in the middle of the night. I logically know that moving and relocating are the same thing, but relocation feels safer somehow. Like I am picking up what I already have and am setting it down somewhere new. Moving feels like Goliath. Big and scary and something new. And well, I'm not David. The story of slaying a giant was never meant for me, anyhow.

The best I can do is trick my brain with synonyms.

And sleep. I should really get some sleep.

I put my phone on my nightstand and tug my quilt up to my chin. Frizzle riots and scratches my arm while attempting to get out from underneath the cocoon, which is perfectly fine with me. I like having the bed to myself.

But then I start thinking of the fact that I will have to sleep next to a person every single night for the rest of my life after I get married. Am I truly ready for that?

I think of Finley's boyish smile and vibrant eyes. I imagine his intoxicating natural scent of incoming winter showers. I hear his voice whispering that he loves me and feel the phantom touch of his fingers trailing down my back. His lips moving against mine...

If it's with Finley, I think I'll be okay.

After inviting Mr. Austen to my regularly scheduled office tea time, I start to prepare water and mugs. More accurately, I demanded he come to tea time today, but that's neither here nor there.

I need to tell him that I have a month of work left.

Because I'm relocating to Korsa.

Where I will no longer practice law but I will use all my accumulated knowledge to serve in philanthropic ways alongside Maria, Johan's wife. Once I mentioned to her that I was a lawyer, she swept me away and showed me her work area, filled to the brim with legal matters concerning family law in Korsa.

She became one of my new favorite people on the spot.

See?

Relocating.

Picking up my legal practice and simply setting it back down in Korsa.

A knock sounds at my door, then Mr. Austen appears in my office. "That was quite the invite, Lorelei," he jests, walking in all the way and closing the door.

"I have quite the news." I snag two elderberry green tea bags from my stash and plop them into our mugs. I chuckle to myself looking at my BAE: Best Attorney Ever mug, seeing it in a whole new light since Finley explained what bae actually meant. Hadley got me good with that little joke.

"And what's that?" He takes a seat, crossing one leg over his knee. I place his cup of tea in front of him on my desk.

"Remember that guy I told you about?"

He thinks for a moment before snapping his fingers. "The one who was supposed to fall for your sister but instead fell for you."

"That's the one," I state, blowing on my tea. "I'm dating him now. Which means I will be moving to Korsa the second week of June because we will be married before Christmas and then there will be the coronation at the beginning of next year."

Panic begins to build in my chest, but I stamp it down with thoughts of my prince. My loving, kind, beautiful, thoughtful, perfectly-matched-for-me prince.

Mr. Austen is silent for a bit, looking at me with searching eyes. "And you're positive about this, Lorelei? You look a little pale."

"Have I ever made a decision lightly or without great thought?" I brush him off. I know I'm pale. And panicking. But that doesn't mean it's not the right decision.

He sighs, "No. You have not. But I must say," he picks up his mug, "I am going to miss you. And tea time. You are one of my best attorneys. When is your last day?"

"A month from now. I have to go to Dallas for a wedding for the first week of June, and then the second week I am moving. I want to spend the last two weeks of May prepping."

"Always have a plan, don't you?" He grins. I smile back at him, but then a sudden sense of sadness grips my heart. I really will miss my boss.

"Thank you for being a wonderful boss and mentor," I pause. Because Mr. Austen is so much more than that. "And friend."

He smiles and taps his fingers on my desk. "You as well, Lorelei." At that moment his phone buzzes. I think he whispers, "Emma Jane" under his breath before letting it go to voicemail.

"Emma Jane Williams?" I ask. "As in the barista at Books and Beans?"

He nods his head and sips his tea while turning his face away from me.

"Is she okay? Does she need a lawyer? Can I be of assistance before I leave?"

He shakes his head and puffs out air. "No, nothing of the sort. We are family friends. Grew up close to each other in our neighboring town of Hartfield. She's trying to get me to help her set up a friend of hers with a friend of mine. Playing matchmaker of sorts."

"Ah, okay. I did get the feeling she was very into love when I spoke with her about... something before."

"That she is." He laughs, looking beyond me as if he is somewhere else. "Well, we will chat some more, of course, but I better get back to work today. It's been a real pleasure working with and knowing you, Attorney Lorelei Spence."

I stand as he does and follow him to my office door. "The same can be said of you, Attorney Knightley Austen."

"Mom! Dad!" I shout as my parents stand outside the apartment door. "Come in." I wave them forward as Lucy runs and bear-hugs Mom. Dad steps around them and embraces me in a warm, strong hug.

"When did you get back?" Lucy asks, wild excitement in her eyes.

"Well, when we heard from Lorelei that you two were traveling to Korsa with Finley, we suspected things might be getting serious between those two, and we needed to come vet the man ourselves," Dad says, turning his hazel eyes onto me. I shrug.

"Yeah, I guess it is serious. But did you really expect me to jump into a relationship half-heartedly?"

Everyone laughs though I meant it seriously. Mom says, "No, we didn't. Which is why we are back." She embraces me in a hug. She still smells like sunshine from Arizona. "We want to meet this guy. And we missed our beautiful daughters."

"I'm glad you both are home," I say with sincerity. "I've missed you both."

"Second that." Lucy jumps in. "So, are you two taking us out for dinner?"

"Lucy," I hiss under my breath.

"What?" She feigns innocence.

Dad chuckles but says, "We have the camper set up at Juniper Creek, but we do need to clean up a bit. We rushed over here because we were dying to see you two. Let us go change and we will meet you at Perry's Seafood?"

"Are you serious?" Lucy exclaims at the same time I shout, "For real?"

"We miss good 'ole Cajun food." Mom smiles, looping her arm around Dad casually. She turns her attention to me. "Would you please invite Finley?"

"Of course," I state. "He mentioned he was working on reports, but I can see if he can spare some time this evening."

"Great!" Mom replies. "Well, we will head on out. We just couldn't wait another second to see our girls."

Lucy and I wave them out then immediately start to get ready to meet them at Perry's. I send a text to Finley asking if he's available, and he responds with "Anything for you, my Queen."

My heart warms at his sweetness. I never thought I'd be one to look for romance or affection when it came to a relationship, but now that I have it with Finley, I couldn't imagine going without that love and care. My heart squeezes at the thought of possibly losing him one day, but I push that thought aside. No sense in wondering about what-ifs.

An hour later, Lucy and I are in Finley's mustang headed to Perry's Seafood. He insisted on picking us up since he finally got his beloved old car back from where we left it at the trailhead in Tennessee. Gabriel and Anders tail us in their black sedan, and according to Finley, they will not be sitting with us tonight even though I said it would be okay.

"You've mentioned your parents are friendly and outgoing and very loving towards one another. How should I behave? Speak to them? Are they going to grill me? What kind of questions should I be prepared for? I've—" he swallows, taking one hand off the wheel to run his fingers through his semi-styled blond hair, "never met a girlfriend's parents before."

Lucy snickers from the back seat, and I bite my bottom lip to keep from grinning. Finley is obviously in a nervous spiral over meeting my parents, and I need to walk with him through it, but it's also kind of adorable.

"Just be yourself, Finley. You are great. They know that I wouldn't settle for anyone that I wasn't comfortable and confident with."

"Right," he says with a shaky voice. He totally does not look convinced by the way he constantly musses up his hair as his leg bounces ninety to nothing.

I place my hand on his thigh, the heat burning through his khaki pants. He ceases the nervous bouncing. "You trust me, right? Believe in me?"

He nods emphatically.

"Well then trust my confidence in you. Trust my belief in you."

"Aww," Lucy drawls. I snap laser eyes at her, and she laughs.

"Thanks, Lorelei," Finley says, looking at me with love in his eyes. "I do trust you. And I love you very much."

"Aww!" Lucy drawls again but longer and louder. This time I laugh with her. This feels good. Right. Light. Free.

Finley, my twin, my parents... It's the people I love the most around me tonight.

We pull into the parking lot, get out, and make our way into the restaurant. It's nothing fancy or huge, but it is one of the higher-priced places in this town. The smells of Creole seasoning, crawfish, and oils assaults my senses, throwing me off balance for a moment.

I forgot how intense the smells of this place were. It's not a bad smell, just a strong and over-stimulating smell. I'll be okay as long as I'm able to step outside when I need to. But for now I want to try and adjust to the environment.

Since it's a Wednesday night, the place is empty. But it does concern me because there are usually a few families here at any given moment.

"Did you rent this place out for the night?" I ask Finley.

"Yes. Primarily so we could eat in peace and try to keep anyone away from discovering I'm still here."

"Ah, that makes sense." I glance at the large hammerhead shark that hangs above the entrance, something that terrified me as a child, but I grew to love it.

I named it Gray.

Because of its gray body.

Creativity is Lucy's thing, not mine.

Just like I grew to love the shark, I can grow to love my new life in Korsa.

Lucy automatically guides us to a circular table in the backroom away from other people. We sit down, and I distribute the menus stationed in the middle of the table. My parents haven't arrived yet, and I keep having to suppress my laughter at Finley. He is constantly looking back behind him towards the doors.

"Calm down," I whisper as I nudge his arm. "I'll let you know when they arrive." Lucy and I both sat in the seats that could easily see the entrance because we both don't like having our backs to people.

The waitress takes our drink orders and as she leaves, Dad walks through the door, holding it open for Mom. I grin broadly and tap Finley to let him know they've arrived. His demeanor instantly stiffens; he very much looks like a crown prince at this moment. He quickly asks, "Is my hair okay? Is there anything on my face?"

I can't stop the laughter that bubbles from me, but I shake my head no. His brows pinch together, but my parents arrive at the table. He stands and reaches out a hand towards my father. "Finley Andersson," he says with an easy smile. "It's nice to meet you, Mr. Spence."

Dad takes his hand immediately and gives a firm shake. "The pleasure is mine. Please, call me Richard."

Finley dips his head in a bow before turning to my mom. "And you must be the beloved mother of these beautiful women, Mrs. Spence."

Lucy snorts, and I cover my laugh with my hand. Finley has definitely been in the South long enough to pick up on southern charm. But using the word *beloved* is a dead giveaway that he's blending his princely manners with the charm.

"Do you welcome hugs?" Mom asks with a hopeful smile and stars in her eyes. Finley grins and initiates an embrace. Mom squeezes him and tells him to call her Janet. Her voice is oozing with and admiration.

Everyone sits down, and while they begin to browse the menu, I lean over and whisper to Finley, "Prince of Hearts, I do believe my mom is enamored with you."

"You think?" he asks, his blue eyes widening.

I don't respond verbally but instead lean over and kiss him on the cheek. Though I initiated the action, my cheeks heat, but when I pull back, I notice his have, too. I once read in a book that initiating physical acts of affection in front of others helps the one whose love language it is to feel loved. By the way he smiles broadly at me, it has worked. He mouths that he loves me before I watch his shoulders relax and demeanor shift to something less anxious and on-edge.

The dinner runs smoothly, and I only have to step outside once, which was after they set our food down in front of us. Finley engages perfectly with my parents, whom I know absolutely adore him based on their expressions, questions that they ask, and conversations that happen. Finley talks with my dad about fishing and topics of law (which I jump into) and my mom talks with him about being a travel writer and discusses Finley's own travels around the globe (which Lucy jumps into). We all discuss a camping trip for mine and Lucy's birthday coming up in a couple of weeks. (Finley is excited for an opportunity to redeem the ending of our last one). When the topic of relocating to Korsa and the responsibilities of running a kingdom come up in conversation, I shut down just a bit because though I'm confident in my decision, I'm still processing what everything will entail. In fact, I realize I've been trying to avoid thinking about the responsibilities I will gain. Maybe it's better to save that part for after I'm in Korsa. Focusing on relocating is enough for now.

By the end of the night, Finley has effectively won my parents over, and they are already talking about inviting him out to their camper stationed on Juniper Creek for fishing, barbequing, and swimming. We plan to go out there next weekend since this weekend he has a guy's night with Mason and Braxton, which we both assume will be the time Mason asks them about being groomsman in his wedding.

Lucy rides home with my parents even though we told her we would bring her back, but since she doesn't tag along, Finley takes me out to the park for a walk under the warm, clear, starry Mississippi night. I have a finite number of these nights left, so I go despite being tired and knowing I have to get up to work tomorrow morning.

We are walking the paved trail, hand-in-hand, when Finley stops me and asks, "I never imagined this would become my life. Can I be honest?"

"Of course."

He blows out air and rubs the back of his neck. "I never imagined I'd actually have to become king one day. I've been trying to process it since I received the news, but everything has happened so fast. I'm frightened, Lorelei. What if I can't measure up to the greatness of my father?"

I turn his question over while I guide him to an old metal bench on the side of the walking path. We sit, huddling close to each other in the center of the bench, the dim glow of the path lights illuminating a small field of vision. The stars are bright overhead, and the moon is a thin crescent line.

"I can't speak to how you will manage kingship. I'm just a small-town girl from Mississippi who likes plants, cats, and law. But the simple fact that you are concerned you won't measure up means that you probably will. You will work hard to be a great king because your heart is in it."

The crickets sing around us, filling the silence. A slight breeze tickles my neck and I snuggle closer to Finley, looping my arm through his. "I'll be by your side through it all, even if I break down and need a moment. I trust you will get me through, and you can trust that I will stay by your side even when your anxiety gets the best of you."

"I don't know what I did to deserve you, Leilei, but man, I am so thankful to God." He kisses my forehead, then I lean my head on his shoulder. We continue to sit there, listening to the bugs around hum and sing and chirp.

After he drops me off and kisses me (very well) goodnight, I spend the rest of the night accompanying my prince in dreamland.

I know he thinks he is the majorly blessed one, but I would have to say I am more blessed. I guess that's what love is—admiring the mess out of each other to where you both perceive yourself to be more blessed.

Chapter Twenty-Six

Finley

"Get it together, people." The wedding planner with a sharp tongue claps her hands three times. Braxton, Mason, Mason's friend, Grant, from Nashville—who took off his tour for the wedding—and I snap to attention, forgoing our spontaneous game of charades with Hadley, Karoline, Lucy, Lorelei, and Karoline's cousin, Chantel.

Apparently the makeshift altar in the Barn, a wedding venue in Dallas, Texas, is not the place for humor and fun.

Maybe fun for Mason and Karoline, but the rest of us are ready to get this show on the road and go eat dinner. As if right on cue, my stomach grumbles. Mason stifles a laugh as Lorelei mouths, "Was that you?"

For over two months now, I've been dating this beautiful woman who is wearing a short olive green sundress with her wild, curly hair in a side ponytail. The Dallas humidity really took its toll earlier when we were taking outdoor pictures in front of the venue and at the location's lake. She looks like a feral lioness, but I'm not complaining one bit about that.

Our love story is a strange one, but it definitely suits who we are. The flirty, once-spare prince who fell hard and fast for the weird plant-obsessed woman. A love story caught somewhere in-between a whirlwind hurricane and steady snowfall.

We finish the rehearsal, the whole gang laughing at the fact that I have to walk both Lucy and Lorelei down the aisle since we are one man short on the groomsman side of things. We get in trouble by the wedding coordinator a thousand more times as we goof off. She feels inclined to constantly remind us that this wedding will be livestreamed to the world on Mason's social media account, but honestly, we couldn't care less. We are here to marry off two beloved friends; who cares if the world sees our less-than-perfect sides.

That's where we are headed as a society, right? Away from the fake and more towards the real. The raw. Reality. Showing not only the good but also the bad, the mistakes, the humorous moments.

"How was it, y'all?" Mason asks, walking up and in between me and Braxton. He throws his arms around us, grinning ear to ear. "Going to be the wedding of the century or what?"

Braxton laughs, "Well, you sang at mine, so..."

"And mine will be royal, so..."

We chortle, and as I look at these men and the group of women huddled off in the corner, a sad feeling sinks in. "I'm going to miss you guys when I leave. In a few short months, you've made this place truly feel like home. More so than this state did while I was in college with Hadley."

"Don't get sappy on us, Fins," Braxton says.

At the same time Mason draws out a long-winded, "Aww, how sweet."

I roll my eyes. "Men, it's okay to be emotionally honest with each other, you know?" They both laugh and shake their heads.

The wedding party gathers, and we all hop into the limo that met us at the airport a couple days ago. It has transported us all around Dallas, warranting a million photographers and fans to chase us around.

Because this isn't your classic limousine.

This is American country superstar Mason Kane's version.

It is a black Toyota Tundra limousine. A "Tundrasine." With a bed attached to the end and everything. The 26-foot long vehicle insides consist of nine leather bucket seats, the middle ones reclinable, with a bench seat in the back. There are air controls for every row and a glossy brown siding along the doors to match the seat colors.

"A redneck man's dream," Mason had said a month ago when he booked it for the wedding festivities.

I sit between Lorelei and Lucy in the backseat. Lorelei wanted to be by the window, so I graciously sit in the middle so I can be beside her. She looks amazing in her olive green sundress, the material soft and flowy. Of course, in typical Lorelei fashion, she's sporting her white sneakers, though she apparently promised Karoline she wouldn't wear them for the wedding tomorrow.

I intertwine my fingers with hers and kiss the backside of her hand. She blushes lightly and plants a kiss on my cheek.

"I'm so ready to devour steak," Hadley says from the front seat.

"You mean you are ready to devour a rubber tire," Braxton corrects her.

"She is still eating steak incorrectly?" I ask. She always ate the meat well-done in our college days when I'd take her out to fancy restaurants. She was the only one besides the president of the college that knew who I truly was during those days. I went by a different name. That all changed after I graduated and decided to date the world in search of adventure and the possibility of finding a love match for myself.

"It's not wrong!" Hadley shouts in defense, turning to glare at me. "Just because I don't want to consume bloody meat like I'm a Cullen doesn't mean I'm eating steak wrong."

We all laugh, and Lucy chimes in. "I'm with Hadley. Why eat a lump of blood?"

Lorelei retorts, "While I don't eat it rare, medium-rare is better because you get nutrients you need."

"Okay, Vampire Girl," Lucy responds.

We continue conversations about food while we head towards the restaurant that's been reserved for the wedding crew. We arrive at the popular steakhouse and are ushered into the main dining area that's been low-lit with candles and string lights on the ceilings. The atmosphere is decidedly romantic. Mason and Karoline's parents arrive, the pastor officiating the wedding, and the wedding planning duo who have put the whole event together.

Mason and Karoline sit at a table with their parents, Chantel, and Grant. The wedding planners sit off by themselves, and then I sit with the twins, Braxton, Hadley, and Pastor Rawls, the officiant.

"This is the end of an era," Lucy says, looking around the table at each of us. Then her attention snags on Lorelei. "I can't believe you are leaving next week."

"Neither can I," Lorelei says softly. "But let's not talk about that. No need to enter panic mode on the eve of our friend's wedding."

"Right," Lucy says, reaching for a buttered roll that the servers just set in front of us. The rest of us follow her lead.

"So, how's everything going at work, Lucy?" Hadley asks with suspicion oozing from her voice.

"Fine." Her tone is sour. She shoves the bread in her mouth and chews.

"Elaborate," I suggest. "I heard there is a bothersome boss. Do I need to use my influence to remove him from your life?"

At that, Lucy giggles. "Ha, no. It's all good. He is bothersome, but it's nothing I can't handle. Thank you, though, King-in-Law."

"King-in-law?" Hadley spurts a laugh. "That's a title."

"I quite like it," I say, winking at Lucy.

Lucy nods in agreement and then sighs. "My boss, Mr. Harper, has taken to asking me out. It hasn't become too frequent, but since we danced together back in February, he's asked me out at least twice a month. He is now asking me out for dinners instead of just lunches."

"Isn't that workplace harassment?" Lorelei asks. "I can take care of that. My former boss is not only a lawyer but is also the mayor of Juniper Grove."

"No, it's nothing like that!" Lucy spews. She continues talking quickly and with her hands, which both contain halves of her buttered roll. "It's just that I know he's a player. He has had many women on his arm in the time I've worked here. He isn't mean or rude or oversteps boundaries. He's just persistent and a natural flirt. I'm a game to him."

"You sure?" Braxton asks. "'Cause I could handle him for you."

"I second that," Hadley jumps in.

Lucy laughs and waves them off. "No, guys. Really. He's a good guy. Very giving of his time and money when it comes to the community. He's just a ladies' man. That's all."

"Well, you have support, Lucy. You're not alone. Even in Korsa, we will have your back," I state.

"Thanks, guys," Lucy says, taking a sip of water.

The rest of the dinner flows smoothly with conversation alternating between sentimental, humorous, and the random interjections of Lorelei's facts when something interesting comes up. I will truly miss these people.

They made a home for me in such a short time.

But one look at Lorelei reminds me that wherever she is will be my permanent home.

Chapter Twenty-Seven

Lorelei

One more sweep. If I do one more sweep of the apartment then I will have finally convinced myself that I am not forgetting anything.

"I don't make a habit of telling you to calm down in the midst of your frenzies, but Lorelei, chill out. I will ship you anything you forget if you will just sit down for two seconds."

Ignoring my twin wholeheartedly, I open the entertainment center and look inside before moving back into the kitchen. Most things happen to be staying here because Lucy will still live here, and well, I'm moving into an actual castle.

It's sufficient to say she needs pots and pans more than I do.

But I don't want to forget little things that bring me comfort and will remind me of home such as the pot holders with plants on them. Will I need them? No. But I will catch sight of them and will remember this little apartment and my sister, and I will probably cry, but I will also smile.

"See." I hold up the pot holders. "I would have forgotten these."

Lucy's face falls blank as she deadpans, "Because heaven forbid you don't have pot holders at Stjarna Palace."

"You gave them to me. They are special. I will think of you when I see them."

Her face softens and she drops her folded arms to her side. She walks to the couch then plops down. "Come sit down, Lorelei."

Taking a deep breath, I do as she asks. I really do need to calm down. The moment my butt hits the dark brown cushion, Lucy scoots over and embraces me in a hug. "I'm going to miss you so much." She sniffles, and I wiggle into a position where I can wrap my arms around her.

"I'm going to miss you, too, baby sister."

Lucy laughs through breathy sobs, squeezing me tighter. After a moment of silence and intense sisterly hugging, we break apart.

Lucy's bangs are disheveled, so I play with them until they sit on her face nicely. "You're going to be okay, you know?"

"I might be okay. But I'm not sure I'm going to be well. I've never lived alone before."

I take her hand in mine and look into her watery, hazel eyes. "You're self-sufficient and a beautiful, capable woman. What fears do you have?"

She looks away from me. "I'm scared that I won't be able to keep up with rent, electricity, and water. Not to mention wifi and other bills. I'm afraid I won't be able to afford food and gas. I'm worried that I will lose contact with you and Karoline. Hadley is here, but she's married. I'll have to hang out with Emma Jane more."

After a beat, I open my mouth to respond, but she begins again. "I'm scared of becoming a lonely cat lady for the rest of my life."

We both glance at Frannie and Frizzle as they laze about in the streaming sunlight.

"Those are valid fears," I say, folding my hands in my lap. "I had goals of being a plant and cat mom for a while. I don't think it's a bad thing. But I know it's not what you desire. And to that, well, Lucy, you can't control the will of God. Please remember that. Don't jump the gun with anything. Take this time to be alone. To learn to be content with it even though I know it is an affliction on your soul. Grow closer to the Lord and find yourself. Write your stories and figure out this life. We are twenty-six. You are not behind in life, Lucy. Do you believe me?"

"No," she says immediately. I grimace, but she turns a soft smile to me. "But I can promise to try."

The response doesn't calm me much, but I have to accept that Lucy is not mine to manage, and she has to figure things out herself. I will pray for her, reach out consistently to her, and support her as I can.

"May I ease part of your fears?" I ask. This is the right moment to bring up an idea Finley and I discussed earlier in the week.

Lucy nods, questions in her eyes.

"Finley and I would like to pay the rent and utilities on the apartment. It's not because we don't think you are capable, because we do, but it was quite sudden of me to up and leave you. We didn't give you much time to save or arrange other accommodations, so please don't take this as a handout but as a severance package."

Her eyes widen as her jaw drops. "Are you for real?"

I nod with finality. "And if you try not to accept, Finley is prepared to promote your books."

She narrows her eyes and scowls. "Fine. But only because I want to build my authordom myself. That is sacred to me."

I grin, and Lucy finally relents, smiling back at me.

"You're kinda the best twin ever, you know?" Lucy jumps on me, throwing us both backwards, falling deeper into the couch.

"How can I be the best when you are?" I respond. We both laugh until our cats decide to pounce, sinking claws into our skin in the name of playtime.

"I'm going to miss this." And right as the words leave my mouth, my laughs turn to a tearful, mourning sound. This change hurts, but I also know that what awaits me across the pond is a lifetime of joy, love, and intellectual stimulation. I mean, I will be governing a country, after all. What better use of my law training, historical facts, and philosophy obsession.

The thought stirs giddiness in me, and my tears quickly dry up. Lucy and I spend the rest of the afternoon finishing packing, cleaning (I won't leave her with a dirty apartment), and randomly crying when we think of memories we've shared together over our twenty-six years.

I won't lie and say I'm not worried about my twin. I make a mental note to talk to Hadley and Emma Jane. I won't share Lucy's fears and worries, but I do want to make sure I have people in place to check in on her. Grandma Netty will look after her, but she's getting old and has been struggling the past few weeks. But maybe Lucy can look after her, which will help my sister retain a sense of responsibility and feeling needed. So many things to consider, so while I dress for my date with Finley tonight, our last one in Mississippi for the foreseeable future, I take my concerns to the Lord and place my trust in Him to take care of my sister in my physical absence.

"It's time we redeem this location." Finley's fingers brush the backside of my arm as he guides me down the stone path that leads to Club Paris, the French restaurant I met him at once upon a time when he believed he was meeting up with my twin for their first date.

As his feather-light touches continue to simultaneously send gooseflesh up my arms and warmth to my cheeks, I'm enamored with the thought that I may never get used to the glorious feeling of being touched by this man.

I hope I don't.

My eyes take in every ounce of him once we get to the door, lit only by two incandescent lights. He's wearing a white collared shirt with three buttons, the top one unbuttoned, tucked into navy pants. Light brown dress shoes round off his classic, easy appearance. Unwillingly tearing my eyes from him, I glance down at my navy ponte cap-sleeve dress with a thin, gold belt accentuating my waistline. Lucy outfitted me with simple, small gold hoops that don't hit my neck when I walk, matching gold sneakers that mirror my white ones, just nicer, and styled my hair into big hollywood-style waves. I did require pulling the mass of red hair into a ponytail, but she said as long as it was a high ponytail, it would be sufficient.

I obliged. And I'm pretty sure it rivals Ariana Grande's.

"What's there to redeem? I thought that first date went okay." I swim in my memories, remembering how horribly I impersonated my sister, and I grimace. "Other than my terrible acting skills, which was odd considering I'm a great masker."

"The Lord must have known you needed to be yourself." He grins a dazzling smile at me as he leads me through the double golden doors of the restaurant. I'm hit with the smell of fresh bread, pasta, and a variety of spices begging to let me taste them. The restaurant still looks the same as last time with one exception: we are the only ones here outside of staff.

Bewildered, I look up at my boyfriend. (And no. I will never tire of calling him that.) "Did you..."

"Rent the place out?" Finley finishes. "Yep. We can have our last date in Mississippi in peace. You don't have to worry about getting overstimulated by a bunch of chattering people, and I get you all to myself." He winks, and a nervous energy stirs within my stomach at his statement. A good kind of nervous. The kind that only my man seems to be able to awaken within me. I'm not at all phased that he's spending money like this on me. He's a prince. What else would he do?

We are escorted by the male host who greeted us last time to a round table in the middle of the restaurant. They've dimmed the lights, lit candles, and have...

Oh my stars.

Chrysanthemums. All over the tables. Of every color.

"Finley..." I gasp his name, my hand flying to cover my open mouth. Water prickles in the corner of my eyes as I turn around to face him. His smile is proud, but not in a smug way. It's a smile that screams his love for me, his appreciation and adoration of me. He takes my hand from my mouth and holds it between his own.

What in the world did I do to deserve this man?

I don't have to be Lucy and all romance-obsessed to know exactly what's going down tonight. "Yes," I sputter out even though he hasn't asked the question yet.

"Yes?" Finley asks with a tilt of his head, an action I'm pretty sure he's picked up from being around me.

"Yes, I'll marry you," I say, stepping closer to him, taking my hand from his and wrapping my arms around him. I place my head against the spot where his shoulder meets his chest. A perfect spot made just for me. "That's what you're going to ask me tonight, right?"

His chest rumbles underneath me, and then fear that I've misread the situation settles.

I groan. "Oh, no. That's not what's happening, is it? I'm sorry. Forget I said anything." I attempt to break away from his hold, but he doesn't let me scurry away like my brain demands. Panic begins to rise, but I remind myself that Finley is not going to judge me or make fun of me.

He loves me.

I breathe.

"Leilei, calm your mind." Finley tugs me back to him, but I position my head up to look at him instead of resting against him. Not a trace of a smirk or a ghost of amusement colors his handsome face. Only a genuine smile and sparkles in his blue eyes, slightly darker in the dimmed room. "That's exactly what I'm doing."

He steps back and slides down onto one knee, holding a silver ring with no jutting diamond.

I could cry.

"Yes!" I say again, this time with more enthusiasm.

Finley chuckles and shakes his head. "Pretty woman, will you allow me to be a gentleman and declare my intentions while showering you with affection?"

Suddenly, a memory from our first date where he asked me to allow him to be a gentleman and get my chair for me resurfaces. I can't help but laugh. "We truly are redeeming this location."

"I was going to ask you after dinner, but you are wonderfully perceptive and unafraid to voice your thoughts, so I will ask you now." He clears his throat, a flicker of uncertainty crossing his face before he smooths out his expression. "I want to thank you for agreeing to stand in for your sister. Without that decision, I don't know where we'd be. Maybe God would have brought us together in another fashion, but I quite like the way it happened for us. Leilei, you are beautiful, kind, intelligent, charitable, loving, protective, and my *myssa.* I've prayed to be loved by and to love a woman like you."

I'm bouncing at this point, biting my tongue to not shout "yes" again like an uncontrolled beast. His words are lovely, but I already know he feels this way. *My emotional man,* I think to myself, grinning ear to ear.

He continues, his expression softening at my obvious joy. "Thank you for being who you are. Please, do me the honor of allowing me to love you, protect you, and date you for the rest of our lives. Be my queen, Lorelei Raine Spence."

I'm about to burst if this man doesn't put that ring on my finger and wrap me up in two seconds.

He laughs, then says, "You can answer now, bae."

"Yes!" I shout, thrusting my hand into his face so that he can put the simple, perfect band onto my finger. He listened to me when I said I didn't want a rock on it because I didn't want to risk it rubbing against my skin. And though I know the kingdom may be confused as to why their queen wears a simple band instead of a gaudy diamond, I am *happy*.

After sliding the perfectly fitting ring onto my finger, Finley hops to his feet and picks me up, twirling me around once in his arms before setting me down and kissing my lips with a tender, slow passion.

When we part, Finley pulls out my chair for me, and I sit. We are immediately served wine and bread and are told that our orders (that Finley had already placed for us ahead of time) would be out shortly.

Finley pours our drinks, sets the bottle down, and holds up his glass of red liquid. This entire time, neither of our smiles have faltered. "From the moment you went on a tangent regarding the history of cheers, I was smitten with you, Lorelei. And every moment since has been nothing short of spectacular. I love you."

I giggle, feeling like the princess I'm about to become. Clinking my glass with his, I exclaim, "Cheers!"

"To a long, joyous, and adventurous life with you." We both take a sip of our wine, and as I reach for the bread, he grabs my hand and kisses it.

Feeling more complete and satisfied than I ever have in life, I beam at my fiancé. Definitely enjoying the upgraded term. "I love you, Finley Andersson."

LUCY'S JOURNAL

SOMEDAY, JUNE SOMETHING. * WHO CARES * VOID OF LIFE

Hadley and Braxton are married. Karoline and Mason are married. As of yesterday, my sister is now engaged to the Crown Prince of Korsa... and I'm stuck staving off my playboy boss's attempted advances. It's not that he isn't extremely handsome and hot. It's not even that I think he is a horrible human being. He runs a community center for disadvantaged kids for crying out loud. It's the fact that I've seen him with so many women on his arm in the short year that I've known him. And he's my boss. And he's two years younger than me. That's why I have to continually push him off. He's just after the chase. He doesn't actually care about me. That much is clear. I'm just another prize for him to win. Once I cave and he "gets" me, he will throw me away. I know his type, and I am at defense level 100 against it... Even if I choose to flirt back with him occasionally because he might be a wee bit fun to play with. But I'll never admit that aloud.

But God...

Where is the man for me? I'm so lonely now, alone in this apartment. This is only the first night. Well, Lorelei left Frannie for me, but it's not the same. Nothing is the same anymore. It feels like a dark, heavy weight is settling on my chest, suffocating me and beckoning me to the edge of a cliff. I don't want to feel this way. Help me... Please, God. Help me. Not to need a man. Not to be so concerned that I'm lonely. Not to feel lonely.

I should reach out to Hadley. Or maybe even Emma Jane.

But why does it feel so hard to pick up the phone?

AFTER

And fall in love she did...

The twin sister of the lovely woman with fair, freckled skin, warm, coppery hair, and a bubbly personality that would rival his own, that is. The flirty prince had finally found the one whom his soul longed for, and it turned out to be a lovely woman with fair, freckled skin, warm, coppery hair, and a stoic and serious personality that, though opposite, complemented his own. The bewitched crown prince whisked his new bride-to-be and her cat away to his palace where they would spend the remainder of the year not only preparing for a grand wedding but also transitioning into their new roles as king and queen of their tiny island country. As he learned what it takes to be a good monarch who ruled in fairness and kindness, she discovered what it takes to serve her country's down and out citizens and families through her philanthropic work. The crown prince and his lady grew in their insurmountable love for each other with every passing day, supported and defended each other's decisions, and slipped away to "practice" every moment they could, preferably in the garden by the newly planted chrysanthemums. Their wedding and coronation was on the horizon, after all, and they had big plans to live happily ever after.

The End... *For now.*

Catch the royal wedding and coronation in the fourth and final book of the *Designated* series, *The Designated Date.* Coming soon!

Loved the Story?

Consider leaving a review on Amazon and Goodreads!

Get the last book in the series, *The Designated Date,* today!

ACKNOWLEDGMENTS

The Designated Twin was an escape. In the midst of crippling depression, I relied on Finley, Lorelei, and the rest of this cast and world to wrap me in a warm hug every time I sat down at my computer to write. That's all I can say about this story—I absolutely needed it, and the Lord put it on my heart to help me through the darkest night I've experienced.

Thank you to my Lord and Savior Jesus Christ for the gift of writing. You know I have struggled against You this year. I've ran and have shouted and have made my anger towards You known. You have loved me fiercely and wholly through my struggles and apathy. *Soli Deo Gloria.*

To my family and friends, I love you all so very much. You have kept me afloat this past year. You all know who you are.

To the Bookstagram community, thank you for loving me well. I'm so thankful for every follow, like, share, comment, message, post created, reel made, and review written. I love the online community you have invited me into.

Thank you to my critique partners—Whitney and Kaitlyn. Thank you to my betas—Cole, Kim, Anna, Allison, and Abby. You ladies helped SO MUCH and were tremendous in your advice and feedback. To Leah, the best editor in the whole wide world, you are such a gem of a human. You are so much more than just my editor; you are dear to me, friend. Thank you for your continual encouragement through this book and through this very tough season of life.

To my street team and arc readers... THANK YOU. I could not be an indie author without your constant love, support, and excitement! Thank you for all that you do to help me promote and market my books. To my readers... What more can I say? I sure can't say thank you enough. A writer is nothing without a reader. You are the lifeline of this career. This book belongs to you now.

I hope you all found a sweet escape as I did when I wrote it.

ALSO BY

DREW TAYLOR

Scan the QR code or click on the link to learn more about Drew Taylor's books!

www.drewtaylorwrites.com

ABOUT THE AUTHOR

Drew is on a personal mission to bridge the gap between "Christian" media and "Secular" media. She believes objects and concepts cannot be Christian, only people can be. She loves to tell engaging and sizzling romantic stories that are wrapped in reality, humor, and wit without the open doors or on-page cursing.

Drew is from south Mississippi but now resides in Alaska where she attempts to engage 15 and 16 year olds in classic world literature. When not teaching or writing, she enjoys reading,

Bookstagram, baking Christmas goodies (even in the middle of June), researching random history facts, watching K-dramas, and spending quality time with the people who mean the most to her. Sign up for her newsletter for important updates in case Social Media decides to kick her off one day: https://mailchi.mp/61fed5b940fb/drew-taylor-author

Follow Drew:

Instagram: @authordrewtaylor

Facebook: Drew Taylor, Author

TikTok: @faithfilledromance

Pinterest: @authordrewtaylor

Printed in Great Britain
by Amazon